GOT YOUR SIX

PLAYLIST:

Tread Lightly – Forest Blakk

I Don't Remember Me (Before You) – Brothers Osborne

Waiting For The Snow – Of Monsters and Men

Must Be The Whiskey – Cody Jinks

Whitesnake Road – Tyler Childers

7&7 – Turnpike Troubadours

Drinkin' Problem – Midland

Women, Amen – Dierks Bentley

2016 – Sam Hunt

All I see Is You – Shane Smith

Put The Hurt On Me – Midland

Dance Me to the End of Love – The Civil Wars

Nose On The Grindstone – Tyler Childers

Let Me Love the Lonely – James Arthur

Ocean – Lady A

The Devil Wears a Suit and Tie – Colter Wall

Your Man – Josh Turner

I Know You're Gonna Be There – Luke Bryan

To second chances.

Don't blow it.

PROLOGUE

Past

"YOU'RE OKAY, YOU'RE okay." My voice quivers with the tears that are lodged deep in my throat, my nostrils burn with the smell of smoke, and I try to suck in a deep breath through my mouth. Something pins my chest; rough canvas rubs my cheek. *The airbag.*

Coughing has me jerking my head to the right and I notice my baby brother is close to me, his moans fill the car and I scramble for my seat belt trying to pry it off of me but the buckle is jammed in the slot and no matter how I strain and pull, it won't budge.

"You're okay, you're gonna be fine," I promise him.

"Ford, my legs." The words pass his lips with a rasp and I cry out for help when I see what's got them pinned. My cry is loud and feral. I know I'm seconds from losing my cool, and the only reason that would ever happen is if I was faced with losing my little brother.

Lights are blinding me, I blink and look around, trying to find the source and hoping it's someone coming to help. When I finally locate it, it's not someone there to help but who put us here in the first place. A truck is pressed—no, lodged face-first into the passenger side of my own truck. Crushing my brother.

"Fuck." My words pass through my lips as I finally register the sound of howling sirens in the distance. "Help is coming, Jack. Help is coming."

"Ford." My brother's face is as pale as the moon, I use my right hand to grasp his arm and hold on tight. His breathing is rough, each gasp of air a challenge.

I just hold on.

I hold on for him. I hold on for me. I hold on for Mom and Dad.

"It's okay," I whisper again and shake my head. My eyes find his and I breathe out roughly. "It will be fine." My tone is deep, demanding, willing my words to come true.

They say it only takes one moment to change the direction of your life; only one moment to alter it forever.

For me, this was that moment.

1

Present

FORD

WHAT THE FUCK was I doing here?

The question keeps filtering through my mind as I stare at the perfect farmhouse that sits across the dirt road from where I sit in my rental car. The house is in a large cul-de-sac style neighborhood, only these houses were all placed on large lots with several acres, giving the illusion of a farming neighborhood. The white farmhouse had a big wraparound porch, a blue door that I remember watching my dad paint while Mom held baby Jack in her arms when I was ten years old. I can still recall the look on her face, the pride that she and Dad both had felt at finally buying the house they'd always wanted.

I didn't know why I was here. I hadn't been home in years. Not because I wasn't welcome. Hell, if my mom knew that I was sitting outside her house right now, debating on coming in, she'd tan my hide.

But something was holding me back. Maybe it was the demons that haunted my every move. Maybe it was the depressing thoughts that seemed to constantly frame my thoughts. Maybe I was just a prick and didn't want to give my family any false hope of me sticking around when I have no intention of doing so.

I was only here because my boss, Gemma James, was forcing me to be here. She was a stickler for the rules, and when I'd broken one too many—for the good of the world, I'll have you know—she told me I was grounded "until further notice."

To say I was shocked would be an understatement. I was pissed. I'd given my life to this organization, to keeping the public safe without ever getting any recognition for it. I was okay with that, but being put on a mandatory leave put me over the edge.

"Gentry, you need a break." I can still remember her cool blue eyes drilling into me. Nobody really messed with Gemma, but in that moment, I wanted to. *"You've been at this so long that you've lost sight of the real cause."* I had tried to protest, but she wouldn't let me. *"You don't get a choice. Go home. Regroup. You can come back to work when your head is straight."*

I hadn't replied to that, mostly because there wasn't anything I could do. She'd halted all of my access across the board. My badge was just a useless hunk of metal now.

I've worked my entire life to get where I am, and then it was stripped away because I was angry about the way things had been going lately, because I'd lashed out. Because I had just become so fucking over it, that I could hardly breathe anymore.

And staring at my family home was not helping matters. I knew if I went in there, my family wouldn't even blink before throwing their arms around me and welcoming me home. They wouldn't dredge up the past. They wouldn't hate me. They would bury the hatchet that I'd wedged between us and beg me to stay. But I couldn't. Not after what I'd done.

Why did I come here?

I'd enlisted in the military straight out of high school, joining hadn't been my first choice, as a matter of fact, it wasn't even on my radar until things had gone to shit and I needed a way to run away.

When I'd come up for reenlistment the second time around, they'd given me a hell of an alternative. Quantico. A brand new challenge. Anyone who knew me, knew that when given a bigger, better challenge, I couldn't pass it up. And I hadn't.

So, I took that head-on and joined the FBI after graduating top of my class. Just barely ahead of my best friend Liam, who was a fucking know-it-all pain in the ass who'd saved mine more than I could count.

When was the last time I'd talked to him?

Fuck. Maybe I wasn't thinking straight.

When you can't remember the last time you'd talked to your best friend of the last ten years, something wasn't quite right.

Rubbing my eyes, I shake my head and duck when I see the front door open.

My mother stands on the porch with a watering can, absentmindedly tending to her flowers hanging in the pots over the arch of the door. She'd always been obsessed with flowers, her house inside and out was filled with them. The smell of flowers still brings a wave of nostalgia to this day.

It makes my gut churn to see her. Her hair perfectly styled, her ritual of getting up at the ass crack of dawn to do her hair and makeup seemingly still intact. Although now, streaks of gray shoot through the brown hair that she'd always had. My mom had aged since I'd seen her last.

When she ducked back inside, I threw my rental into drive and got out of there as fast as I could. Despite how much I wanted my feet to carry me to her, I just wasn't ready to face my family.

And I wasn't sure I'd ever be ready for that.

2

FORD

AFTER DRIVING AROUND to clear my mind, I park my car outside the local bar. It used to be the only spot in town when I was younger and it was where everyone went. It's been years since I've been back and maybe I was a glutton for punishment being here. But part of me, the sick part, had hoped that the familiar setting would bring me a form of comfort. Given that the previous owners were the parents of one of my best friends. Though, that was another lifetime ago. After a tragic accident struck the family and her mother was shot in an armed robbery, things fell apart from there. My own mind wasn't in the right place when things went down and unfortunately, I'd fucked-up not only my relationship with my family, but with my best friends too.

When I pull up, the old *El Abrevadero* sign lights up the dark window. I walk up to the old bar door and pull it open, walking in to see only a couple of people milling about. Of course, it was only two in the afternoon, so there was a good chance everyone else was still at work.

Old country tunes play from the speakers above, and I take that as a good sign and continue walking into the bar and find an empty barstool. I can't see anyone in here, but I can faintly hear humming coming from the back. I holler out to whoever it is, hoping I can avoid some familiar faces for a while before word gets out that I'm back in town. It's been a long time since high school and I'm hoping I can get by without being recognized for as long as possible.

When someone emerges from the back, my stomach drops when I see the familiar face. Delaney Torrez.

I'd come here hoping I wouldn't run into her, but that was a pathetic excuse, there was always a chance I'd find her here and maybe part of me was actually hoping for it.

I haven't seen Laney in years. The last time I did, it didn't go well. I wouldn't be surprised if she threw me out on my ass. I wait for her to notice me and when she does, her feet catch and she teeters forward, catching herself at the last minute.

I'm halfway out of my stool before I stop myself when she gains her balance again, there's a hesitation from her. For a moment, we stare at each other and I brace myself for the hate that justifiably should come my way, but in a blink, her face goes blank. If I hadn't been watching, I would have missed it all.

I clear my throat when she doesn't say anything. "You got any Coors?" I spit out, hoping she might go easy on me while at the same time, kind of wishing she would do anything but stare. I'm not sure where to go from here. I came here to just sit and drink in peace. And the first person I run into is one of four I'd been hoping to avoid for a while.

Her eyes assess me. Without a word, she gives me a nod and cracks me open a bottle. I take it cautiously, yet gratefully and take my first sip of the ice-cold brew. Before I can say anything more, Delaney gives me one last cool look, turns on her heel, and disappears from sight. I ignore the pang in my chest as I watch her walk away.

It was so bitter-fucking-sweet being back.

I'd never hated living in Texas, everything here was shit that I loved. I loved driving the old dirt roads in my truck. I loved the late-night bonfires and getting drunk off cheap beer we weren't supposed to have, I loved playing Friday night football and hearing them chant our team name as we won the championships.

High school was my castle and I was the fucking king. Until everything around me came crumbling right down to the ground. Every brick I'd used to build that castle, wiped out with one single night.

Remembering all of that has me looking to the doorway where Delaney disappeared. That girl… Fuck. Talk about the one who got away. Or rather, the one I left behind.

Our lives were meant to be so much simpler than they turned out to be. We were going to be the friends who stayed that way, always having each other's back. Me, Delaney, and Bobby, our other best friend. We were thick as thieves. Then shit hit the motherfucking fan and our lives took a nosedive.

But the accident, the one I can barely even speak of, it flipped my world completely upside down with no warning.

It got so bad that I dropped football, leaving the team and keeping my head low. I never went to another bonfire; I didn't hang out with anyone. I finished school the best I could and the second I finished my last class, I joined the military.

I left for basic immediately after I was done and tried so fucking hard to never look back. It hurt everyone, I knew it. My parents were heartbroken, and my brother… fuck. I wouldn't be surprised if he never spoke to me again. I couldn't handle the pressure of sticking around. Of being the fuck-up that I was and facing that every single day. And if I couldn't do that for myself, or my family, the least I could do was pay it forward and serve in the only way I was capable.

I DON'T THINK I'm drunk. But I'm not exactly sober. I have

no clue what time it is, it's been a while since I came into the bar. I'm oblivious to most of my surroundings except I do notice that there are servers running from table to table, and now that I look closer, there are many more tables with customers than there was before. Each server is walking around, taking orders, filling drinks, carrying trays of actual food, not just bar food. Like good fucking smelling food. Attempting to get my eyes to focus, I peer up at the sign above the bar that holds a small inscription that says *"El Abrevadero, Bar & Grill"*.

Well, that answers that question.

It was packed in here now, much like the way it used to be when I was young. Everyone still seemed to frequent this bar more than any other place in town. Even though there was now a green juice bar down the road, along with other pointless, overly populated crap.

Fuck. I was rockin' a serious buzz.

A body sidles near me, trying to get Delaney's attention for another round I'm sure and I tense, turning my head and pulling the bill of my hat down so the guy I used to call my best friend wouldn't recognize me.

Bobby doesn't seem to care though and talks with Delaney like the old friends they are. The urge to join in, to slap him on the back and pull her into a hug is so strong that I have to take a deep breath. She smiles at him in a familiar way that makes my stomach lurch.

Out of the corner of her eye, I see her peek at me, but she

keeps her body aimed in Bobby's direction. Even drunk, I notice the maneuver and she's doing it for my benefit. I don't deserve it.

Bobby and Delaney were the only two who tried back then, tried to break me out of the shell that I'd burrowed in. Tried to help get me past my own thoughts and mistakes. But none of that mattered. I was broken long before they saw I needed mending.

Delaney comes over near me again and sets a plate of food in front of me. "Eat," is all she says before turning her attention to someone else, flitting around and filling people's orders, delivering that smile again. I'm so distracted by her that I don't touch the food in front of me, and when she's near again, she sees I haven't touched the burger and says, "Eat that and I'll get you a whiskey." Her voice is still that husky tone that I used to love.

It sends a jolt of nostalgia through me, but I swallow that down and reply, "Make it a 7&7 and you've got it."

When she winks and walks away, I allow myself to relax a little. Maybe coming home won't be as bad as I expected. Maybe it will even bring the healing that I so desperately need.

3

DELANEY

THE PLACE WAS packed tonight and I felt myself get a rush of excitement just seeing it in front of me. It was booming compared to how we'd done the last few nights, and I sent a silent thank you out to the universe for turning my luck around.

I'd been fighting for this place to do well for months, hell, *years* if I'm being honest and finally, it was paying off. Maybe I'd get to take home an actual paycheck after I paid the bills this month. Talk about a true American dream.

This bar was my family's legacy, and the last thing I wanted was for it to flop. I wanted, *needed* to make sure my mother's hard work didn't go down the drain. She'd fought tooth and nail for this place, working all hours of the day to keep up with it. She couldn't fathom the thought of losing it, and her father hadn't been in the right state of mind when he'd said he was going to sell after her death.

After my mother passed and my father started getting older, he'd shown less and less interest in the restaurant. I was truly hoping if I could get it running smoothly on its own. If I could get a good manager in here to run it without me. If I could save just enough money, I could keep Mom's legacy and have my own dream too.

I'd dreamed since I was in high school of owning my own business, but I never wanted anything to do with the bar. While it was a great place, it wasn't *mine*. It was a place I'd always be able to work if I had to, but it wasn't ever supposed to be permanent.

When my mother passed my senior year of high school, I knew that my plans for college were going to be put on hold. My plans to open a flower shop were no more, at least, until I could help Papá get back on his feet. He was a stubborn old man though, and he hadn't wanted to let me leave at all.

Being a martyr was something that my father had eternally exceeded at and up to this point, I'd let him have that control over me. But I was about done with allowing it. It had gone on long enough, and I was ready to finally start living *my* life.

Running a business was tiring, but when we were having a night like tonight when it seemed almost everyone in town wanted to be here, it filled me with pride to know my mother's hard work hadn't gone down the drain. That everything I'd worked for hadn't been for nothing.

I finish serving a table their food and wander behind the bar, nodding at a couple who raise their glass for a refill and serve them before going down to the end of the bar to find an empty plate and a patient gaze locked on mine. If anything shocked me tonight, it was seeing my high school best friend sitting in my bar. It was startling, to say the least. I hadn't seen Ford in years. The last time I did see him, he was not the person I'd once known. Before Bobby or I could figure out how to reach him, he was long gone. It was hard not to hate him at first. He couldn't have picked a worse time to do it. One week after my mother's funeral and several weeks after Ford had had his own tragedies strike, he had basically ignored my very existence. Nowadays, what he did would be called 'ghosting.' Back then it was just avoidance.

I'd been heartbroken, truly. I was seventeen, madly in love—or what I thought was love anyway—but at the same time crumbling at the loss of my mother. He was right beside me through her funeral and wake, through having to accept "I'm sorrys" from the town, from the few family members that we did know. A week after her death, he'd unexpectedly taken off. Barely an excuse, and then he was gone.

Sixteen years though, that's way too long to hold on to a grudge. Somewhere around year three, I'd decided to let it go. To move on. We never heard from him, never saw him, and it was pointless to hold on to something that he so obviously didn't care about.

Running a restaurant and keeping my dad from destroying his liver with alcohol was a full-time job, two full-time jobs really. I didn't have the time or the energy to hate.

Now, seeing him here after all this time? It brought back those memories. They were—for the most part—good ones. All the way up until that car accident, things between Ford and I had been nearly perfect.

One thing was for sure, Ford Gentry had grown up good.

Not that that was a surprise to anyone, he was the classic boy next door. He had the killer grin, the built-by-football body, and he was the kindest human to walk the halls of Midland High.

He was always helping other people out and I guarantee he learned that from his mother, Melissa.

When Bobby Nelson came up to the bar, I knew he'd recognize Ford immediately. The three of us were best friends all through high school, and after Ford disappeared, Bobby was the only one I could lean on. He never left town, but instead stuck around working for the mill that his father owned. When Ford dropped off the Earth, I knew that Bobby was hurt. So while I was keeping him engaged in conversation to distract him from the stranger at the bar, I couldn't decide if I was doing it for Bobby's benefit, or Ford's.

That was a mystery that me and my heart weren't willing to uncover just yet. But even as I knew I shouldn't get involved, I also knew there was no way him being home would be a secret for much longer.

LETTING A FRUSTRATED sigh escape my lips, I start the count over again. There has to be something I'm missing. Since I'd taken over Mom and Dad's bar, I'd done a complete one-eighty with not only the bar itself, having turned it into a restaurant, but with the financial part as well.

I didn't mind the hard work, I had the ambition, the hope, and the work ethic to make it happen.

And I knew we needed a change. Putting in a family restaurant that served everything from your classic burger to authentic Mexican was a place everyone could come and get their fix. We were especially popular with young families. I was proud of what I could do for my mother's legacy.

After some time, and paying off debts I'd gotten us into just making the restaurant happen, I'd been able to not only give us a hefty nest egg, but I'd been able to use some of the money earned to put myself through business school. It wasn't exactly what I had in mind when I had thought about college, but it was a hell of a lot better than nothing.

Now here I am, counting out the night's earnings and coming up short. Again. There was absolutely nothing more frustrating than missing money. Except maybe hormonal acne, nobody liked that.

But missing money only meant one thing, someone was skimming some off the top and it illogically hurt my feelings. I'd vetted every one of my employees, I'd never wanted to have people I couldn't trust. And aside from our latest addition, Matteo, everyone else had been working here for a year or more.

Matteo was a bit young; he was still in high school and only worked nights and weekends. But he was sweet and ambitious. He was saving for college. I couldn't imagine him being stupid enough to steal from anyone.

Stretching out my shoulders, I look around the empty restaurant. It was nearing two in the morning and I'd just watched Ford stumble out the door after I called him a cab. I offered to help him home, but he waved me off. Given that we weren't exactly speaking, I let it go and continued to pretend his presence didn't rattle me to my core.

It was going to make a stir when people found out he was back. Still, I got the impression that he really didn't want anyone to know. At least not yet, I just didn't know the reason and a little part of me was wondering if I'd ever find out.

I lock up the cash in the safe and grab my purse, ready for my bed and some much-needed sleep before starting over again tomorrow.

Arriving home, I flip on the hall light and throw my stuff on the bench I'd picked up at a garage sale, thinking it was a good buy that I could redo as a DIY. Alas, it still sat unpainted and chipped from wear. It was on the never-ending to-do list.

"*Mija*, is that you?" my father's gravelly voice calls from the den he often frequents.

"Si, Papá." I walk into the den to see his form lying back on his recliner where he often sleeps.

"How was work?" He leans to sit forward, and the chair pushes him slightly. I grab his shoulder to help balance him and sit on the small ottoman he keeps beside the chair. I used to sit on it as a kid and listen to his and my mother's stories. I think he keeps it here just so I'll sit close.

"It was busy." I smile and give him a reassuring pat on the hand, not wanting to give him grief over what I concluded with this week's earnings. He's still in the restaurant every single day, though his duties are more office related work anymore, he does occasionally serve a table or two, wanting to keep up with the town and the people.

He's a beloved figure and makes a point to know everyone who enters his restaurant. I swear it's the reason that we are so popular. It took a bit for him to get back to it after Mom, but once he did, it was like no time had passed.

"Everything going okay on the night shifts?"

"Yeah, it was busy, but the staff handles it like champs." I smile and stand, giving him a kiss. "But we both need sleep."

"I will, soon." He gives me a smile and looks back to the show on the TV. One of the soap operas my mom used to love. It was her guilty pleasure.

"Okay, Papá."

I turn and leave him be, silently wishing I could help him move on, and knowing that a love like theirs isn't something he could move on from.

HE WAS BACK. For the third day in a row, Ford Gentry graced one of my barstools and drank away whatever worries were eating at him. It was sad to witness. I knew for a fact that drinking feelings away wasn't going to help him. Something was clearly bothering him; it wasn't like anyone who was watching couldn't figure that out.

Ford sat with his back to the rest of the restaurant, his hat pulled low and his face hidden by a propped hand. This wasn't the man I remembered. The Ford I knew was peppy, a jokester, a guy who only wanted to make everyone else happy.

Maybe there was more to him than I'd ever thought, knowing that there was so much time I didn't see him, I realize there could have been things that had happened in the last sixteen years to make him this ghost of a man. God knows the years had changed my demeanor.

I was walking back over to his side when he spoke for the first time. "Do you remember me?" The question was guarded and low, like he wasn't sure he wanted me to.

I hesitated, not sure what to tell him when he locked eyes with me. They were pools of brown that made it impossible not to stare. His eyes held so much pain that I suddenly felt like crying. Or hugging him. Instead, I shrug my shoulders and give him the most honesty I can. "I never forgot."

His eyes widen slightly with surprise, but quickly, his mask slips back on and with a nod, he turns back to his drink without another word, while I stand there for a moment confused. I open my mouth to say more, what, I don't know, but something along the lines of "Where the hell have you been?" or "What are you doing here?" Before I can ask either of those questions though, Lizzie, my best friend, calls my name and drags my attention away.

I turn to walk away with a quick glance over my shoulder at Ford's slumped form. Lizzie gives me a wide-eyed look, and I suspect she's finally realized who's camped out at our bar. I take her arm and guide her to the back, while she finishes fastening her apron for her shift.

"What the hell? Ford Gentry is back?" Her words tumble out excitedly. I wasn't the only one captivated by him back in the day. Like I said, he was popular.

"Uh, yeah," I reply. "But look, you can't say a word, okay? He's not ready." I don't know why the defensive words tumble out, why I'm trying to protect him, but I do it anyway.

"Um, okay?" Lizzie looks at me like she's trying to figure me out, her blue gaze digging into my brown like she can make me break. She can. She's done it a million times, but I hold steady. "Whatever you say, boss." Her snarky response makes me laugh at her.

"I'm not your boss." The familiar response to the barb relaxes my tense muscles.

She follows me out of the back room and back into the restaurant where people wait to be seated, we've officially hit lunch rush and the door starts opening as a fairly steady stream of people filter in on their lunch breaks from wherever they've come from. "Except that you kinda are…"

"Whatever." I smirk. "Get to work."

With a loud laugh, Lizzie gets busy, and I try to keep my gaze discreet when it strays to Ford Gentry.

4

FORD

THREE WEEKS SINCE my return and the only thing I've reacquainted myself with is Delaney Torrez's gorgeous self. Though not as well as I'd really like to.

She's been my secret angel, hiding me in plain sight away from the prying eyes of everyone in this town. It was surprising how little they seemed to care, but I stuck to my side of the bar while keeping my hat tugged low.

The only day I wasn't at this bar was Thursdays, and that was at Delaney's insistence. I wasn't sure why, but when I hadn't listened, thinking it was something stupid, I'd nearly run smack into my parents. Apparently, it was their new tradition to eat there every Thursday night.

It had caught me off guard because when I was home they never went out to eat, that was always a treat for the family, only something we would do after a big event or a celebration.

I didn't know how Delaney figured out I hadn't yet seen my parents, though my life was pretty pathetic right now. Practically living at a bar, lusting after a woman I'd never have and pining over my life.

It isn't hard to remember when things started to change for me. It was, however, not something I had accepted.

I didn't want this asshole to tag along with me. I could pick her up myself, from what we knew, she wasn't even a threat but just someone who'd gotten mixed up with the wrong people. I knew that she was one of the good ones, so I personally made it my responsibility to pick her up. My best friend had turned her over with the intent and knowledge that I would be there, and I didn't intend to let him down.

But Perk was here, and he was a grade A douche who didn't know how to talk to anyone without using blunt force.

"Are you Margaret Davis?" he yelled as he stormed out of the car. Fucker. I got out and made my way around the vehicle, trying to put myself between them, but by the time I was there, he was already shoving her in the back seat.

"Chill the fuck out, Perk. She's not a threat."

"You don't know that." He spit back in my face. In front of anyone else, he was a model citizen. But I knew better. He was just an asshole who deserved to be put in his fucking place. I swallow down what I want to do

to him and hop in the front seat, taking us back to the safe house.

When we arrive, Margaret knocks me on my ass. Not really, because she really doesn't stand a chance. But her snarky response to shooting me has me grinning for the first time in weeks. I can see why Liam got caught up with this firecracker.

This whole incident was ridiculous but that was because I knew Liam personally. I knew he wouldn't turn his back on his country for anything. Not money, not people. This girl was just in the wrong place at the wrong time, and I knew she hadn't had anything to do with what was actually going on. I'd bet my life he sent her here knowing I'd be around to help run interference. In all the time I'd ever known him, he'd never shown interest in being with anyone for more than a night. It was why he was a perfect candidate for undercover ops.

I lead her into the house, intending on helping her get us to Liam, to get my best friend on the right side of the law again. When she reveals what she knows, we immediately move for the door. And that's when everything went to hell.

The memory of the first time I'd seen Margaret, and failed her, swaths me in a cloak of guilt. I know now that what I'd been feeling wasn't really attraction to her, it was attraction to the idea of a partner, to this power of protecting someone I could actually care about more than surface level. It was jealousy that Liam had found that person who could put up with his life, who would do whatever she could to help him. He had found someone who'd love him no matter what he's done.

I sigh and rub my eyes when I feel someone watching me.

"Want another?" Delaney's kind voice asks me. She doesn't judge the fact that I've been here damn near every day. And when I nod my head, she just gives me a kind smile and refills my glass.

And not for the first time, I wish I could get myself together. If not for me, but for this woman in front of me who could be the answer to a lot of my problems.

I COULDN'T BRING myself to do it. I watched from afar as my mother watered her plants. She had a specific time she watered them every single morning and I'd found myself parked down the road to see her each time.

Desperately, I wanted to walk up there and let her put her arms around me. Her fresh flower scent that has always accompanied her would envelop me and finally I would be able to breathe normally again. It's been too fucking long since I'd been able to do that.

Leaving the way I did, knowingly putting my family's hearts on the line. I'd broken their trust, and I had no doubt about that. But I couldn't stick around. After the accident that had nearly ruined my brother's life, the guilt was too much to take. Maybe they didn't hate me, maybe in the last decade and a half, they had moved on, but I wasn't ready to chance that they hadn't.

Now, I just couldn't bring myself to go back in there. To the home that was my comfort zone, that was the place I swore to my mother I'd never leave, which made her laugh and tell me, *"Honey, I'd be glad if you stayed. But you're still gonna have to learn to do your own laundry."*

That was who my mama was though, she'd adopt a hundred children if they needed her to. Our house was that one house that was the place to be, the place to hang out when we were stupid teenagers and thought we knew everything.

I beat back the achy feeling in my chest and refocus when I see my mom go back into the house. Sighing, I let my head fall back onto the headrest. I wasn't even sure why I'd come back here. I could hardly breathe in this town, so why was I torturing myself? When did my life go to shit? It wasn't all of a sudden, I know that. I've been struggling with this for years.

It had all started with the accident. It was a stupid, never should have happened kind of accident. I can remember every detail like it was playing on the TV. Mom and Dad were out of town, not far, but about an hour south in Houston celebrating their anniversary and I was in charge of Jack, my little brother who looked up to me far more than he should have.

He was eight, old enough in our small town to hang out home alone for an hour or two so I could go hang out with my friends. We were nearing the end of our senior year and most of my friends were heading to college. Time was slipping away and while I was ready for the next chapter of my life, I was also a little sick thinking about leaving the home I'd known for every day of my eighteen years.

When he'd begged me not to leave him home alone, I had begrudgingly decided to bring him along and cursed the fact that I had to. I'd wanted some time with my friends, with Delaney. Taking my little brother was not on the top of my priorities list.

But I knew my mom and dad would kill me if they found out I left him home and they would also kill me if they found out I took him, so I'd stupidly chosen the latter choice.

I should have just stayed home.

We only made it two miles from home when it happened. I was driving through an intersection on a green light, and from the corner of my eye, I saw the headlights. Before I could do more than grab on to Jack's chest with my arm, pinning him to the seat even though his seat belt was on, we were plowed into, spinning us through the intersection. Jack's screams were piercing the air and even now, I have to squeeze my eyes shut at the sound that runs through my head. By the time my parents had arrived at the hospital, Jack had been in surgery for four hours, the driver of the other car had been arrested for drinking and driving, and I had nearly lost my damn mind. All I'd gotten was a broken fucking wrist, and they were in there performing surgery on my brother's spine to see if they could repair it enough for him walk again.

My mother came in, tears already streaming down her face. My father was stoic. He put his arms around me and my mother, holding us both tight, and for that moment, I allowed myself to feel grief. Even though all I deserved to feel was guilt.

Eventually, Delaney had shown up, her mother with her to

comfort my parents. And I'd numbly allowed her to hold my hand while we waited. I didn't say a word and thankfully, she didn't push me, not even once. Just sat there and waited with me while my brother's fate was resting in the doctors' hands. Eventually, Bobby was there too, sitting on the other side of me and silently showing his support. We were eighteen. This shit wasn't supposed to happen this young.

Finally, after hour eight, the doctor emerged telling us that with the severity of the damage, Jack ever walking again would be a miracle, but the good news was he was alive.

Yeah, he was alive, but he may never walk again. So what living could he really do? After seeing my brother lying in that hospital bed, my whole life had flipped upside down and shaken sideways.

The second I was done with high school and officially eighteen, I'd signed my name on the dotted line and never once looked back at my horrid senior year. I wasn't myself anymore. I wasn't happy-go-lucky Ford Gentry. I'd been through shit I couldn't handle and I needed out.

My parents were informed of my well-being from year to year. I wasn't a total asshole; I knew that mom would die if I never told her I was still living. Hurting my folks though wasn't an easy pill to swallow. It was hard to do it, but there wasn't a choice when you were solely responsible for paralyzing your little brother.

And that's why I turn the rental car back on and headed back the way I came. I wasn't ready.

I wasn't sure I'd ever be.

5

DELANEY

HE WAS BACK. And I was ready for him to talk. It wasn't my place, probably, but the fact of the matter was he was in my bar, my space, and had been for a month. The only nights he didn't frequent the barstool was Thursday nights, and that was when I had to bald-faced lie to his mother whenever the question, "What's new?" crossed her lips.

Melissa Gentry was a kind woman who would quite literally give you the clothes off her back to help a person in a bind. I wouldn't lie to her anymore, not for anyone. As much as I sympathized with Ford's need to ease into this town again, his parents were an entirely different case.

"How ya doing?" I asked casually as I wiped a glass and stacked it with the rest. The mundane task held my emotions in check when impatience tried to rear its ugly head. *Why are you hiding from your family?* I wanted to scream the words, but one psychology class I'd had to take in school was weaseling its way through my brain, reminding me that forcing an issue on someone was the wrong way to get through.

Ford eyed me warily and sipped the whiskey he favored. His glazed eyes told me enough, that the whiskey was still doing a bang-up job in letting him forget and relax, but I was ready to help him push himself out of this nasty slump he'd climbed into. "Fine." His voice was so low if I hadn't been staring at his lips at that moment, I wouldn't have been able to tell what he said.

"You do anything fun lately?" I ask, continuing to work on random things on that side of the bar. The restaurant only had a few patrons tonight, it was Tuesday and not our busiest night, so Lizzie and Matteo were able to take care of everything else while I interrogated my best customer and old friend. I was crazy for doing this, you don't have to tell me.

"No." It was almost comical the way he was grunting out his answers. Honestly, the fact that he was even giving me anything had me surprised.

"How's your mama been?" I wasn't very subtle, but around here, asking about someone's mama was customary.

"I don't know, Delaney. How's yours?"

I pause in my movements and look at him then, I'm sure my expression was less than friendly. He gives me a smirk before returning to staring at the bar. That was a low blow, especially since I hadn't even started with the hard-fucking questions yet. I felt my temper rise and swallowed the anger that wanted to explode out of me. Tears prick my eyes in anger and hurt. He knew, he *fucking knew,* how much my mom meant to me and if I could find the words to hurt him back, I would…. *Hell.* No. I wouldn't. Because that's not me. But none of that meant I had to put up with him sitting in my bar.

Turning, I picked up the bar phone and called the number for a cab. It was time for him to go. As badly as I wanted to be the one who broke back into my ex-best friend's hard shell, I wasn't going to suffer the abuse from him to get it done.

Before I could finish dialing the number, I heard the apology slip from his mouth. "Delaney," he says, trying to get my attention again. I hang up the phone and turn.

"What, Ford?" His name hasn't been said aloud from me since he came back, but I had been doing that purposely so that I wouldn't slip to anyone who came in with questions on their lips.

"I'm sorry. That was a dick thing to say." His eyes held mine and their sea color held me for a moment before I shook my head and replied.

"Yeah. It was."

Another song filters through the speakers and we stare at each other for a moment, listening to the lyrics, coincidentally about a broken heart being healed by whiskey, before he opens his mouth again. "I haven't seen them."

I'd suspected he hadn't, otherwise he'd have been here on Thursdays as well. I almost dropped it though, why should I even care? If his family found out, it had nothing to do with me. And at this point, his attitude was more getting on my nerves than enduring. But, the old Delaney, the one who wanted to fix everyone's problems but her own, the one who at one point loved this person, couldn't hold back. "Why not?"

A shrug and a shake of the head was all he wanted to five me, but it wasn't enough. "Why not, Ford?"

Sighing, he looks past me like somewhere on the wall of liquor is the answer he so badly seeks, but that's the issue, that's what's gotten him this far. "I'm not ready."

I furrow my brows and lean on the bar, not directly in front of him, because despite being a full-grown woman, I wasn't ready to admit that I was still highly attracted to him, even given his current state. "Ready for what, exactly?"

"I'm not ready for the disappointed look from my father, or my mother, or my brother. I'm not ready to apologize."

"Apologize for what?" I ask, genuinely confused.

"For *everything.*" His voice cracks on the word and my eyes heat with compassion for him. "For abandoning them. For hurting my brother. For not coming back."

His answer has me pausing, I wasn't expecting that. "You haven't been back, like, at all?"

Ford looks at me then, and I hold his eyes. "Not really, no."

For the first time that I can remember, I'm speechless. This man hasn't been home since high school? That doesn't seem even remotely possible. I mean, I know I was out of it with my own tragedies, but damn, we're thirty-four years old. High school wasn't just a few years, it was forever ago. I try to imagine just leaving and not looking back. Not seeing my father for that long, I honestly can't picture that. I would be heartbroken. *Poor Mrs. Gentry.* She was probably devastated.

"You need to go home, Ford."

He shakes his head again. "I can't, Laney. I'm not ready."

I shake off his use of my nickname before I let it take root. "Ford." I say his name sternly and wait for him to look at me. "You need to go home." Holding him with my stare, I try—in the gentlest of ways—to get him to understand me. I'm not being mean, I'm thinking of his family. They need him.

"Laney," he replies. And then, like the asshole he is, he taps his drink.

"You're cut off, Ford."

I should've done it hours, hell, days ago, but this time it's for real. He needs to pull his head out of his ass. I'm not about to sit around and watch this man drink himself to death. He has responsibilities that he needs to take care of, and I'll be damned if he doesn't buck up and do it.

He throws down a wad of cash, one far too big for what he drank and stalks out of the bar without another word. I sigh and stand there for a moment. I wish I could help him with whatever was bothering him.

But you can't help someone who doesn't want to be helped.

I'VE OFFICIALLY SCARED him off. It's been four days since Ford has stepped through the doors of *El Abrevadero* and I can't help but wonder where he went. His family had been here Thursday night, as usual, this time with Jack in tow. Must be the end of his school year, I knew he was in graduate school, but other than that I was clueless.

I'd put on a cheerful face for them as I always did and served them myself, call it punishment for pushing their son too hard, but I had felt like I owed them something. I knew logically I wasn't the reason that Ford hadn't gone home. My pushing wasn't like I was pushing him away, I'd truly wanted to help.

But I won't lie. I was worried about where Ford had gone, since I hadn't seen him in the bar, I wasn't able to keep an eye on him and I didn't realize I'd been that concerned until this moment when I waited restlessly for him to walk through the door.

"Just go." Lizzie startles me from behind and I turn, giving her a questioning glare.

"Go where?"

She snorts. "Please. To Ford, obviously. Don't think we haven't noticed that he hasn't been gracing our barstool the last few nights." She hip checks me and waves her hand, reaching under the bar for my purse and shoving me toward the door. "Go find our boy and make sure he's okay."

I hesitate for a moment, but then I let her words push me through the door. Her nudge was the permission I'd been waiting on. Because despite the harsh words he'd spoken, or the ones I shoved down his throat, I was worried about him.

Being the one to help him get home many a time, I knew where he was staying. At least, it was where he'd been the last time I had to give a cab driver an address. The motel parking lot is mostly abandoned except for a black car that sits untouched in front of door '34'. The car was familiar because I'd seen it left behind in front of the restaurant many of the nights he was too drunk to drive it home. I couldn't for the life of me understand why he was staying in one of the most run-down motels this town had, I wondered briefly if that was why he was so down on himself. Maybe he'd run out of money and that was why he was home. Maybe he was washed-up from the military and didn't have a dime to his name. Maybe he was dishonorably discharged. But glancing at the sleek vehicle he drives around town when he was actually sober, I knew that wasn't true. He had money, the truth had to be that he just didn't want to be found.

I walk up to the door and raise my hand to knock before I notice a sliver of light spilling through it. A pool of dread swirls in my stomach. There's no reasonable explanation for this door to be cracked.

Shoving it open and peering inside, the smell that attacks

my senses is overwhelming and I lift a hand to cover my nose to protect myself from its rancidness. The room that had probably once been in okay shape is now trashed, *literally*. It's littered with bottles and fast-food wrappers, and I notice a suitcase spilling over with clothes both clean and not.

The only indication of life in the room is the light snore coming from the bed, Ford—at least, I hope—is lying there completely unaware that he has company. It rattles me that he's passed out and his door was irresponsibly left wide open for anyone to come inside, though, responsibility hasn't exactly been his strong suit as of late.

I have no doubt that he's drunk as hell. It shows in the half-empty bottle of *Seagrams—ick—*sitting on the rickety nightstand. The TV is on at a low murmur, the news broadcasting the weather for the coming week, and if the circumstances were different, I would say that he was just relaxing.

Walking to the side of the bed he's closest to, I reach a hand out to nudge his shoulder. When he doesn't budge, I whisper his name. Again, he doesn't move and I sigh before giving a heavier shove. "For—" My voice is cut off when he's suddenly up with his hands against my shoulders, holding me firmly to the wall.

"Ford," I whisper, trying to get him to focus. My eyes tear up and I grab hold of his wrists that press against me so hard that pain shoots through my shoulders. I say his name again and again, trying to calm him down enough to realize where he's at. His eyes finally clear enough to tell me he's fully awake and he stumbles away from me, shock and confusion covering his face.

"Laney." He slurs out the nickname. All of a sudden, his eyes turn hard and accusing toward me. "What the hell are you doing sneaking up on me?"

I open my mouth to answer, but I can't. The man I knew when he was just a teenager, had never looked like this. The anger in him overpowers the space, and I suddenly feel a trickle of fear racing down my spine.

Like he can sense it, his eyes widen in realization and he steps back even farther, standing up straight before taking a step away. "You shouldn't be here."

I rub my neck subconsciously. "I wanted to make sure you were okay."

Ford looks around the room and looks at me with a snort. "Just go, Laney."

Ford stumbles over to the bed and sits, or falls, back onto the bed. I see a key card to the room on the dresser and snatch it up, knowing the only way to reason with him is to get him somewhat sober.

"I'll be back," I say, waiting for him to reply. When he gives me a wave, I take it as "okay" and not "go away" and rush out the door. I don't know why I'm making this my responsibility, it's not like I don't already have a million things in my own life to worry about. Despite that though, I add 'Make Ford talk' to my ever-growing list.

6

DELANEY

I DECIDE TO wait until morning before going back, considering he was passed out before I'd even left the room, I figured the best cure for a nasty hangover was sleep. He was in a bad way last night. I don't know what is getting to him, what demons are hovering over him like a dark cloud, but I know that the Ford I once knew isn't the one who's back.

Maybe it's childish to want to find that person again, to bring back the happy-go-lucky guy I once knew. Despite that, I find myself back at his motel bright and early the next morning.

The door is still shut, so I take the card I stole and after a quick unanswered knock on the door, I let myself in. He's still in the same position I left him in and a sliver of panic hits, I rush to him and check his pulse, sighing with relief when I feel one.

This guy is going to give me a heart attack.

I take several steps back and call out his name until he stirs, not wanting to risk him panicking and pinning me to the wall again. That may have been the scariest thing I've ever experienced.

"How you doing, bud?" *Bud? Really, Delaney?* I shake my head at myself and look him over. He looks like absolute hell.

I hand over a large coffee with the works and tell him to get to drinking the good stuff. "That's what got me into this mess."

Letting out a laugh, I say, "Nah, this is the real good stuff. Whiskey can't hold a candle to coffee."

Working in a bar, I could easily succumb to the easiness of drinking all the time. But I've seen far too often the people who let themselves get too far gone with that stuff. Maybe that's why I was here, maybe I didn't want to see Ford become like the rest of them, letting this sickness take control of his life.

I give him a minute to wake up and look him over, despite the fact that he looks like he's in rough shape, he's still a sight. I remember like it was yesterday the first time that Ford talked to me for real. We'd known each other forever, from the time we started kindergarten to our senior year. Somehow, he and I were thrown together more often than not and Bobby was our third stooge. We all worked so well as friends together.

It was junior high when my feelings started to feel like more than just friends. But I never said a word, not to him or anyone else. It was the Sadie Hawkins—yes, we did that in our small school—and I had a big ol' speech to give him.

However, I was a little slow. Sandy Wilson beat me to it and he was smitten. For about three months, but it still broke my poor little heart. Luckily, Bobby took pity on me and went with me so I could still feel like I did the right thing. I'd be lying if I said that as Bobby led me around in a circle on the dance floor that I didn't watch Ford blush when Sandy whispered in his ear, they left and never came back.

It was short-lived when she started telling him he couldn't hang out with me or Bobby. So everything went back to normal pretty quick. I went to his and Bobby's games, to Ford's parents' house, they came to dinner at mine, we did our homework in the bar together, anything we could do together, we did. Falling in love with Ford was easy, it was the falling out that had hurt so damn bad.

Which, once again, makes me question my sanity in why I want to help him so damn bad.

"What are you doing here?" Ford's voice breaks me out of my thoughts, and I refocus on his eyes, they're so blue it's hard to focus on anything else.

I clear my throat and look around the room. Shrugging, I answer, "I'm here to help."

A scoff leaves his lips. "I don't need your help."

I stand straighter and give him a look. "You need to stop, Ford."

"Why the hell do you care?"

I try to ignore his words, trying to steer him away from that conversation, knowing that the answer isn't so black and white. I grab one of the trash cans and start throwing his bottles, empty or not, into it. He protests weakly at me throwing his alcohol away, and I ignore anything from him. "You need a shower," I say pointedly, channeling my inner mom-look toward him, going for intimidating. "Then, I may just reward you."

"Reward me, huh?" I didn't realize he'd gotten up from the bed but feel his hot breath on the back of my neck.

I fight down the blush I know is gracing my cheeks when I realize what I said, with as much confidence as I can muster, I turn to face him, looking him straight in his eyes, I say, "With food. Don't get too many ideas."

He stares for a moment before slowly backing away, on the tip of his tongue, I know there's a retort waiting to be set free, but instead, he spins around and heads to the bathroom.

FORD COMES OUT of the bathroom with a billow of steam trickling out behind him, nothing but the towel wrapped around his waist that barely covers anything and I have to force myself to look away from him. I continue my straightening of his room and turn from him when he bends to get clean clothes out of his suitcase.

I nearly swallow my tongue when he turns away slightly and just drops his towel to the floor. "Ford!"

A chuckle sounds behind me and I can't fight the smile that slips onto my lips. "What? It's nothing you haven't seen before."

While this is true, it doesn't stop the blush that spreads up my neck and into my cheeks. "Not without a little foreplay first." The words leave me before I have a chance to censor myself.

"Oh really?" Suddenly I'm surrounded by the scent of him, that hot guy musk that only they can have after a shower. How do they do that? "I think I can help out there."

I don't turn, but I can feel his smile from here. "Get dressed, Ford. I'm hungry." With another chuckle, he makes his way back to the bathroom, leaving me to try to catch my breath and calm down. He's definitely going to give me a heart attack.

7

FORD

DELANEY TORREZ WAS trying to save me.

It was adorable and pretty fruitless, but it was fun to watch her try, nonetheless. I'd been holed up in this motel for the last week… at least, I *think* it's been a week. I'd stopped leaving it ever since that night at the bar when she started pushing, started prying, and I didn't want to hear it. Not after she'd been offering me solace for the last few weeks, my safe place had suddenly become the one place I didn't want to be.

I'd thought she just didn't care that much, that she didn't give a shit why I was getting drunk nearly every night at her bar, as long as I paid my tab and didn't cause any scenes.

Boy, was I so fucking wrong. Looking back, I remember

her watching me, looking out for me. Always serving my third whiskey with a glass of water, every fifth with a plate of food. She was playing the long game and I don't even know if she knew she was doing it.

Showing up last night was quite the surprise, though it's a bit of a blurry memory today, but I remembered her coming over, I remember what I did and I don't think I'll ever be able to let go of the regret I feel when I think of the way I treated her.

When I come out of the bathroom, this time fully dressed, she's hanging up her phone and waiting by the door, purse over her shoulder and looking flawlessly beautiful regardless of the fact that the woman works more hours than anyone I've ever met.

"Ready?" she asks, not looking me in the eye.

Swallowing a bit of my pride, I say, "I'm really sorry, Laney." She looks up in surprise and furrows her brow slightly. "For last night," I clarify and her eyes soften toward me.

"It's my fault, I snuck up on you."

"It's no excuse." I wait for her to say something about how scary it was or how she thought I might kill her, but she doesn't, just shrugs her shoulders in a way that lets me know she's okay and opens the door with a gesture for me to follow her.

I pull the door shut and she walks us to her car. "Let's take mine," I say when she reaches the driver's side.

She gives me a scrutinizing look. "I'd rather drive, if that's alright."

Realizing she's referencing how much I've been drinking, I

nod and go for the passenger side and try to hide the shame that I feel welling up inside me. She doesn't even trust me to drive her, when once upon a time, she trusted me with everything.

We ride in silence to a diner that's outside of town about ten minutes, it's a breakfast and lunch diner that people frequent constantly. Sometimes we'd get up early before school and come here. It brings back memories I'd forced myself to forget.

We reach the diner and I rush around, trying to open her door before she can do it. She tries to hide her surprise and thanks me with a mumble. After we're seated in a booth, we both silently read over our menus, I try to focus on the words, on picking food but my eyes keep going up over the top to get a glimpse of her. Delaney grew up into this radiant person. It wasn't just the fact that she was beautiful, and she is, but it was how she acted, how she treated people that I think drew me to her in the first place.

My phone starts to vibrate on the table and I glance at it, seeing Gemma's name pop up, I groan, reaching over to silence it. The last thing I need is Gemma James to give me a fucking lecture about finding myself.

"What'll you have?" The waitress rushes over and asks with a wide grin pointed in my direction. I direct her to Delaney who hides an eye roll and orders, stifling my chuckle, I rattle off my order and turn my attention back to Delaney who looks more perturbed than I've seen her before.

"You okay?"

"Nothing's changed."

I quirk my brow, enjoying watching her face grow annoyed. "What are you talking about?"

"Getting special treatment because you're a pretty boy." She lays it out so flatly and with the most serious face that I can't help but bust out laughing right there in the middle of the diner. Patrons look on with amusement on their faces, and Delaney looks so embarrassed right now that it makes me laugh harder.

"Damn, I missed you busting my balls," I say without thinking. I expect a retort from her but she just shrugs and we sit there in silence for a while longer. It's not uncomfortable, my little outburst having broken the awkwardness. I have a headache from hell still, but past that, I'm pretty pleased with where I'm at right now.

Coming back was a scary decision, but if I can get this back, this wonderful person whom I was an idiot to leave behind, who should absolutely hate my guts, then coming home will have been worth it.

"So," she starts, breaking the silence. "What made you come home?"

"Just diving right in, huh?" I tease. I'm not ready to break and tell her about my demons, I'm not ready to face everything that has my chest constricting right now.

"Well, you've been here for some time. I figured you might have been ready to work things out by now." Delaney pauses and looks at me like she's trying to figure out my story without me voicing anything. "Why haven't you seen your mama yet?"

Her Texas twang—slight as it is—distracts me for a moment

before I can think of an answer that won't sound like some sort of excuse. "I'm not ready."

"Ford," she starts, thinking about what she wants to say if the bite of her bottom lip tells me anything. "I don't even know what to say. I know that before you left, both of our lives kind of went to shit… I know that. I also know that you've needed time to come to terms with… whatever it is your dealing with. And I just wanted to give you that peace."

I shake my head in question. "Why have you been protecting me?" The question's been on my mind for days. Delaney doesn't owe me a thing and yet, she's been my biggest saving grace since I entered Texas territory.

"I don't know." She runs her finger over the lip of her coffee cup. "I guess I would want someone to help me out if I was drowning too."

An emotion I'm not used to hits me at her words and I swallow hard. This woman still knows me better than anyone. She can see through every layer I've ever built around myself, she doesn't buy any bullshit I try to spew.

Our food coming interrupts our conversation, and I couldn't be more grateful for that than I am now. Delaney doesn't ask any more questions and I don't say anything about it either, we fill the silence with easy conversation, with the good memories of high school, with who from high school is left in town and who got out as soon as we graduated.

It's easy. Delaney makes everything easy. She makes breathing easier. Not once does she push me about my family and I'm grateful for her understanding.

But I know Delaney won't let it go forever.

8

DELANEY

IT WAS FAR too early for me to be up, but thoughts about life wouldn't let me get back to sleep. The sun was just starting to peek over the horizon and I was in our family den looking through old things. Maybe I was just being nostalgic, but I loved looking at old pictures. It reminded me of good times.

I admit, part of it was just trying to find pictures of us as kids. We have millions of them, it seems. Dating back to five years old. Me, Ford, and Bobby. Me standing in the middle while the other two stand there, Ford leaning forward, a cheeky grin showing off his dimples, me with a shy, more subdued smile on my face, and Bobby with his arms crossed and a scowl on his face. I smile at it, it's a perfect depiction of who we once were.

I find pictures in one of our yearbooks of him with one of his high school girlfriends in his arms, Amy was her name and she's married now with her fourth baby on the way. I wish I could say I hated her, but that would just be jealousy speaking when truthfully, she was a sweet person.

These photos make me sigh, they were pictures of good times. Of happier memories. It feels like the last decade or more we've been in this motionless bubble, unable to move forward. At least I feel that way anyway.

Yesterday he was finally starting to show his true colors, his laid-back side that I hadn't seen since he'd come home. It would be a shame if he lost his true self. Whatever was really bothering him, it was holding him tight in its grasp. I only hoped I could help him get out of the funk he was in.

Closing the yearbook, I look at the pile of photos I pulled out to get to it and pause, seeing one of my parents, one that I assume was before I was born. My mother was gorgeous, there's a reason my dad was smitten with her. They're standing with a man between them, one I've never seen before, and I furrow my brows. He's a handsome man, wearing a suit and from the photo, you can tell that the man exudes confidence, he's got his arms around my parents and my dad smiles at the camera, but Mom is stiff, her smile is forced and I wonder who the man is. Whoever it is, he made her uncomfortable.

I take the photo and put it in my pocket, reminding myself to ask my dad about it later.

With a sigh, I heave myself off the floor and grab a to-go coffee, ready to head into work.

Another day, another struggle.

NEARLY GROWLING IN frustration, I close the lid of my computer and put my head in my hands. No matter what I do, or how hard I work, we're still barely making ends meet. It doesn't help that I just had to dole out a huge chunk of cash to a plumber for the women's toilet. It was the last thing I wanted to spend money on, but I was left with few options.

I try to think about where the money could possibly be going. The numbers aren't adding up and haven't for months now. I need to have a serious conversation with my father.

I've been at it a few hours now when the door to the restaurant opens, it's nearly lunchtime, so it wouldn't be a surprise if we had a couple early guests. Sean, our resident chef is already in the kitchen with his staff, prepping. I get out of the chair I've been in all morning, glaring at the screen in front of me, and go to greet the new customers.

What I do find surprises me. "Ford," I say, my voice sounds breathless and I scold myself to keep my cool.

"Laney."

"What are you doing here? It's a bit early." I don't mean to scold him, it's not like I'm responsible for him but I don't like seeing him sit here day after day, drinking himself away.

"I was wondering if I could help out today?"

I raise a brow. "Help out?"

"Yeah, you know, serve food or clean or I don't know… something." He stuffs his hands into his jean pockets, I recognize a nervous gesture when I see one.

Ford needs something to stay occupied. And I'm not one to turn down help. "I can't really pay you."

He waves a hand at me. "I don't want that. I just want to help out. You've helped me. I want to return the favor."

I nod and give him an okay. He follows me to the back, and I get him an apron and a shirt with our logo. "Get changed and get ready to work." I give him a smirk and walk out toward the front, trying to tamp down the excitement that rises over the fact that he's here.

He just needs my help, I remind myself. He's not here for me.

SMOTHERING A LAUGH, I turn my back on the situation and try, try really hard, not to embarrass him any more than he already is. Ford is a hard worker, really, truly, he is. But waiter, he is not. Ford has spilled more food and drinks than anyone else has in the last year, he's messed up so many orders that I swear he's paying for their meals with his own money.

It's not necessarily funny, but for some reason, his determination is comical. After his eighth spilled drink though, I throw him a lifeline and call him over. He looks at me sheepishly. "I guess waiter won't be going on my resume."

I shake my head at him, a chuckle spilling out of me. "No, I don't think so."

"I'm so sorry." Though he's apologizing, he's laughing along with me.

"I have some kegs that need to be replaced, I think we can put that muscle to use instead." I lay my hand on his arm without thinking and direct him to where the kegs are. When he bends to get the empties, I stay stuck in my spot until I hear a throat clear. I whip my head up to see Lizzie, who gives me a look.

Rolling my eyes, I get back to work, and when my eyes stray to the six-foot two man on his knees behind the bar, I tell myself it's to make sure he didn't break anything. Not for any other reason.

"What's going on here?" My dad's voice startles me and I turn toward him, he's looking to where Ford is changing out the kegs and I wave a hand.

"Oh, he's just helping out today."

"Ford Gentry," he says, his eyes still on him.

"Yeah." I shift on my feet, suddenly feeling the need to justify his being here. "Great that he's here, right?"

My dad looks at me and takes my arms, leading me a few feet away. "His mother talks about him. Says he's in the FBI now. I thought you two had drifted apart." If I didn't know better, I would say my father was anxious about something. I shrug and look back to where Ford is still installing the keg.

"I don't really know what's going on, honestly. But he needs some help right now."

"I don't like it. Plus, we can't afford more people." He takes a handkerchief out of his pocket and wipes his forehead.

"He's working for free, Papá."

With a grunt and a rare glare, Dad heads back toward his office and I stand there, confused and intrigued as to why my dad is bothered by Ford's presence. Our families used to be tight until my mom died, after that and Jack, everything seemed to crumble.

9

FORD

IT WAS SIMPLE, really. I couldn't get her off my mind.

It wasn't that she said or did anything in particular that made me feel this way, it was more of just her presence that I enjoyed. Delaney had a way about her that made me comfortable, she always had. There was something that called me to her that said, *'home'*.

I was ashamed of my actions. Allowing anyone to see me in the state I was in the other night was despicable. But letting her see me that way? It was downright wrong. And I swore I wouldn't let it happen ever again.

Having her as a distraction was both a blessing and a curse, I'd never failed at any job before but I couldn't focus on a single task she gave me. It was almost worth every screwup because every spilled drink and messed up order, she let loose a laugh I couldn't get enough of.

Finally, when the restaurant closes down and the last of the staff leaves, I linger around, waiting for her. It's not like I was planning on working here all day, but once I got into a rhythm, helping sling drinks and restocking the kegs, I found I didn't mind the work. It also felt good to be in her company, it felt almost like old times. The days we'd hang out here in this very place and do homework, laughing and distracting each other from our work.

Watching Delany was a highlight. She smiled at every customer, she was friendly and engaging. No wonder everyone was here every night, it was the place to be and that was all because of the gorgeous woman who ran the place.

Her father was here too. Until the time before he went home, and every time he saw me, he gave me a glare. I'd gone up to reintroduce myself, which was met with a brief head nod and a nervous shuffle toward the back. It had my hair standing up on the back of my neck.

In my line of work, I could tell when someone was hiding something from a mile away. It was kind of my specialty and came in damn handy. Liam called me the human lie detector for years. That is, when we were working together. I missed that dude.

My thoughts are interrupted when the beautiful brunette comes out from the back, bag slung over her shoulder. The smile on her face is tired but relaxed, and I give her a smirk of my own. The girl I'd left behind all those years ago was now replaced with this gorgeous woman standing in front of me, and I found myself more intrigued by her than ever. I expected myself to panic over that little thought, but the only thing I wanted to do was follow that thought with promises I wasn't sure I should be making.

"Good night?" I ask, following her out the front door.

"Great night." A happy sigh leads her out the door I hold for her, and I wait for her to lock it before she turns to me. "Thanks for the help."

I let out a laugh. "You mean once I started helping you make money instead of spend it?"

A laugh escapes her and she shakes her head at me. "Yeah, I guess so."

We fall into a comfortable silence and I can't get the smile off my face, not that I care to anyway. "What?"

Her voice wakes me out of my trance and I just shrug. "Nothing." I look around for another car and only see my rental. "You need a ride?"

"Oh no, that's okay. I'm not far."

My eyebrows furrow on their own. "You walk home every night?"

She gives me a wide-eyed look. "Yeah, when I need to. Dad needs the car."

I can see her testing me. She's seeing if I'm going to give her a lecture, so being the wise man I am, I keep my mouth shut and go to open my passenger door. "Come on." I nod toward the door.

Delaney looks like she's considering arguing with me but decides not to, quickly jumping into the car with a suffering sigh. "I'm not forcing you to," I say, peering down at her from where I'm standing holding the door.

"Oh sure."

"I'm not, here." I stand back and give her room to get out, holding back the smile that wants to break free.

She looks like she's about to get out when I shut the door and round the front. A laugh breaks free when I see her stunned look and hear the shout from her.

When I get in the car, she's giving me a look of disbelief. "What?" I question innocently. She may think she has some sort of control, but I wouldn't have let her walk home alone this late.

"What, what? You know exactly what." She sits facing forward and I can see a smile trying to break out but she does her best to keep it in.

"I have no idea. I'm just giving a beautiful woman a ride home in the middle of the night, so she doesn't get jumped on the side of the road." I don't even try to hide my smile.

"Beautiful woman, huh? Boy, that charm just pours out without you even tryin', don't it?" Her murmur is quiet and I just keep my comments to myself. In a short time, I've realized that I think more of Delaney than any woman I've ever known. It's not just attraction, though that's there as well, but it's respect. The woman works harder than anyone I know and does it with a smile on her face.

Even when I was a complete asshole to her, she still went out of her way to make sure I wasn't trying to kill myself.

We pull up in front of her house not even five minutes later and she sits silently next to me, her head is leaned back and her eyes are closed and she looks seconds away from falling asleep. "You alright, Laney?"

My voice rouses her from her almost slumber. She gives me a sleepy smile that does more to me than even I want to admit. "Yeah, sorry." A chuckle escapes her as she unbuckles her seat belt. "I could drop at any second."

"Well, we don't want that." I hop out of the car and open her door, she gives me a confused look and says, "You don't have to open my doors."

I cluck my tongue. "My mama raised me better than that."

"What about the whole, let a woman take care of herself thing?"

"I personally don't think that's got shit to do with it. You could be the most feminist woman on the planet, that doesn't bother me. I believe, and have seen, you do everything for yourself. But I have little belief that me being a gentleman takes away from that." I pause when we reach her door and she looks up at me. "Me opening a door for a woman doesn't mean I'm in control of anything, if anything, it means you're the boss and I'm just the willing servant."

She opens her mouth to respond and then surprises me with a

laugh, it's loud and I can tell she's a little delirious from a lack of sleep but I wait patiently for her to get a hold of herself. It doesn't take long and she looks at me again, a smile still on her lips. "You surprise me every day, Ford Gentry."

"That's my aim, Delaney Torrez." We're close now, maybe closer than we've ever been, and I see in her eyes the thing she wants. I want it too, I can't deny it, but in the back of my mind, I know that I need to work a few things out before I start something.

Because when I do, I won't be able to walk away.

A FOREIGN FEELING hits me when I find myself behind Laney's bar again; I'm content for the first time in months. I mean, I was used to top-secret missions, having a gun on me twenty-four seven, scoping out some of the most dangerous people in the United States. But here, at the restaurant, I was almost happy.

I had a feeling it was more to do with the woman constantly busting my balls than actually liking making drinks and replacing kegs. Which was fine with me.

The worst part was I couldn't hide that I was back in town anymore, it was official, Ford Gentry was back and apparently it was news. People from my high school days came in just to confirm the rumor.

I knew it was only a matter of time before I needed to get

home, to tell my family I was back and beg for forgiveness. Delaney was my constant support in that, and I needed her to have my back more than I could say. I needed *her*. Every night I'd insisted on driving her home since that first night, and our talks had gotten more and more extensive. I'd learned how she was after her mom passed and how vital my own mother was in her healing. Apparently, my mother was still her amazing self, even at the time that I was pulling away.

Delaney was the one encouraging me to go see my parents. She didn't think they'd ever hold anything against me, but my fear was holding me back. Being rejected by my family scared the shit out of me, so I did the only logical thing, I avoided it.

"Ford," Delaney calls my name and I swear I melt just hearing her say it, but the tone is off and when I turn to look at her, the smile on my face slides away at the look on her face, it's one of empathy.

"What's up, Laney?" I ask once I'm closer. Before she can answer though, my name is called from another voice that instantly has my hair rising on the back of my neck. When I turn, I see my mother standing by the front door of the restaurant. The look on her face is hard to decipher, it's somewhere between sadness and disbelief.

"Mom," I say back, before I can even make a move, she's behind the bar and hugging the daylights out of me. I squeeze her back just as hard and look over her shoulder to see Delaney smiling at us, her eyes are misty but she gives me a nod as if to tell me it's okay.

"I can't believe you're here." My mom's voice is muffled, I can tell she's trying to hide from the onlookers. She's a strong woman who hates when she cries.

"I'm sorry, Mama." My voice unexpectedly cracks on the whisper. She leans back and looks me over; her face is shining with a happiness I wasn't ready for and relief courses through my veins.

"Oh baby," she says, clutching my cheeks. "You don't have to be sorry."

"Ford," Delaney gets my attention and I look over to her, embarrassed that she's seen me cry in my mom's arms, but at this point, she'd seen everything already so it didn't really matter. "Why don't you go home with your mom, catch up?"

I nod my head and look to Mom who looks beside herself happy. "Oh, please do. Your father didn't believe the rumors, he'll be so happy."

"Okay." I dig in my pocket and retrieve the keys to the rental and hand them to Delaney who looks at me confused. "Here, take the rental tonight. I want you to be safe."

"Ford," she scolds, grasping the keys. "I don't need your car."

"Neither do I." I look to Mom. "You'll give me a ride, right?"

She looks at me, surprised. "Oh, of course."

I smile at Delaney. "See, problem solved. I'll be back tomorrow."

Delaney pauses. "You don't have to." She clears her throat. "I mean, not now anyway."

I look her in the eyes and make sure I have her attention. "I'll be back tomorrow."

She tries and fails to hide a smile. With a small 'okay', I walk out with Mom and take a breath. One down, two to go. I just hope my dad and brother are as forgiving as Mom.

10

DELANEY

THE RESTAURANT WAS busy, as per the new usual, which didn't make any freaking sense. The till still wasn't adding up, and there wasn't any indication that anyone was stealing. I watched every single person, carefully. I vetted them all before hiring them. Well, except Lizzie. But I've known her since grade school, and she wouldn't even think of it.

I had to turn to Dad. I didn't want to, but he was partially responsible for it and now it had been going on too long to actually turn away from.

I found him in the back office, which is where he almost always stayed during busy hours. He loved being here, I think part of it made him feel closer to mom, but his inattention to detail and lack of caring made it hard for me to leave him here to take care of these things on his own.

It was why I knew that I'd be here forever, even though I had my own goals, my own dreams, I knew that it was more important for me to keep the Torrez family dream alive.

"Papá," I say when I enter the room. He greets me with a warm smile and looks away from the order sheets he has on the desk.

"*Mija.* How's it going out there?"

"Good. It's busy tonight."

"Good, good." He regards me and asks, "Something wrong?"

"Um, well, I've been noticing some of the numbers are off." I see him visibly stiffen and I wait.

"Don't worry about that, *mija.*"

"You know about it? Where's it going? We're barely making ends meet here." My voice rises and I can see him about to put up a fight. My talking back has never really been allowed and I've tried to keep things civil for the sake of our relationship but when it comes down to it, I'm the one running the restaurant and I'm the one who needs to know where every penny is going.

"Yes, it's a necessary expense. Soon enough, everything will be fine."

"Papá—"

I start but am cut off by his near shout of, "Enough!"

I shrink back a little. I may be a grown woman but I still don't like being scolded by my father. I sigh and open my mouth to respond when he cuts me off again.

"You don't need to worry about it, *mija*." His voice softens and I see that it took everything out of him to yell at me.

"Okay, Papá."

I leave but with the intention of coming back later. Despite the fact that he's now told me to drop it, I won't be able to. Not until the bills stop piling up and I stop being behind.

IT'S LATE, TOO late for customers to be coming into the restaurant, but that apparently doesn't stop the man who does. He moves across the restaurant to where I'm standing behind the bar closing up for the night. I give him a quick glance in the eyes before returning to my task. I'm too tired to deal with some drunk wanting a drink.

"You must be Delaney." His voice is low but certain and he leans against the bar like he owns it. I pause my end-of-the-night ritual and give him a look.

"We're closed, I'm sorry. You'll have to come back another time."

His chuckle is deep as he rises to his full height, his suit is pitch black and sharp. It looks expensive. "Not for me." I try to keep my cool, but chills scatter across my skin at his gaze.

"Rafael!" My father's voice startles me and Rafael, as I just learned, stands up straighter and his once alluring gaze turns stony at the presence of my father. He stayed later than ever, and I get the uneasy feeling this is why.

"Joaquín." His voice is steel toward my father and Rafael gives me a pointed look. My father takes the hint faster than me and shoves my purse into my arms.

"Go on home, *mija*."

"Papá," I protest.

"Delaney." His hard voice just adds to my confusion and I turn away from the man who's making my father uneasy, more questions than ever filter through my mind and I plan on waiting up until he gets home to start grilling him.

IT'S LATE, OR early, depending on which way you look at it. Papá still isn't home, and I can't seem to stop the pacing my feet need to do. My brain is in overdrive. He's never, ever been out this late before. I don't know who Rafael is, but there's no way they're just old buddies catching up. Their short exchange told me that.

He had a look about him that showed power, the vibe that came off of him was one that said not to fuck with him. He was terrifying. And the fact that he is alone with my father right now was not a good sign.

I didn't know who this guy was or why he was suddenly

commanding control over my father. But I knew that when I found out, I wouldn't like the answer.

11

FORD

THE MOMENT I stepped through the door to my childhood home, my father had his strong arms wrapped around me and despite myself, despite all the shit I've ever been through, I broke. I broke down right there in the living room of the home where I learned everything about life, about being a kind person, about taking care of people who you love, about being a decent human being, about showing your emotions and never being ashamed of it.

And I was ashamed. Not because I was crying on my father's shoulder, my mother's hands pressed into my back, giving me silent support. I was ashamed of how I'd treated my family. The people who loved me and whom I loved back.

A banging of the front door hitting the wall jolts us apart and with shock covering my face, my brother's flushed face appears. Standing in the doorway. Standing.

Though I didn't think it was possible, I break further and before I know how or what's happening, we're both moving toward each other, embracing. He's almost my height, his strength he uses to hold me up as I lean on him, allowing myself to feel every single painful bit of this reunion with my little brother whom I abandoned.

He should hate me. *Hate* me.

Instead, he lets me lean on him, lets me cry until I can't anymore and when I pull back, I see his own green eyes staring back at me, tears on his face as he stares like he's memorizing me and I sigh.

"I'm sorry." The hoarse apology feels like shit. It's not enough.

"Ford." He shakes his head, looking like he doesn't know what to say. I take stock of him, looking over how strong and capable he is. The only thing noticeable about his trauma from his eighth year of life is a cane that he seems to lean on.

My mom clears her throat and we both look at her, tears seem to be streaming steadily down her face and my father wipes his face with the palm of his hand. They come near us and we're all hugging then. All leaning on one another as emotions overwhelm us.

For the first time in years, I can take a big clear breath.

DELANEY WAS RIGHT, they would love me no matter what. Even after I'd spent years away, years without communication, without telling my mom I loved her or asking Jack how he'd been. None of it mattered to them.

I spent the night at the house, in my old room that hadn't changed. We ate dinner together and Jack stayed over late and we talked all night. It was amazing. But even during all of that, I couldn't get Laney off of my mind, wishing she was beside me during my homecoming.

I wondered how she was, if she got home safely, what her night was like. I felt like an idiot for not getting her phone number, but I'd been with her every day, it didn't really seem necessary when we were so close, and before I'd decided to get my head out of the bottle and man up, I wasn't ready to give anyone a way of contacting me.

I'd just woken up to the smell of bacon and cinnamon and knew Mom was making her famous homemade cinnamon rolls. They were a staple Saturday morning tradition in the Gentry house and something I'd forgotten that I missed.

Stumbling down the stairs, I find her at the stove and grin. My mom was seriously the best, and I vowed to myself to get my shit figured out and be a better person for the people in my life. "'Mornin' Mama."

She spins around and pins me with a grin. "Good morning, son."

I walk up to her and kiss her on the cheek before I grab a cup of coffee and sit at the small kitchen table, it's as old as me and well-loved. My parents don't believe in replacing old things, they just believe in taking care of what you have.

"What are your plans for the day?"

I clear my throat. "Uh, I think I'll head over to the restaurant."

Mom smiles like she's in on some secret. "Delaney Torrez, huh?"

I can't hide anything from my mom, so I just nod my head as she sets the fresh food in front of me. "Where's Dad?" I change the subject before she can get more out of me.

"Oh, he took a couple cows in, he'll be picking up some calves this afternoon."

My parents make a small living off of growing cows and trading them in to the butcher. It made a small amount, but enough for them to live off of comfortably. "Gotcha," I say as I finish up my food. I stand and kiss her cheek. "I'll be back later."

"I love you, Ford." Mom grabs my hand and looks me in the eyes. I know I hurt her, I know I hurt them all, but I vow to myself that I won't ever leave them like that again.

"I love you too, Mama."

FUCKING GORGEOUS. IT'S amazing how after only one day apart that I missed the sight of Delaney as much as I did. She's already buzzing around getting ready for the beginning of the lunch rush and I love watching her in her element. She truly was meant to be around people. I study her the way someone studies the planets and see her tuck a pen into the bun on top of her head and shove her notebook back in her apron before smiling at the couple that gave their order and then she scurries in the direction of the kitchen.

When she spots me, she pauses in surprise. We move toward each other and she tilts her head back to accommodate the height difference. "I didn't think I'd see you today."

"Miss me, Laney?" I smile at her and wait for the answer I'm dying to hear.

"No." She's quick to reply and her face gives nothing away. "Just thought you'd stay home with your family." I follow her back behind the bar, the kitchen is loud with the cooks firing off orders and the waiters all shuffle back and forth, but I block it out and grab her hand before she can get too far.

"You can admit you missed me," I murmur close to her ear.

She finally gives me her eyes and I see the defiance before she can give the smart-ass answer. "I can't afford..." She pauses, baiting me. "To lose as much food as I have with you around."

I laugh and grip her hand tight. "Oh really?"

"No, seriously," she answers with a chuckle. I take a chance and reach with my other hand to brush my fingertips across her cheek, she blushes. It takes everything in me not to pull her into me and kiss her full mouth, but I know better right now. Laney and I were never romantic back in high school, I'd never looked at her like that. She was my best friend, nothing more, ruining that would have hurt me. But I can't deny the pull I feel to her and not trying, not pushing for something now. Well, that's impossible.

"Well," she starts and reaches under the bar, grabbing an apron for me. I smile at her. "If you're here, get to work, Gentry."

"Yes, ma'am."

I'M TAKING A small break behind the restaurant when my phone rings again and I let loose a sigh, already knowing without looking who it will be when I pull the phone out. Gemma's been hounding me about the one thing I don't want to do; therapy.

"Hello," I answer the phone with another sigh, Gemma is my superior now, but that hasn't always been the case. I've never let her forget that at one point we were not only on the same level but competitors.

"Gentry." Her tone gives off a similar vibe. "You've been avoiding my calls."

"Oh… no. What makes you think that?"

"Ford." Sigh. "You have to take this seriously. You won't be allowed back into the field until you are cleared."

I pinch my eyes closed. The reminder of why I was actually in Texas in the first place stings. I'd reached a breaking point. I was 'unfit to serve' in simple terms. They could have fired me for what I did, and they maybe should have. But Gemma worked her magic, and with a string or two pulled, I was put on leave instead. I didn't have a clue how damn bad I needed the break until I had stopped working.

"I know I do. I'll start this week. But…" I hesitate, trying to think of ways to say I don't want to go back yet.

"Gentry. You need more time?" Her question sounds ludicrous, and even she knows it. Gemma is the type that lives and breathes the job. It's her entire life, much like it was mine.

"Yeah, Gemma, I need time." I sigh and turn toward a shuffle behind me. I see Delaney walking back into the building and frown at her retreating form. "I gotta go, Gem."

"Next Tuesday, three o'clock. Dr. Reis."

"Got it." With a click on her end, I shove my phone back in my pocket and walk into the building, Delaney's at a table working her charm on another set of customers when Mr. Torrez rushes past me. "Whoa."

I didn't mean to draw attention but when her dad looks at me, I'm slightly taken aback at the bruising that surrounds his eyes and without thinking about it, I grab his arm to steady him. "Mr. Torrez, you alright?"

"I'm fine." He pulls his arm away and starts to walk away,

which I should take as a sign to leave him alone, but I can't stop my feet from following behind him. "I said I was fine. Get out."

Joaquín sits there with a large sigh and I think back to the times I'd come here and see him with his wife and daughter. He was the ultimate family man, he's always been a friendly guy, the entire Torrez family always has been, but since then, it looks like Joaquín has aged twenty years.

"Mr. Torrez, what happened to you?" The agent in me wants to get down to the bottom of what the hell happened. The man part of me wants to know what happened to someone who is close to a woman I've grown to care for, and if she's in line to be next.

"It's not a big deal. Just a run-in with an old buddy." He looks tense and tired. I get the feeling that backing off will be the best for the time being.

"All right. Well, if you need any help, I'm not far."

I take my leave at that, wondering who this 'old buddy' could be and knowing it's not as innocent as he claims it is. But right now, it's not something I have time to pursue, I need to focus on other things.

Like the woman I can't get off of my mind.

Or therapy.

"WHAT ARE YOU doing?" I must have spooked her because Delaney jumps out of her skin. She turns her flushed face toward me and gives me a weak smile. Sitting with her laptop open, I see a spreadsheet that looks like it counts out all of the expenses of the restaurant and bar.

"I'm trying to get expenses together." She rubs a hand through her hair.

"Not going well?"

She shakes her head like she's trying to ward off her stress. "No, no, it's fine."

"Okay," I say without really meaning it.

I wanted to push, I want her to let me help her. Another part of me, though, knew that I wasn't ready to push her yet, and I knew that before I could take that step I had to figure shit out for myself. Somewhere along the way of my life, I'd fucked my head up so bad that I wasn't ready to jump in with the first woman I'd really wanted, the one I craved, and *fuck*, I hated that. I hated that I couldn't brush what I was feeling under the rug and just go for it.

Delaney was worthy of someone who could be there for her, and I wasn't deserving of her heart. Not even close. And until I could get my head put back together, until I could feel like I was able to live this life without questioning why I was here, I had to back off.

12

FORD

THE COOLNESS OF the room was probably supposed to be comforting, but instead made me feel like I was on my deathbed. It was ridiculous that someone could make a room feel like the arctic in the middle of Texas—any time of year.

"Let's start from the beginning," the therapist, Laura was her name, asked me, her legs folded Indian style in a retro chair. She wasn't holding a pen and paper, she didn't have a pensive expression on her face, she was relaxed and calmly sipping her cup of coffee as she waited for my answer.

"The beginning of what?" I ask, my fingers twisting and manipulating the threads of one of her pillows, I didn't doubt it was probably pretty pricey. Stupid expensive pillows.

"Of when you started to feel like you weren't in control of... your mind. Your actions." Laura knew little of the truth, she knew I was in the FBI and couldn't disclose everything, but she didn't know the truth of why I had to be here.

"I don't know. That could be a broad answer."

"So, this has been happening over time then?"

"You don't just do the things I do and come out normal," I scoff.

Laura eyes me, not in a I'm-studying-your-behavior kind of way, more in a you're-being-an-ass-and-I'm-going-to-find-out-why kind of way.

"Tell me what happened to put you here today."

"Here, as in Texas? I got put on probation."

"No, not Texas. Here, as in your state of mind. What's eating you?"

I bite back my smart-ass comment and sigh. "I can't tell you details."

"Just do your best. Consider me Fort Knox, I won't repeat a thing."

"Except to my superiors." Once again, I curse Gemma in my head.

"No. The only thing I'm required to say to them is if you're fit for duty or not."

A suffering sigh leaves my body as I think back all the way to what happened that brought me here. I guess it started on a mission down in Mexico. I think it was too soon for me to be back after the whole Liam and Margaret debacle. The minute that bullet wound had healed, I was back to work.

I didn't even pause to think about my mental health before I returned to the job. Guys like me don't think of that shit, we just *do*, we just work. I'd had to turn in my life to get a new one, an undercover op that I'd been working toward for years that I'd suddenly felt wary about doing. I saw what happened to my best friend after he had been undercover for as long as he had. It hadn't been good for him, it took him a long time to get his shit together and let people in again.

But I wasn't a quitter and I wasn't about to admit that I wasn't feeling this mission.

It was when I found out the details of the mission that I was unsure. The men I was tracking down were human traffickers, they didn't discriminate either, men, women... children. It was the worst job of my entire fucking life and I wanted to go in and blow their fucking heads off.

I couldn't though, Gemma was my boss and she was in control of what I did, she was the one who called the shots, I was just the body that moved on the chessboard. It was infuriating because I was feet away from scum for months, pretending that I was part of it, watching despicable things and hating my life.

I'd almost ended it.

Only because I couldn't sit back and watch. I couldn't do it. Not after everything. And so I'd decided. I'd do it. But first, I was going to end them.

"This was where you went wrong, right?" Laura's voice interrupts my story and I close my eyes and rub them. I feel this weight that pushes against my chest every time I think about it.

"This was where you disobeyed your orders?"

"Yeah, I did." It wasn't hard to admit that I defied Gemma or even my director. I didn't give a fuck at that point, I'd been in this for months, almost a year and I was fucking *done*. I couldn't stomach any of it anymore. In my opinion, we had more than enough to drown these fuckers.

"What happened?" I hear her ask me, but my mind is lost in a sea of red, the blood that's on my hands was too much.

"I can't." My voice cracks with my answer, and I blink hard and clear my throat. I can't talk about it, the eyes staring back at me haunt my fucking dreams. It's the entire reason that drinking was the only way I was comfortable. It was the only way that I could forget the fucking terror that lived in my head.

"That's okay." Laura uncrosses her legs and leans forward. "I want to see you in a couple of days. Okay?"

I nod my head and stand, not looking back as I head out the door. When I'm outside, I breathe in a deep breath of the Texas humidity and curse. I didn't know it was going to be that fucking hard. And I can't blink it away. I can't get the eyes staring back at me to go away.

So, I do the only thing I can to get rid of it, I get a handle and I head back to my motel. Away from prying eyes and concerned

family, away from the brunette I'd thought I could have.
Away from the demons that haunted me in the day.

13

DELANEY

FIVE DAYS. NOT that I was counting, but it's been five days since Ford last came to the restaurant. I hadn't reached out because I assume that he's with his family which was wonderful. But I couldn't deny to myself that I definitely missed him. It was so weird how easily I had slipped back into that best friend role, how he had become some sort of constant like it was just like old times.

Get a grip, Delaney. I scold myself as I smile at a couple after delivering their food.

I had bigger fish to fry than worrying about Ford, he was an adult and he was going to do whatever he wanted. Hell, maybe he wasn't even here anymore. Maybe he'd gone back to... *shit.* I never even asked him where he was living.

We didn't have a lot of talks about the last sixteen years, I mean, I'd opened up about Mom and his mom helping me through that but other than that we didn't really get any further, those times that we went through in the years we were apart were hard on both of us. Any time I brought up his work, he shut it down in such a way that I was distracted enough that by the time I realized he'd done it, we had completely moved on.

The door chimes with a new customer and I plaster a smile on my face and turn to greet whoever it is when my feet falter.

Rafael is standing by the bar—too close to me—with a smile of a predator, his impeccable suit in place and his Cheshire grin smeared across his lips. His presence brings a dark cloud over mine and I hide a shiver from him. "Can I help you?" I ask, my voice breathless. He probably thinks it's for another reason but it's truly because I think he's terrifying.

"Delaney, how are you, *reina?*" I cringe when he calls me 'queen' and move away from him behind the bar, to get some distance in case he gets any ideas.

"Fine. Can I get you something?" I try to keep the chill out of my voice but since I know for a fact that this man beat the shit out of my father, I'm not exactly on this guy's side. Even if my father told me to mind my own business.

"No," he says and straightens. "Except your father. He and I have business."

"Is that code for beating him?" I ask with ice in my voice. I didn't mean to actually ask the question but now it was out, and I couldn't take it back.

He chuckles and rubs his lips. "Ah, that was just a small misunderstanding."

"Really? Because I feel like we're old enough to use our words." My sarcasm is going to get me my own set of bruises, but my anger overpowers my common sense.

"You're right," he replies, raising his hands in some sort of surrender. "How can I make it up to you?"

I scoff and roll my eyes, his narrow at that and I have to check myself. This man, whoever he really is, is dangerous and I'm treading on thin ice. "How about you leave us alone?"

Clicking his tongue, he gives a slight shake of his head. "Sorry, *reina,* no can do there. See, your father and I are in business together."

"What kind of business?"

He shakes his head at me. "Oh, don't worry. I won't hurt you." With a cryptic wink, he leaves, leaving me more confused than ever.

"What the hell just happened?" I ask out loud to no one.

Hours later I'm still mulling over what happened with Rafael when Ford's mom comes in with a pensive expression on her face, I walk over calmly and lay a hand on her arm, "Mrs. Gentry? Everything okay?"

"Oh." She chuckles slightly. "Probably nothing. Is Ford here?"

I squint in confusion. "No, sorry. He hasn't been in in a few days, I assumed he's been with you."

"Oh no, no he hasn't been. And he's not answering his phone. I'm a little worried."

I worry my bottom lip. It's not a good sign and the last time I hadn't heard or seen him; he was on a binge at that motel. "I think I know where he is."

WE ARRIVE AT the motel and I see the rental car sitting in the same spot as last time. I sigh when I realize I was hoping he hadn't left; the problem is, he's not going to be in good shape either way. I hop out and reach into my purse, I'd accidentally kept the key card from the first time, and I give a half-assed excuse to his mom who eyes me with suspicion. This definitely doesn't look good for me.

"Let's knock first," I suggest. He could definitely just be sleeping. *Definitely*. At least, for his sake—though I'm not sure exactly why I care—I hope he's just been busy, been working or something. My gut tells me that's not the case as I grip the card in my hand.

Ford's mom knocks on the door roughly, not in an angry way but definitely in a way that tells me she's worried about her son. I get angry at him just for this, for making his mother worry again after so many years of constantly having to, it's not fair. It's selfish.

We wait a good minute before I can't anymore and I push the key card into the slot. At the green, I push the handle down and open the door. I smell it before I see it, the putrid smell of puke that I've learned well after working in a restaurant for so long. It's a bad freaking sign, as is the fact that I don't see Ford anywhere.

Rushing into the room with a hand over my nose and mouth, I spot his sock-clad feet between a wall and the bed. "Shit," I say before I can think better. I look over to his mom who gasps at the sight. Her shock is quickly replaced with urgency and we both grab a side of him and try to roll him over. I reach for a pulse, the worst-case scenario running through my mind before I have a chance to really take in the situation.

When I find it, I release a breath I was unaware I was holding and look at his face, he's still out cold and I work with his mom to heave him off the floor. When his body hits the bed is when he comes to. I was waiting for it, I knew that he wasn't going to take us being in here well and before I can stop myself, I push his mom out of his line of sight and take her place, it works because before I can get a word out, he has me against the wall again. A thought hits me that makes me wonder what on earth could have happened to him that makes this his reaction whenever he's woken, or maybe it's a bad reaction to the alcohol he's been consuming.

"Ford!" His mother is appalled, I can hear it in her voice, but since I was expecting it, this isn't a surprise to me at all. "Ford, you let go of that girl right now." Her voice is commanding and I'm surprised when it works. He lets me go and I lean against the wall, taking deep breaths.

"Ford," I start, ready to assure him I'm fine before he turns on me.

"What the fuck are you doing here?" Anger radiates off him, his whole body is tense with it.

"I'm just here to help, Ford." I use the most soothing voice I can, trying to connect with him with my eyes. The last few weeks haven't been for nothing, we'd talked, we'd reconnected. Surely that's not all wasted.

"I don't want your help."

"Ford Michael—"

His mother is cut off when a roar toward me rips out of him. "No! Get the fuck out. Now."

I stare in shock at the man in front of me, not only have I never seen him that mad, but I've never, ever had someone talk to me that way. I snap my gaping mouth shut and stand straight.

"Mrs. Gentry, please give me a call if you ever need me," I say to the woman who's in just as much shock as I am, as a matter of fact, she looks downright pissed. But she gives me a nod and turns her fiery gaze on her son.

I will away the sudden tears that hit me once the door closes, I won't cry because a man yelled at me. And I damn sure will never cry over Ford Gentry.

14

FORD

MY HEAD FELT like it weighed a million pounds with a campus band pounding its way through it, I didn't even remember what I drank, all I know is that when I woke up, it wasn't because I wanted to, it was because I was disturbed.

I could feel my mother's glare from here, her icy steel was something that some moms probably envied. One look from her and you knew exactly how much shit you were in before she said a single word.

"Ford Michael Gentry." The mom-tone may just be worse than the look. But with what's coursing through my veins right now, I can't find it in me to really care. "How you just treated that young woman was absolute shit."

I turn my head to her too fast and the world spins. With a groan, I slouch onto the bed and hold it. I've never heard Mom curse before. "I'm not in the mood, Mom."

"Well," she huffs. I feel her move in closer and I wish it wasn't against everything in me to push her away. "I don't much give a crap what mood you're in. What makes you think you have any right to treat someone that way?"

I scoff and let out some sort of bitter chuckle. "You have no idea what I've been through."

She sits beside me; my eyes are still closed tight, but I can feel her close. "You're right. I don't. But whatever it is, no matter how horrible, never gives anyone the right to treat others poorly."

"Mom," I groan, the sound coming out like that of a petulant teenager. "I can't deal with this right now."

"Ford, you don't understand. I thought maybe you needed a couple days, I get that. It's been years and heck, I thought you were into Delaney there for a minute, Lord knows we all thought that would happen when you were kids. But you not communicating after so long, well frankly it scares the shit out of me."

Guilt settles in thick and I look up to see the tears that I know she won't let fall gathering in her eyes, I may still be drunk as shit but no one, no matter what state, wants to see their mama cry. "Mama," I start and gingerly place an arm around her shoulders. "I'm sorry."

"Oof, I love you son." She moves my arm and looks at me in

the eyes. "But you smell like the ass-end of a chicken."

A chuckle leaves me and I look around the room, it's a mess; again. *Fucking A.* Delaney has literally seen the worst of me, and I just keep letting her.

"Hop in the shower and I'll get to work here, but you won't be staying here anymore."

"Mom, you can't hold me hostage at the house."

"You don't have to stay in the house, you can stay in the loft."

"The hayloft?" Last I remembered the hayloft was, well, full of hay, and dirty.

"You haven't been home long enough to see the improvements. We've done some work since you left." She stands and starts grabbing the bottles around the room. "Do you need help in the shower, son, or can you handle it yourself?"

I give her a side-eye. "I've got it." I'm not weak enough to let my mother bathe me, that would be a new low. And I'm not sure how much lower I can get without putting myself in a grave.

THE NEXT DAY, after many lecturing words from my mother, I'm standing in the newly renovated loft that looks like it's had a complete makeover. The once uninsulated roof is now covered in drywall and wood over that to keep the barn look, the floor is a gleaming wood that I find out is laminate, which seems to be a sore spot when I bring it up to Mom and Dad. There's a big bed in the middle that's decorated for guests and any other furniture I could need; it even has a brand new bathroom with a shower. That had to have cost a pretty penny to get up here.

"This is incredible." I look at my dad, Michael, who stands proudly. He's not a man of very many words but he says more with his facial expressions than most can. "You guys did a great job."

"Well, we thought what with the booming trend of *Airbnb* that we could make a little cash on the side, people love staying in a barn." She lets out her infamously loud chuckle. "Who would have thought!"

I smile at her and set down my one bag and start checking out the room as Mom tells us she's going to make supper for everyone, Jack is bringing his fiancée by, something the surprised the hell out of me, but I was happy for him. He deserved that. We still needed to have a serious talk, but for now, we were taking it all one day at a time.

"Son." I turn to my dad's gruff voice. He may not be a man of many words, but his lectures were golden. He walks up to me and gives me a stern look. "Your mother told me how she found you."

I hang my head, ashamed, fighting back the sting in my eyes that hits me at the thought of not only disappointing my family but the reason I went on the bender in the first place.

"I don't want you drinking," he says. I'm thirty-four, technically speaking, I shouldn't just take his word and lie down, but my parents mean the world to me, and hell, I can't let myself let them down. "Not here." He continues. "If you need a drink, you come to the house, and I'll drink you under the table until you puke." Dad puts a hand on my shoulder and shakes slightly. "You don't leave here and hurt yourself, you've been gone far too long to leave us forever, you hear me?"

I sniff and nod my affirmation, the tears slipping out before I can stop them and he pulls me into a one-armed hug with a pat on the back. He pulls back and looks me in the eye. With a nod, he leaves me to myself and heads back into the house. I sit back down on the bed and hang my head; I can't believe I'm here. I'm more grateful to be this close to my parents than ever, I came back to Texas thinking they'd hate my guts, that I wouldn't ever get through to them and explain why I was gone for so long, but of course, they aren't those people and they welcomed me home with open arms.

Remembering the day before, I pull my phone from my pocket and punch on the name of the other person I've hurt, a simple apology probably won't do it, but I can't help but try. The way I spoke to her yesterday, it was shitty. I could blame it on the alcohol or the demons that were haunting me, but truthfully, I was so fucking embarrassed that she saw me that way again, that I fucking pinned her to the wall, *again*. I make a mental note to talk about that when I go back to therapy, which I missed again. No doubt they charged me regardless.

The phone rings twice before it clicks over to her voicemail, it's just the automatic thing so I can't even hear her voice. Hoping it's a fluke, I hang up and try calling her again, with the same outcome, I realize that Delaney isn't going to just pick up and forgive me, so I vow to go over there tonight to make it right.

JACK'S FIANCÉE IS fire. Michelle has the kid on his toes the entire time we're having dinner and she has my parents falling at her feet. She has a charm about her that makes her easy to get along with.

I'm sure she knows how absent I've been, hell, she's been around more than I have in the last couple of years, but she doesn't say a single thing about it. She just takes it in stride and welcomes me back as much as my family did. I'm grateful, because she has a right to be pissed at me.

Dinner passes slowly and when I check my phone, it's past nine. The restaurant will be open for a while longer and I plan on making my way over there before Delaney is gone for the night. With a quick goodbye to the family and Michelle, I pop into the rental and head toward the restaurant.

I think about how to apologize to her; I know I should have reached out sooner but my own selfishness kept me from doing anything for anyone. I hate that I've treated her so badly, I know deep down I don't mean it and all she was trying to do was help me out of the hole I was putting myself in.

She isn't one to back down, she's been trying to help me since I stepped foot into her bar, but maybe I've finally done it, maybe I've finally pushed her far enough away that she won't care to try anymore. Not that I'd blame her.

When I pull up, I frown. The restaurant is dark, the open sign turned off. I can see a light coming from the back and there's two cars in the lot, her and her dad's and another one I don't recognize. I step out of the car and walk up to the restaurant, the door is locked so I knock, hoping Delaney is still back there and I can still, at the very least, apologize.

She comes from the back, she looks frazzled and for a minute, I wonder if she was back there with someone. I swallow down the jealousy and wait for her to open the door. Her wide eyes take me in and she sighs, not in an exasperated way, more like she is just trying to catch her breath.

Fuck, there's definitely someone back there.

"Hey." My voice cracks and I clear my throat. "You didn't answer the phone."

"Sorry, I've been uh… busy."

"Reina." A man comes from the back, his suit missing a jacket and sleeves rolled up. She looks back at him with wide eyes, worry or guilt marring her expression, and I nod my head.

"Ford… I—now's not a very good time." I can't decipher her look, but I take it and move away. Even if she is sleeping with that dude, it's not any of my business, even if it does burn.

"Right." I shuffle my feet and say, "Have a good night."

Just as I turn, she grabs my arm and turns me around, I look down at her and raise a brow in question. "Come back tomorrow, okay?"

Swallowing, I nod my head again. What is with the nodding? "Okay."

I get into the car and watch her walk back into the restaurant, an uneasy feeling about what that was all about and why she's still here with a man this late, why the restaurant is closed, and why I feel like I have any right or reason to care at all.

15

DELANEY

LAST NIGHT WAS bizarre. I don't know how to comprehend exactly what happened, mostly because I don't even know. It was early when Rafael showed up. His presence was commanding and despite my best efforts to resist him, I followed his order when he told me to get everyone out. My father was insistent I listen, that I obey this stranger that held some weird power over him, over us, apparently.

My father told me what was going on, finally. Well, at the insistence of Rafael, who seemed to want me at every meeting they were having now. I didn't know why he was so fascinated with me, but it gave me the heebie-jeebies. I hated it. He made me feel out of control which was my least favorite feeling in the world.

Apparently, years ago, when we were drowning in debt, not able to make ends meet, my father got a loan. I remember it, I was working nights at a Walmart in the next town over, mostly just to keep the mortgage paid, when he finally got a big enough loan to help us get ourselves out of debt. The one thing I didn't know, was that the loan was from none other than Rafael Guerrero, whose name I learned last night when he was bringing me into the fold.

But Dad was behind in payments, it wasn't good. That was why I was missing money nearly every single night. How good we were doing didn't matter when you were in debt so bad the man you owed showed up in person.

We sat down together to make a plan to pay him back, as Rafael said, he'd give me a chance. Insinuating that it was now my burden and mine alone, saying I wouldn't be happy with the other things he had in mind to pay off the debt.

I hid the shiver that slithered across my skin.

When Ford had showed up, we were in the middle of negotiations and Rafael was pissed that I was checking the door. So, it didn't surprise me that he'd followed me out to the front. I didn't want Ford to get any ideas, but I saw it on his face the second he saw him.

Which was exactly why I wanted him to come this morning. I knew why he was there, our little episode a few days ago wasn't good. I was still unhappy with him, but I wasn't someone who purposefully hurt people, or didn't forgive. I was a grown woman and I was in charge of my own emotions and actions.

But I didn't have an explanation for him, I had no clue what I was going to say if he asked about Rafael. It's not like I can tell him the truth, it's too embarrassing. It's not that I'm worried he'll think badly of me, it wouldn't matter if he did. We weren't anything to each other, and frankly, after this many years of nothing happening between us, I knew we wouldn't ever be. He needed to focus on things that had nothing to do with me, but everything to do with recovering from what was bothering him.

Ford was a good guy, but it was no mystery that something haunted his every move. It didn't make him any less appealing to me, but it did make me want to fix him.

"What's up, buttercup?" Lizzie's voice pulls me out of my thoughts and I turn to give her a small smile. I can't exactly be blunt about the things that are plaguing my thoughts, though I'd love to.

"Just getting ready for the day."

She cocks her head to the side. "Mm-hmm. Anything else?"

A sigh escapes through my pursed lips and I decide that it can't hurt to confide in her. Not about Rafael, I can't tell anyone about that. But Ford... she may be able to help me work through that mess.

"I'm just thinking about everything that's happened, ya know? I haven't had this much drama since high school."

"What's so dramatic right now?" she asks with a confused look. I know why she's confused, it's not like my life is really unpredictable, like at all. I'm probably the most boring person on the planet, and that's just the way I like it.

I tell her about Ford and what he's been doing since he's been back, not every detail, but enough to give her a good idea of what's going through my head, I think she already knows where I'm headed with it because she shakes her head slightly. "What?"

"Nothing. It's just." She pauses to shrug her shoulders. "You always want to save everyone."

"I do not," I protest, though it's weak at best.

"Yes, you do." She grabs my hand and I can already tell what she wants to say, I'm not going to like it. "It's not a bad thing. But it's who you are. You do it for me, for all our friends, you do it for your dad most of all, I mean, look around, your dream was opening a flower shop, not being the manager of your parents' bar."

"I don't mind it."

She shakes her head. "I'm not saying you do. I'm saying, you have to be everyone's savior."

"I don't want to be Ford's savior."

"Then what do you want?"

"I just want to… help him." I sigh. "I feel like I failed him all those years ago."

Her smirk tells me everything. I get it, I'm the hero. I'm the one who has to fix everyone's problems, I've always been that way. "So, what do I do?" But before she can say anything, the door jingles open and Ford strides through.

"Just follow your heart, girl. It knows what it's doing." With a pat on my shoulder, she leaves the room so I can talk to Ford. The advice is simple, the problem is, I don't even know if my heart knows what it wants.

Ford stands away from me, I know he's doing it for a reason, and I wonder if he thinks I'm scared of him. Technically, I should be. I should be terrified of him, but I can't make myself feel that around him. I cross my arms and wait for him to speak.

"Hey." His voice is clear and when I get a good look at him, his eyes hold clear.

"Hi." I want to comment on the obvious sobriety, but I don't want to embarrass him. "How are you doing?" I settle on instead.

"I'm… okay." He gives me a smirk that shows off his adorable dimples and I smile back. "I've moved out of the motel."

Raising a brow, I say, "Oh?"

"Yeah, I'm staying with, well, not with my parents, but in the barn out back."

A memory of them talking about redoing that flicks through my brain and I nod. "That's great, Ford."

He sighs and I see the seriousness on his face. "Laney, I owe you an apology. I can't even fathom what you must think of me. How I acted… well, I didn't ever want you to see me like that." He takes a deep breath. "I have some trauma in my past, it's not an excuse, but that's why I've been acting the way I have. That's why I did… what I did."

I nod and open my mouth to respond, but he pushes on. "What

I said to you, it was way out of line. All you've ever done is look out for me. So, I'm truly sorry for how I acted and what I said."

I let a small smile lay across my lips. It's kind of fun to see him so humbled. "Apology accepted."

A relieved look crosses his face and he smiles. Damn, it's not fair that he looks that good just by smiling. *Damn dimples.* "Great, thank you, I don't deserve it, but thank you." He sighs and glances around, noticing how slow the restaurant is and says, "Now that that is out of the way, I was wondering if I could take you to lunch."

"Oh." I hesitate long enough that he rushes on.

"I realize, now, that you have a boyfriend, so I just wanted to take you to lunch as a friend."

I hum but don't correct him. I wonder if that's for the best, that he thinks I'm taken and we just be friends. My head says that's the best way to handle this, that being his friend is the best option. So, I ignore the ping in my chest and smile. "I'd love that."

16

FORD

PEOPLE OFTEN DON'T give me a lot of credit. I've dealt with it my entire life. Going through high school I was the jock, nice, got good grades, but other than that, no one had a clue what I could actually do. The army was more of the same. My sergeant pushed me at every turn, trying to break me, but I wouldn't. I kept my head down and pushed my way to the top and when that wasn't enough, I got out and went straight to Quantico.

The FBI is challenging because no two cases are ever the same, maybe they have similar patterns, but there are always elements that change no matter who's turning the wheel. And regardless of all that, I was always able to tell a difference, to figure out who was doing what and for which reason.

Which was exactly why I knew that Delaney was hiding something from me. I didn't know exactly what it was yet, but she and her father had some big secrets that they were trying hard to keep. I know that everything they're hiding was going to lead me to one person, the man from the restaurant. And that's why, hours after I took Delaney back to the restaurant, after I'd conned her into having lunch with me, I was following up some of my instincts and tracking down the man that had made her slam the door in my face, and if my suspicions were correct, a man that was responsible for the marks left on Joaquín's face.

My phone rings and I answer on the first ring, it's the call I was expecting. "James, I need you to look something up for me."

"Ford." A long-suffering sigh escapes my handler's throat and I grin at her annoyance. I shouldn't be pleased with myself for annoying her but sometimes it was icing on the cake. "I can't help you with anything while you're on leave. You know this."

"Come on, it's just something tiny."

"What?"

"I just need you to run a plate for me, it'll take you five minutes."

"Ford, what are you up to?"

"Nothing, just a hunch." My shoulders shrug on instinct and I rattle off the plate number, knowing she'll catch it without having to write it down.

"Fine, I'll let you know." The line goes dead and I toss my

phone onto the passenger seat. The building I'd found that I knew used to be used for some of the local gangs is empty, so I turn the car on and head home.

Gemma won't be in any hurry to get back to me with that plate information, she still thinks I'm suffering, she won't even entertain the thought of me going back to work and it's infuriating as much as it's a relief. I think if I could work, I could get my mind off of things that have been plaguing me.

I have no doubt that's why I'm investigating this situation. It gives me something to do and justifies my need to watch out for Laney. If this guy is her boyfriend—she didn't correct me when I suggested it—then I need to know she's going to be safe.

"YOU SEEM TO be in a good mood today," my therapist says with a soft smile on her lips. At least she's not the typical therapist. I think I might shoot someone if I had to deal with some old man asking how I was feeling all the time.

"I'm doing alright."

My vague answer makes her smirk and then I see her fall into serious mode again. "Seriously, Ford. How are you doing? You missed last week's appointment."

I hesitate, mostly because I don't want to admit to her that I was on a bender, that my mother and a woman I've come to care about had to come and pick me up—again—and tell me to get my shit together.

"I had a rough week."

"What happened?"

I sigh and explain what happened. Her face gives nothing away, no disappointment, no anger, no sympathy. She just lets me tell her everything without a single judgment.

"This Delaney," she starts, looking over her notes. "She means something to you."

It's not a question, she can tell just by the look on my face, just by how I speak about her. And it's true. As much as I shouldn't, as much as I can't, I do care about Delaney. More than I should, for sure. She deserves more than some suicidal, temporarily fired FBI agent.

"She does," I answer honestly, it's not like she's going to find her and spill all of my secrets.

"And how do you think she feels?"

Pausing, I think about how she's acted and treated me. "I think… she cares, a lot. Not many people would do for me what she has. But I think she's fine with staying friends."

"And you're not?"

"Not what?" I question.

"Not okay with staying friends."

I shake my head with a chuckle. "That's not what I meant."

"What did you mean?"

"I just meant; I think she'll stay my friend. Even after

everything." I swallow down a lump that suddenly claws its way up my throat.

"You don't want more with her?"

"I can't. I'm not good for her, I'm not good for anyone anymore." My weak voice makes me want to scream, I'm not this person, I'm not weak, I'm not scared. I'm not worried about what others think, that's not who I am. And yet, I can't stop acting that way.

"That's not true, Ford. I think you're more than good enough for the right person."

"Well, I guess we'll find out if I ever meet her." Despite my words, I can't shake the visual of Laney out of my head.

"Let's get back to where we left off last time."

I shake my head again, and sigh at her. "I'm not ready to talk about that."

"I understand. Let's start with something simpler then. How about what you were going to do when you got out?"

"Out of what? The mission?" She nods her head and I think about it. "I guess I'd see where they assigned me next."

"You weren't going to come home, have a vacation or just visit family?"

"My family and I weren't exactly... on speaking terms back then."

"But you've made up since then?"

"Yeah, we're working on it. My parents forgave me." *Thank God.*

"Tell me about that."

We're not even fifteen minutes into this session and I'm already exhausted with her questions. I don't want to talk about me or my family or anything relating to me. I want to get a call from Gemma telling me who that bastard is, I want to know what the hell is going on with Delaney, and frankly, I want to see her too.

I tell Laura everything that happened with my family, with the accident and my past. About my leaving them behind for the military and then not feeling like I had any right to come back after what I did to my brother.

By the time we're done with our session, I'm toast. All I want to do is go home and crash for eight hours and block out the world. I'd kill for a whiskey right now, but then I remember what happened the last time I drank anything, the look on my mother's face, and I can't bring myself to give in to the temptation.

Right as I lay down on the bed in the loft, I hear the sound of footsteps entering the barn, I also hear the holler of my brother coming to disturb me. He's been around a lot in the last few weeks since I've been home, and I'm grateful for his presence. He's a damn godsend.

"Yo," I yell back. I don't move from my spot on the bed, my head too drained to really entertain my brother right now.

"What are you doing, slacker?" Jack appears in the doorway, leaning slightly on his cane, and I throw him my middle finger. "Did you just get home?"

"Yeah," I reply with a sigh.

"Where were you?" he asks innocently enough, but I can tell that he's curious about what happened today. If I know my mother, she vented to Jack about me going to therapy and probably unnecessarily made him worry about it.

"I was at my session." I sit up and gesture for him to sit on the chair in the corner facing me. "It's kind of draining."

"I bet." He picks at invisible lent on his jeans and I wait patiently for him to spit out whatever question is brewing.

"What's on your mind, Jack?"

"Damn, man. I have a million questions." Jack's always been a little more on the vulnerable side, it's what my mama always loved most about him. His good humor and sensitive nature drew people to him constantly. It seems that carried over from his childhood to adulthood, and not for the first time, I regret that I was away for so long and missed everything. "I got your card, you know."

I furrow my brow and look down at my hands. "What card?"

"Dude, I know it was from you." He sighs. "My high school graduation, I got a card from overseas with a thousand bucks inside. Wasn't that hard to put together."

"You tell Ma?"

"Hell no. It wouldn't have helped anything."

I nod, mulling over in my head what I want to say, where I want to start, "I missed a lot."

"You did." Jack seems to be thinking over what he wants to say. Finally, he looks at me and tells me straight. "I fucking hated you."

I flinch, but I don't reply. Any anger he has, any hurt, is completely warranted, and it's time I take responsibility for my actions.

"When you left home, you left everyone. You left me and I hated you for so long for it. I couldn't understand how my big brother could just abandon his family, his brother, especially after everything that happened. It hurt, man."

Shaking my head, I rest it in my hands. "I can't say I'm sorry enough. I fucked-up, and I was fucked-up, hell, I'm still fucked-up."

"No, you're not."

"You don't know, man."

I see a spark of anger in his eyes and he stands in front of me. "You're right. I don't fucking know because you won't tell me. You don't talk to Mom or Dad. Mom suspects you tell Delaney Torrez everything, but I don't think that's true. I think you're ready to punish yourself for as long as it takes. Even if that means punishing those around you."

At the end of his speech, I stare for a moment. "Jack, I don't know how to be better."

"Just spit it out."

"Spit what out?"

"Whatever happened to you. Just say it. One time. Just say it out loud." He gets in my face and I stand, regardless of how big he got, I'll always have him by a few inches.

"I can't, Jack."

"Bullshit. You're making excuses, yet again, for things in your life. For once, just own up to it and spit it out!"

"I killed people!" The words leave me without permission, and I watch a flash of surprise hit my brother's face before he quickly conceals it. A sob catches in my throat and I fall onto the bed. "I hurt people who didn't deserve it, I didn't think I'd have this guilt, then I thought I could make it go away."

Jack's voice asks in a whisper, "How?"

"By ending it."

The words are out and I can't take them back, I can't fix the way that Jack will now forever look at me, I can't take away the image he's probably worked up in his mind. I can't fix anything. I've never said it out loud. Some people in the FBI of course know this is what happened, minus the kill myself thing, but they know I've done horrific things, but having my own flesh and blood know makes it so much worse.

"Shit." Jack takes a seat next to me and stays silent for a few minutes before he opens his mouth to speak. "I'm so damn glad you didn't."

A scoff leaves me before I can stop it. "I don't know sometimes."

"No, stop. You can't talk that way." He puts a hand on my shoulder and I relax slightly. "You being back here, in our lives, reminds all of us how much we need you. Mom, Dad, and I, we've been strained for years and now we're not and we know why. You're the missing piece, man. We're family. And when you were gone, yeah, we had happy moments and lived and everything, but there was always something missing. And it was you."

A tear escapes me before I can stop it and I wipe it away with a quick sniff. "I don't know."

"Well, fucking listen to me. I'm smarter than you, so you should know to listen to me."

Laughing, I throw his arm off my shoulders. "Fuck, man." I look at him and shake my head. "I've never… told anyone that."

"Damn. I can't imagine it's easy to keep that in but it's better to get it out." He sighs and shakes his head. "Look, that kind of thing will poison you. You can't keep it in forever, getting it out, even just to me, will help you. But if you ever need someone to vent to, you come to me. I'll always have your back, man."

"Thanks, Jack." I let myself get lost in thought for a minute, I hated having this constant feeling of hopelessness. Every time I think I'm moving forward, I feel like I take three steps back.

We sit in silence for a couple minutes before he stands up and claps his hand on his leg, I know whatever he's about to say is going to probably be shot down by me, but I wait anyway. "Well, I'm starving. And it's Thursday, so let's go." I furrow my brow at him and he sighs. "It's *El Abrevadero* night!"

At the prospect of seeing Delaney, I don't hesitate and follow him out the door. "I knew that would get you moving."

I smack my brother on the back of his head and let out a carefree laugh.

Maybe things are finally looking up.

17

DELANEY

THANKFULLY THE NIGHT is busy enough that the personal drama of my own life is in the very back of my mind. I love when it's so busy at the restaurant that I don't have to think about anything but getting the job done. The best part of this job was being able to interact with everyone in town.

I'm so busy filling drinks at the bar that I don't notice when the Gentrys come in for dinner, and if it hadn't been for Lizzie's terribly indiscreet job of trying to get my attention, I probably wouldn't have even seen them until I ran by their table.

It doesn't escape my notice that a very tall, very handsome

stranger is accompanying them this time. It's the first time the entire family has been here in years, and I can see by the look on Melissa Gentry's face that she is on top of the world tonight.

"Hey, a very specific table is requesting a very specific server." Lizzie's voice makes me turn away from the group but not before a very pretty set of blue eyes catch mine and hold for longer than necessary.

"Oh yeah? They really like you, Liz," I tease her while she rolls her eyes and gets back to her tables. I walk around the bar and to the opposite side of the table from where Ford is seated. For two seconds we make eye contact before I refocus my attention on Mrs. Gentry. We always chat when she comes in and tonight will be no different.

"Did you make these arrangements, Delaney?" She points to the small centerpieces I threw together this morning, a pretty set of sunflowers and roses to spruce up the table. It's an unusual pairing for sure and the flowers came from the discount rack at the local grocery store, but the fresh flowers make me grin, nonetheless.

"I did, just thought it'd be a nice touch tonight."

"Well, they are just beautiful. When you finally get your shop, I'll be sending Mr. Gentry over there often."

I pause at the mention of a shop, it's no secret that I wanted to be a florist, but what everyone else also knows is that I haven't been able to with the family business. "Well, if I ever get there, I'll be happy to make sure he picks out only the most beautiful of colors."

After our small talk, I take the family's drink order and leave them to pick up their menus. They're a predictable sort, so I doubt that their choices will be much different from any other Thursday. I pause when I feel a presence behind me. After recent events, I've been a little more tense than usual.

But when I turn to see Ford, I soften visibly, and he smiles at me. His eyes are red-rimmed and for a moment I think about asking if there's something wrong but I keep my thoughts to myself. "You don't work here, Mr. Gentry."

"I have some special friend privileges with the manager." His smirk shows his dimples off and I stop myself from swooning too hard.

"Is that right?" *Shit.* That sounded a lot like flirting. Am I flirting?

"That's right." He leans in a little closer while I continue to fill the drinks. "How have you been, Laney?"

I try to hide a shiver when his gravelly voice hits my ear. The nickname brings a wave of nostalgia over me that makes me want to reach out and hold on to it. "I've been okay."

"Just okay?" He tilts his head and leans an arm against the backside of the bar. "That boyfriend of yours not treating you right?" He says it jokingly, but I sense if he got even a tiny signal that someone wasn't treating me right, he'd find a way to take care of it.

"I don't have a boyfriend."

"Oh?" he asks with a lift of one brow. He shifts his stance until he's a little bit closer to me and I chuckle at his move.

"Why do you care so much, huh?"

"Laney." He looks at me seriously and I raise my brows, amused. "This is serious stuff. I have to know what kind of competition there is."

"There's no competition where men are concerned because I'm not interested in dating."

That takes him down a peg or two and he thinks over what he wants to say, then he starts nodding his head and says, "Fine. That's fair. But everyone's in the market for friends, and I'm willing to bet I can be your best one."

"My best friend," I state with a cocked brow, ignoring the puttering of my heart at those words.

"That's me!" Lizzie says happily, stumbling into the conversation. "Why are you talking about me?"

Ford answers for me. "I was just informing Laney that I will be taking over the role as her best friend."

Lizzie gasps like he just said he wanted to kick a puppy or something else unfathomable. "You will not, sir!" She stands straighter. "I already have to compete with Bobby, I refuse to compete with you too."

I laugh at their antics and wait for them to battle it out. I don't comment on the Bobby statement, avoiding Ford's questioning gaze. While they're still arguing, I take the drinks over to the table and set them down, ending by Ford's spot and taking their orders, when Ford finally comes back over and gives me a wink and a kiss on the cheek. "Lizzie thinks we're going to be competing, but I already know the truth."

I let out a breath, thankful that he's not trying to bring up old stuff right now. "Oh? And what's that?"

"Come on, Laney, you can't resist me." He says it so plainly with a shrug of his shoulders.

I chuckle and nudge him into his seat. "Yeah, we'll see, hotshot. Now, what are you eating?"

"Surprise me."

His cheeky attitude leaves a semipermanent smile on my face as I head back to the kitchen, and I shake my head in wonder at how I ended up with the attention of Ford Gentry. The guy's guy, the man teenage girls fawned over for years, and quite possibly the nicest man in the universe.

He has skeletons, I know it, he knows it, his family probably knows it. But I don't doubt he'll overcome them. I know how hard he must be trying; I see how well his family is getting along and how happy his mom is.

And, not for the first time, I wonder if Ford could maybe make me happy too.

—

I'm pissed. My skin is crawling, and I can't stop looking over my shoulder waiting for the black Audi to show up again. Rafael shows up only when he wants to, no warning, no calls or threats, he just… shows up.

And it seems I'm his newest favorite victim. There's not a lot I can do about it, I've gone to five different banks basically begging for a loan that could cover what we owe him, but no one was willing to give me anything. I knew it was a long shot, but if I could only owe a bank and not the scariest man I'd ever met, then I wouldn't have to worry every night.

We were due to pay him again tonight, and I barely had enough 'extra' money to pay our loan for this week. It just meant I'd be going without any sort of paycheck for the foreseeable future. I was okay with that as long as I could get him off of my back. My father wanted us to sell. Sell the restaurant and just give him the profit. The only problem—well, one of several—was that if we sold it, we would both have to get jobs, and my father wasn't in any shape mentally or physically to start over now.

So, I told him I'd handle it, I told him that I would just be the one who paid the debt and we could move forward.

Lights shine through the front door and I know that he's here without having to see him, I've already memorized the way his lights look so I can be prepared or hide, I don't even know.

The bell jingles and I stand still, tall and strong as I wait for him to approach. Just his presence makes me shudder, and not in a good way. Rafael approaches slowly, gauging my reaction to him, but I keep my expression neutral. He feeds off of my reaction,

I learned that quickly after our first meeting with my father, he read every emotion on my father's face and used it against him. It was easy to pick up on.

"*Reina,*" he starts, moving toward me the way I imagine a lion would its prey. "And how are you this evening?"

I sniff at his question and say, "Fine." I reach under the bar for a bag that holds this week's 'rent' in cash. I toss it onto the counter and fold my arms across my chest. "Here's your money."

He doesn't even look at the bag, just holds his gaze with mine, and if I didn't know any better, I would think he was offended at my tone. "Is that how this will be?"

"What?"

"I'm not going to hurt you, Delaney, I'm merely collecting a debt that's owed to me."

I don't reply because I don't have one for him. I'm not in the mood for chitchat for someone who would try to hurt my father, who would threaten me with more than just taking money from my family, from ruining my dreams one dollar at a time.

Rafael sighs and comes around the back of the bar, he opens the bag and counts the money. When he looks back at me, I feel the panic seize my chest. No longer is there the playful—at least, playful for him—look in his eye, it's now replaced with a glowing hate. "I thought I made it clear that you wouldn't skimp on rent."

"What?" My voice is choked as I ask, and I look back at the bag. "It's all there, I checked."

"Maybe the dollar amount is... but there's a certain incentive that I expect from my clients."

The tension in my body is so tight, I swear some of my bones are going to snap in two. "And what's that?"

A slow, deep breath inflates his chest. "Just… more. And if you can't give me that, I'll take it in other ways."

A scoff leaves me before I can think better, and I spit out words I should have never let out. "Not in a million fucking years."

That hate I saw before only grows and without warning, his fist meets my cheek and blinding pain slices through me. I've never been hit before, and I can't breathe properly with this pain being at the forefront of my mind.

"*Reina,* I don't want to have to hurt you again." I don't look at him when he walks away. My hands hold my body up against the bar and I let my hair hide my face that has tears falling down my face involuntarily.

The pain is more than I can bear, but I try to steel myself. I try to take the pain and turn it into anger, because the last thing I want is to let this man, this devil, get to me.

The devil may wear a suit, but he's no gentleman.

18

FORD

"FORD, WHAT THE hell are you up to?" Gemma's no-nonsense voice comes through the line and I smirk on instinct, knowing I'm going to have to be as nonchalant as possible.

"What are you talking about?"

"That plate you had me run. It was registered to a business LLC, one that has us tracing it back to someone we've been watching for years. How did you find him?"

"He found me, more like," I hedge, not wanting to give away everything off the cuff. *"Who is it we're talking about?"*

"His name is Rafael Guerrero, he's a notorious crime lord from Mexico. His family has been on the FBI watch list for decades, but we've never been able to find him."

"Huh." My answer doesn't satisfy her, but all I have running through my head is the question of why Delaney is mixed up with this guy.

"Ford," Gemma starts. "Whatever you're thinking, don't. You're still on leave and you're not supposed to be mixed up in anything."

"I'm not trying to be."

"Stay out of it, Ford. Whatever you want to do, don't. Just..." Gemma sighs and I bristle, she doesn't show emotion very often, the fact that she is, catches me off guard. "Take care of yourself." I don't hear anything after that, and when I pull the phone away from my ear, I see that she hung up.

The phone still rests in my hands while I think over what to do. There's the obvious choice of warning Delaney, telling her that under no circumstances should she be hanging out with this guy. But if I know anything, it'll come off as more jealousy than concern for a friend.

The best choice at this point is to follow through with what I said I would do, and that's be her friend. At least if I'm that to her, I'll be able to watch everything, track any moves this guy makes and make sure that Delaney keeps her head down and out of trouble. I've always been the guy who wants to save everyone, I could never figure out if it was why I was so good at my job or why I'd essentially failed at it.

Delaney was different. Wanting to help her wasn't just for my own ego, but it was more because I'd never want her to get hurt. Knowing I won't be able to do anything about my feelings for her only makes them want to grow more, I know I'm not in any position for a woman in my life right now, my demons are still in every shadow of my mind and I can't seem to get them out, no matter how hard I try.

I make my way to the restaurant and for a moment, I sit there and stare, letting memories of my childhood and teenage-hood swamp me. This street holds everything that we all did as teenagers. Every business owner on this street is one I've known since I could walk.

I shake away the memory when I see Delaney out my window hauling a massive black trash bag around the side of the restaurant where the dumpster is. I jump out of my car and rush around the back.

I see her struggling with the bag and rush to her side, I can't see her behind the giant bag, and I give a shove to help her get it in the dumpster. I slip a smile on and turn to face her, but my smile is quickly replaced by a frown. "Laney, what the fuck."

Across her face is a bruise the runs from below her right eye and past halfway down her cheek. I reach up and gingerly touch the skin, but she flinches away from me. "Ford." Her voice cracks, and she clears it before trying again. "What are you doing here?"

"Laney. What happened?" I demand, my fists curling at my

sides.

"It's nothing." A forced laugh tumbles out and she says, "I was just cleaning last night and slipped, hit my head on a table. Really, really dumb of me, I know." Her smile falters but I force myself to calm down, yelling at her isn't going to get me where I want.

With the acting skills of Tom Cruise himself, I put a mask on and give her a smile, one that hopefully says that I believe her bald-faced lie. "You gotta be more careful, that face is too damn pretty to hurt."

A blush rises on her cheeks and I file it away in my memory bank, making Delaney Torrez blush may just be my new favorite thing.

Following along behind her, she lets me into the restaurant, there's only a few people here at this hour and Matteo is the only waiter right now. He gives me a chin lift when he sees me and returns to his customers. I slip behind the bar after Delaney and reach under the bar for an apron I left there the last time I was here. After tying it around my waist, I start the process of cleaning glasses and checking the stock of the bar for the night ahead. I feel her presence behind me with no doubt questions on her mind. "What are you doing?"

"What's it look like?" I smirk at her. "I'm working."

"Working."

"Yeah, didn't we already talk about this?"

"Well, no. Not really."

I sigh and turn my whole attention to her. "I need something to do with my free time, I happen to enjoy this kind of work and I don't intend to be paid. So, if you don't mind, I'd like to continue helping out when I can."

Delaney bites her bottom lip and makes my life harder than it needs to be when she tilts her head to the side, contemplating her words. "It doesn't seem fair. Not paying you," she clarifies.

"I get that, but frankly, I've worked a lot of years and have a nest egg that would support me for a long damn time. I don't want to be paid; I want to help you out." *And keep my eye on you,* I add silently.

Her eyes waver, I can tell she wants to argue about this. And then all at once, the fight leaves her. "Okay."

"Okay."

With a smirk and triumph boosting my ego, I go back to my job with just a wink thrown her way. Though the plaguing thoughts follow me until the end of the night, wondering who would hit her. Her father or Guerrero. Those are the only options that come to mind, I've been around long enough to know there aren't that many other choices at this point.

We're walking out to my car—again, I don't let her have a choice about riding home in my car, no one should have to walk home this late at night—when I come up with an idea.

"When's your next day off?"

She laughs good-naturedly. "What's a day off?"

I smile at her and ask, "Okay, when's the next day you can take off?"

"Um, I have no clue. Why?"

"I want to do something with you."

"Oh, and what's that?"

I scoff. "You don't want to ruin the surprise."

"Okay… I guess I could get Lizzie to cover me one day."

"Perfect." We pull up to her house and when she hesitates, I want nothing more than to pull her across the console and kiss her. I've been dreaming about her lips more than anyone should ever dream about lips and I know without a doubt, someday I won't be able to stop myself.

With a sigh that showcases the weight of the world on her shoulders, Delaney lets out a yawn before tossing me a wave and opening her door. "See you tomorrow, Ford."

"Tomorrow, Laney." I smile at her assumption of seeing me tomorrow and find that I'm looking forward to doing the same thing tomorrow as I did today. All of that due to the woman who seems to be plaguing my thoughts with every passing minute.

19

DELANEY

I GLARE AT the sun that seems to be trying to melt me to the top step of my front porch, it's nine a.m. and already hotter than hell outside. Sometimes I wish I lived in a little town up north where rain was the typical weather for the day instead of this sauna we call Texas.

It's not necessarily early for me, but considering the reason I'm standing out here, wondering what the hell is in store for me today, it makes it that much worse to be out here in the first place. The grumpy, disgruntled thoughts leave me the second I see Ford drive up in his fancy rental car. He's the reason I'm out here and just judging by his face, I should already be regretting letting him talk me into taking off a whole day to hang out with him.

I can't even remember the last time I took an entire day off just to have some fun. Hell, I wouldn't be able to tell tourists what 'fun' things there are to do because I just never get around to it. When people do ask, I direct them to Lizzie. She's always talking of new things to see and do; her wanderlust knows no bounds, and she's proud of that fact.

Ford exits the car as I come up in front of it, he's wearing black tactical pants, boots, and a tight black T-shirt. "Are we going on a mission for the government?" I joke.

His grin spreads on his face and he pulls me into a bone-crushing hug. I breathe deep through the hug and get a whiff of his cologne, it's too good. How does a guy's cologne always smell so dang good?

"To answer your question, no, we're not. This will be much more fun."

"Yeah? And what is it that we'll be doing?"

Ford's eyes light up and he looks at me seriously. "See, I could tell you, but then I'd have to kill you."

I see a flash in his eyes, maybe regret at his words after the things we've been through already. I'm not naïve enough to believe he couldn't do that, but getting to know who Ford is, I scoff and nudge his shoulder out of the way, trying to put him at ease and make my way to the passenger side. "Please. That's the oldest line in the book. I'm supposed to be intimidated?" I question.

He leans against the driver's side, arms crossed, and says, "Something tells me nothing I can do would actually scare you."

I don't reply with anything but a smirk and slide into the car. Little does Ford know, just being in his presence scares me.

"YOU ARE KIDDING me." I stare in horror at the sight in front of me. The buildings are haphazardly thrown together with old boards and screws, most covered in splotches of paint that weren't planned. The whole thing looks like *George of the Jungle* come to life. Except, instead of monkeys, there are about fifty men dressed head to toe in gear, running around screaming out commands and curses.

"I'm not. Not even a little, actually." Ford walks up to what I'm guessing is the sign-in and I look at all the various guns displayed behind the man. Tubes filled with colored paint balls are lining the shelves.

The man hands over two helmets and protective vests. "This is a joke, right? You know how uncoordinated I am," I state as I hold up the vest to my chest, I wait for Ford to drop the punchline but he just keeps staring at me. He and Bobby tried to talk me into this shit all the time and I never had any wish to join them. Ever.

"No, this is fun. Haven't you ever had any fun, Laney?"

"If this is your definition, then no. No, I have not."

Ford laughs and the sound somehow sets me at ease. "Well then, you are in for quite a treat. Not only is paint balling epic fun, but I'm a hell of a teacher. Just stick with me, kid."

He's not kidding either.

The man running the little booth has me sign a waiver, it's intense for paint balling and there's even an "In Case Of Death" clause in it. I hesitate on that one, eyeing the man behind the wooden counter. "Seriously?"

The man gives me a bored look and just shrugs. I sigh, but sign anyway. What's life without a little risk?

Once we're 'geared' up as they tell me it's called, he leads me to the side and shows me the best way to shoot the gun. I follow his instructions and yelp when a paintball comes flying out, hitting the dirt right beside his foot. "Maybe wait until we're in the arena before you pull the trigger."

I give him a sheepish look and listen carefully to what he expects me to do. I'm dying in this heat, the gear only adds insulation to my already sweltering body and I curse Ford right then and there for making me do this. But it's when the horn sounds, and the next wave of people enter the arena that I really start to hate him. Immediately we rush to a hidden area that's supposed to 'protect' us, but the paintballs are already flying toward us.

"Ford," I yelp as one zips past my head.

"Just stay low, they won't get ya." His good-natured humor on the subject makes me scowl at him.

"That's your great advice?" I let out another yelp as more hit the board that my head leans against.

"Oh yeah, and…" He lifts his helmet up, letting me see his smirking face. "Don't forget to shoot back."

I open my mouth to let out a protest, but Ford is gone and shooting his way through the hordes of people. And now, I'm on my own. "Ford, you bastard," I mumble before throwing my helmet back over my face and taking aim. If I have to be in this stupid game, I won't go down without some sort of fight.

It's not hard to find people to shoot, basically last man standing is the rule of the game, no teams like I've seen before in movies or shows. I'm wishing I'd taken the time to do some practice shooting sometime in my teens like almost every one of my peers. Growing up in Texas, and so far out in the middle of nowhere—at least at the time—every parent took their time to educate their kids on the safety of shooting a gun.

But I'd been too busy, I'd been occupied with my dreams of being a business owner, and now, I was regretting it.

Spying a guy through the tiny hole in the wood, I rise up and aim, I mean, it can't be that hard can it? After shooting from my peek, they quickly figure out where I am. "Shit," I say as I duck out of the way, the pellets hit the wood with thuds and I steady myself, taking in a deep breath.

Ford is nowhere in sight, and I make a note to give him shit for leaving me alone in this. I follow the trail that leads down some steps and to another perch. I take my time moving through it, not wanting to feel the pain of one of these things hitting me. When

I reach the lower level, I check my surroundings again and find a guy turned away from me, eyeing another player.

I don't hesitate when I pull the trigger, hitting him in the back, I hear him curse and he turns toward me but I hide myself from view again, not wanting him to retaliate, even though he's not supposed to, I'm guessing that he wouldn't care for those rules much.

When I think it's safe, I move along the ridge and slowly, I see guy after guy leave the arena, tons getting eliminated from the game, heads hanging low. The sounds of the air soft guns letting pellet after pellet out of their chambers echoes all around me and I start moving again, by chance I see a guy come into my sights, he sees me and raises his gun but I drop down and shoot in his direction, knowing the likeliness of actually hitting him isn't very good.

"What the hell," I hear him curse and open my eyes that I hadn't intended to close, seeing that I got him square in the chest.

"Uh, sorry!" My apology doesn't exactly seem to warm him up and he walks off with the rest that are getting shot.

I keep my head low, not wanting to get shot, not wanting to be spotted by anyone and praying this thing will finally end, my nerves are shot. I swear I'll never go anywhere with Ford ever again.

"Laney!" I hear him call my name and the first reaction I have is relief, but then I see him standing out in the open. "Laney, it's over! Come on out."

It's over? And he's still in the arena... which means he beat everyone else. Except me. A smile takes over my lips.

His helmet is still covering his face, and he's resting his gun against his right shoulder. He's turning in circles and watching for movement, so as slow as I can, I readjust my grip and aim straight for him. I know my aim probably isn't that good, but if I can hit him, it's at the very least payback for bringing me here and abandoning me. "Laney!" Right as he calls out, I pull the trigger and hit him in the arm, once, twice, three times until he's cursing loud enough for me to hear from at least two hundred feet away.

I'm giggling when I stand and reveal myself to him. He rips his helmet off and stares in shock, without meaning to, a smile overcomes his face and he shakes his head. "You fuckin' won, babe."

Babe. He's never called me that, but I file it away in my memory bank.

I shrug my shoulders like I'm not at all surprised and give him a smile. "Well, you shouldn't stand out in the open for all your enemies to see then, Gentry."

Without warning, he walks to me and picks me up, laughing, he spins me in a quick circle, I don't think he even realizes what he does when he places a soft kiss against my lips, but when I pull back, slightly shocked and a lot ready for more than that, he's got a look on his face that says he knew exactly what he was doing.

"Let's go, hotshot. I've got something else up my sleeve."

20

FORD

TO SAY DELANEY shocked the shit out of me is an understatement. I was not expecting her to be able to wait everyone out and win the whole damn thing. The fifty guys that were in there with us were definitely more than a little shocked at the turn of events. But it really only solidified what a truly special person she is.

Am I too old to have wanted to impress a woman with my paint balling skills?

Probably. But it didn't stop me. She never went when we were teenagers, but this was a place that Bobby and I came frequently.

I drive us out of town a ways, with a cooler full of food and drink. I go to a place that I've loved since I was a kid. It was kind of *the* place to be, especially as a teenager, but after spending the morning in the hot sun, it was the perfect place to spend the afternoon.

Delaney doesn't say anything, but I can tell she wants to question where we're going and what I've got in mind. She gave me a little punch in the shoulder for me leaving her alone in the arena, but I knew she'd be fine, I frankly thought she would follow me and see me do my thing. Paint balling was amateur hour compared to what I've been doing for the last sixteen years of my life.

I find the road I'm looking for and turn down the dirt drive, it's a bumpy ride and makes me wish I'd rented a four-wheel drive but I manage okay and make it to the end where the lake comes into view. From what I can tell, there's not a soul in sight.

Kissing her in the arena had been spontaneous, but now there wasn't anything that was going to stop me from taking this a step farther. Being around Delaney was the only thing keeping me sane and though I could hear a voice in the back of my head telling me to back off, telling me that I needed to leave her be, I wasn't sure I could—or even wanted to—listen to it.

She hops out of the car excitedly, probably remembering the many days of summer we spent right here at this very lake. The sun gives it a glistening appearance and for a moment, I just watch her look at it. I take a moment to breathe in the fresh air, to try to appreciate where I am and most of all, who I'm with.

I set the cooler down and spread out the blanket on the grass.

The cooler holds cold water and when she wanders over to where I've set everything up, I hand one to her and she guzzles it down. I do the same and then I start the process of taking off my boots. "What are you doing?" I look up to see her eyebrows pinched while she watches me undress. "What's it look like? I'm getting in."

"What?" She laughs at me and shakes her head. "You brought a suit?"

I wink at her as I pull off my pants and she turns slightly, I would swear she blushed if she wasn't already flushed from our earlier activity. "Underwear counts, right?"

"Ford, jeez, no warning?" I can tell she's trying not to laugh at me as I take off toward the lake, I don't wait for her, I just dive into the water, being that it's a million degrees, the water is fucking refreshing. I swim a ways out and when I pop back up through the surface and clear my hair off my face, I don't see her anywhere. I furrow my brow and call out her name.

And suddenly, she's right in front of me. Wearing nothing but her bra and, I assume, panties. My control slips when I imagine what she'd look like spread out on a bed in the same attire, and I have to think of nonsexual things to get myself under control.

"What?" Her voice is small and indecision wars in her eyes. I lean in closer, treading the water slightly, it's just enough that I could barely touch the bottom without going under. Grasping her hand in mine, I push us to shallower water, gaining ground so I could hold her and not drown. I keep my eyes locked on hers.

This isn't territory we ever entered before. This is new, this is two former friends finding something completely different, and I'm not willing to let it slip through my fingers. Timing be damned.

When my feet touch the ground, I give her a small grin and grab her other hand, her eyes watch me expectantly, I can't tell if she's desperate to run or to be pulled in. Without waiting to find out, I pull her to me and let my lips tap hers. I don't push it, I wait for her to respond and when she does, I let our lips do the work.

Her arms wind around my neck and I lift her up, her legs wrap around my waist and I hold her steady to me, tasting her for real this time. She responds generously and I let myself enjoy this moment. I've kissed plenty of women in my life, but none could compare to what it feels like to kiss her. I don't know if it's because it's been so long or because of who Delaney is as a person. She's someone who has fought to push through a wall I'd buried myself behind, she's fought for me in a way no one ever has and a clarity like I'd never known hits me out of the blue.

I almost wish I'd paid better attention back when we were kids. But this thing between us, it's been marinating. It's been waiting for this time in our lives for us to be able to explore what it is we're supposed to do, what we're supposed to be. Me being on leave, her being right where I needed her to be when I didn't even know I needed it. It's all fate coming together.

When we pull away, both of us are trying to catch our breath and I take in every detail of her face. Her freckles that lightly dust her cheeks, her dark brown eyes that seem to drink me in,

I watch for any kind of negative reaction to what we've done, about how we're holding each other now and beam when she just gives me a small smile. Before I can ask her anything, her stomach rumbles, making me laugh out loud and raise a teasing eyebrow. "Hungry, huh?"

She looks at me with a look that I don't know how to decipher, but before I can add an innuendo or two, she nods her head and uses my stomach as a kick board, flinging herself back into the water and to the shore again. I shake my head as I follow behind her.

"HOW DID YOU know that this was my favorite food?"

I raise a brow. "Sandwiches?"

She opens her mouth for a big bite and nods her head at me as I let out a loud laugh. Delaney isn't like anyone I've ever dated, not that I've dated much in the last decade but her carefree attitude is sexy as hell.

"Well, I'm glad I could give you such a gourmet meal then."

"Oh yeah, you got it right."

We're silent for a while after that, eating our lunch and watching the sun move across the sky as afternoon blazes above us, the breeze off the lake giving us a brief but welcome reprieve. Eventually I let myself lay out on the blanket and just relax for the first time in a long time.

Delaney follows suit and stretches out on the blanket next to me, our shoulders barely grazing but enough that I can feel the heat radiate off her body.

I clear my throat. "So, tell me, that wasn't your first time paint balling, was it?"

She huffs a chuckle. "Oh my God, yes it was. That was terrifying."

"Please, you were the smartest one in there!" I turn toward her at my teasing, catching a flush hit her cheeks. It still surprises me how modest she can be, she works her ass off and does a smart job running her family's restaurant, but she'd never gloat or tell anyone that.

"I was not, I was the biggest coward in there."

"Nah, it was a tactic. We wear camouflage in the military for a reason, so we can blend in and hide in plain sight. One misstep, one shiny object, can take out a whole team of people."

I'm still looking over at her as she rolls to her side, she has a small smile gracing her lips that I love. She looks over at me, that soft look still in her eyes. "Tell me what the army was like."

A sigh escapes me as I think about what to tell her, my time in the army was far better than my time in the FBI at least. "I loved the army." She keeps that smile and waits silently for me to gather my thoughts. "I had a family of brothers there that I was super tight with, we were all in the same unit, wherever I went, I knew they'd be there right alongside me. It was really the only reassurance we had."

"Was it hard?"

"Yeah." I laugh. "I always thought summer football camp was hard until basic training happened, and then I realized what a pussy I was." A giggle comes from Delaney and I continue. "But it was good too. It gave me a purpose to help people and fight for our country."

"God bless the USA."

I raise a hand for a high five. "Damn straight, baby." When her hand hits mine, I grasp it tightly and interlock our fingers. "So, what about you? What have you been up to these last few years?"

She gives a little shimmy of her shoulders in a casual shrug. "Not as much as you'd think. Life doesn't change much around here."

"Come on, something had to have happened."

"Seriously, I've just kept the restaurant running. Renovated that, went to business school, took care of Dad." She gives a little shy smile at me.

"And nothing's changed? What about…" I pause, wondering if I should bring up our old friend Bobby. Then I decide, someday, I'll have to face him too, so I might as well get it over with. "Bobby?" I finish.

"Ah." She huffs out a laugh. "Believe it or not, we are still pretty close friends,"

"Just friends?" The words are out before I can think them over, I know I'm not prepared enough for the answer to be no.

"Well, yeah." She shrugs, casting her gaze back to the sky. "After… school, we were able to lean on each other, me more than him. He helped me get through losing Mom and…"

She doesn't have to finish the sentence for me to know *"and you"* is the end of it. I squeeze her hand. "I'm sorry about your mom," I say instead of bringing up my absence again.

"Thanks. Your mom was a huge help to me back then."

"She was?"

Delaney smirks at me and says, "Well, it was only a few months before we graduated. She brought us meal after meal when she could. Though she was back and forth to physical therapy for Jack, she didn't have much time on her hands. She gave me someone to lean on. Dad was a mess, as you'd expect, and he just wasn't himself for a long time. And well, after that, I knew that whatever I did, I was going to have to help Dad out until things were steady again."

"And what happened? It didn't get better?"

"No, it did. When I was working at Walmart to help us out, we were able to get ahead. So much so that I was able to go to night school and get a business degree. Once I was through, that was when I was going to put down a payment on a new building to open a flower shop, but things got in the way." A deep sigh comes from her and she shakes her head. "We got robbed one night. They took everything in the safe." Her eyebrows scrunch together.

"What is it?" I ask with a squeeze to her hand.

She shakes her head again and refocuses on

me. "Nothing, I was just thinking about something." I don't pry because I'm sure that sharing all of that with me wasn't easy, something tells me she's not used to being able to share her feelings with people and I swallow down the want inside to tell her I can be that person for her.

"I'm really glad you gave me today."

Her words catch me by surprise, and I give her my signature smirk. "I'm glad you gave me a chance."

"I don't think I could ever not." Delaney's eyes drift down, hovering over my lips, and before I know what move to make, she's leaning in, pressing her lips to mine in a sweet kiss. One that I'd never thought of having with her when we were kids, but now, I can't understand how I couldn't have wanted this back then.

I release a low groan and nudge her lips open with my tongue. I taste the sweet strawberries on her tongue from her drink and reach my hand out to grasp her hip. It meets practically nothing with her still in only her underwear. She skims her hands up my chest and I break out in chills when her nails scratch lightly on my skin.

I reluctantly release her lips but not before I press another chaste kiss to her lips. "As much as I'd love to continue this, I don't think out in the open is the place to do it."

She laughs and looks around. "PDA ain't your thing, huh?"

"Well, not when I'm protective of the person I'm with."

We gather up our clothes and put them back on before packing up the rest of the picnic, grabbing our belongings in one hand and Delaney's hand in my other, I lead us to the car all the while thinking of the ways I'm going to make this woman mine.

We may have just found each other again, things aren't perfect in my life. Living without this woman in my life though, that's not an option now. She's the air I need to breathe and without her, my oxygen is gone.

21

DELANEY

THE BREEZE IS fresh as I make my way to the restaurant that day, and for the first time I don't feel the normal frenzied rush to get there. I stroll, taking in Main Street and the shops that surround our place. Every shop has been there for years, each with its own unique history. Some owned by elderly now, some passed on to the younger generations or bought by others from out of town. The latter being the people who desperately wanted to have that small town Texas life. Everyone loves the old town feel, and our town is definitely in that category. We're as old as it gets.

I wave to Miss Edith when I get to the restaurant, she runs the bank down the street and is a perpetual bachelorette, says no one has caught her eye for long enough to make her settle down, which, until recently, I'd been able to relate to.

I open the restaurant to silence and take in the cleanliness that we left it in the night before. My team never lets me down, they take pride in their work, making it even easier to leave it in their capable hands. *I should take more days off.* I think, noting the perfect reset of the restaurant.

I toss my bag in the office and sigh. I check the notebook I keep of payments due and see we're actually up-to-date. Despite the fact that Rafael has been taking a good chunk every week, we're managing to stay afloat, I think it has something to do with our new two-for-one margarita special.

For the first time in a long time, I actually feel like things are coming together. That pressure eases off of my chest for the first time since my mother passed. The second she was gone, I felt like something was always missing and I could never figure it out. I thought if I got the restaurant off the ground, I would feel a sense of pride and know she would be proud too. But even after I thought I had; I didn't feel that relief.

Ever since Ford stepped back into town, that relief I'd been aching for was finally there. I was able for the first time in years to breathe, to relax, to finally lean on someone other than myself. Of course, maybe that's not fair. It's not as if I couldn't have gone to a number of people over the years for help or to talk. But I'd never felt free enough to do so.

With that relief came an unexpected since of fear, of

apprehension. Ford was hiding something. Whether it was just his past, or someone who'd hurt him, something lingered behind his eyes that had me begging him to let me help him through it.

Then there was a new shift in his demeanor, a new light to his eyes that had me wanting to ask questions I didn't think I had a right to ask. But he never stopped me when I asked those questions, and I wondered if he was waiting for someone to come in and push him into letting all of those demons come out.

Since our first date—where I hadn't had a clue that I was actually on one until the time in front of the lake, I'd seen Ford nearly every day. I never gave myself a lot of time off, but Ford managed to see me regardless. I felt like a teenage girl all over again. Giddy and excited nerves fluttered in my belly each morning at the thought of seeing him again.

I'd been a shell of myself for as long as I could remember, and suddenly, with the reappearance of my best friend, I'd found that happy person I had been in high school. The one who looked forward to each day with a renewed sense of purpose, with excitement buzzing in my veins.

And while we hadn't had much talk of me being his or vice versa, there was something silently passed between the two of us that made me sure of it without having to voice a word, and that both exhilarated and terrified me.

"DELANEY, TABLE FOUR needs waters."

Something was *in* the damn water, that was for sure. The restaurant was packed full and people were demanding orders left and right. It was pure chaos, and I wasn't sure if my staff was fully prepared for this kind of work.

Some tour busses had come in this afternoon that were unexpected, apparently everyone on those damn busses had fasted for the last day with the way they were demanding food.

"Got it!" I rush behind the bar and grab a plethora of drink glasses, quickly filling them with ice and pouring water over them. I don't have a clue how many people are at the table, so best guess is to grab more than you need.

"Busy much?" The voice behind me makes me jump and I turn to see green eyes smiling down at me.

"Ford," I breathe and give him a smile on instinct.

"Need some help?" My shoulders fall a little in relief when he asks, and as much as I don't want to take advantage of him, I can't say no to help.

"Please." I turn back to grab the tray, but he grabs my hand.

"Well, I'm going to require some payment this time." My breath catches when I think of having to pay another person, I can't swing that. Not this time. Maybe a few months ago, but now with Rafael and everything else, there's just no possible way.

Before I can reply, I feel him push me against the bar slightly and press his lips to mine. My eyes close and my eyebrows rise in surprise. I melt against him and let him take his time even knowing there are people watching; most probably getting impatient when I should be hustling their food to them.

"Yeah, that'll do it." Ford's voice breaks through the fog in my head and I laugh a little. "I've got the bar."

"WE DID IT!" Lizzie's voice raises over the after-rush chatter and we cheer with her, all of us spread out around the restaurant for our first break of the evening. When the rush cleared out, it only left one couple who were too engrossed in each other to actually focus on eating.

Ford comes up behind me and grabs my hips, I spin to meet him and let him give me a soft kiss. "Thank you," I say to him and let him grab my hands in his. "I couldn't have done that without your help."

He raises an eyebrow. "So, what you're saying is you can't live without me then." There's something lingering behind his eyes, an unease after he says the words. I don't pick at that thread though, giving him an out by letting the teasing words fall off my lips.

"Mm, I didn't say that…"

"I'll bet I could get you to," he challenges, and I don't have a retort because I know he's right. He could get me to admit that because hell, breathing is easier with the man around.

"Well, I guess you have a challenge on your hands."

"Challenge accepted."

22

FORD

I SERIOUSLY HATED being here. It wasn't as bad as I had thought it would be, truthfully. But now this woman knew every little thing about me that no one else did. She knew the horror that was my life just a year ago, she knew that I was struggling with living with myself over what I'd done, what I'd seen. There was a small voice in the back of my head that made me wish that I had been telling this to Delaney and not her.

Things with us were slow, and that's the way it needed to be. We've only ever been friends, and not as adults. The things that we went through in high school were horrific, but the shit in my head? That was stuff I had to work up to. I couldn't just spit it out.

Plus, it didn't help my case that whenever I was around her now, I was having a hard time thinking of anything other than getting her curves into the palms of my hands. Holding her close to my chest and pressing my lips to hers, the softness melting against me while I held her up.

"So, tell me your plan."

"My plan?" I blink the image away, trying not to let my neck redden when I realized where my brain had just gone in front of my therapist.

"Yeah, when I give the go-ahead, your bosses will reinstate you. Where do you see yourself going?"

I lean back from resting my elbows on my knees and realize what she just said, that she's getting ready to give the all-clear for me to work, to get back to the FBI and to my career. I feel a rise of anxiety in my chest and clear my throat. "I don't know."

"Well, before you were benched, you were taking on some seriously dangerous missions. Do you think you can handle that again?"

"I—" I didn't have a very good answer. I think I could easily go back to being an undercover agent. It was something I was damn good at, the training I'd undergone to get this far was intense and only made me want to be the best.

Things had started to change though, and not only because of that last mission, but being home had made me consider other things, other people as well. Did I want to be that and go back to how it was before, no family, no friends, no Delaney?

Fuck no. I didn't want that.

"I don't know what I'm going to do."

I LEAVE THE appointment, feeling more confused than ever, I almost want to convince Laura to extend my treatment, so I don't have to choose. So I can stay home and continue living the way I have been. For the first time ever, I've been actually happy.

I make my way to the restaurant knowing Delaney is there and needing to see her to get myself out of my own head, I can't stand to be stuck in there for very long. It's too much, too many thoughts and memories. Too many demons to haunt the ever-loving shit out of me.

The front is eerily empty and when I call out, I don't hear anything. I make my way behind the bar, ready to start cleaning to give myself something to do when I hear someone behind me, I turn and reach for the gun I used to keep on my person, only to come up empty and see Joaquín coming at me, anger vibrating off of him and a pinch between his eyes, directed at me.

"Mr. Torrez." I give him a curt nod when he gets close but don't budge. I may not know exactly what's going on with Guerrero, but I do know that he was responsible for leaving marks on Delaney and her father did nothing to stop it.

"Why are you here?" His question throws me off and I squint.

"I'm here to help Delaney."

He scoffs, "I'm not stupid, boy. What is your real reason for snooping around my daughter?"

This man in front of me is not the man I used to know. God knows I know time can change a person, but what shit was he into that would make that sweat beading on his forehead so severe, that would make the panic and fear in his eyes at my presence so obvious? "Why are you worried about my being here?" I stand casually and cross my arms.

Joaquín flushes and wipes his forehead with a rag from his back pocket, "I'm not worried, but I am confused why all of a sudden you are home."

"I was sent home." I shrug. I don't have anything to hide from the Torrezs, I'm not officially investigating anyone, and I don't have any reason to believe they're doing anything illegal. It's not illegal to take a loan, but it is illegal to collude with criminals.

"That's it?" he asks, his eyes wide as if waiting for the punchline.

"That, and the fact that your daughter is the most amazing woman I've ever met, and I'll be damned if I ever give that up." I stand tall and intimidatingly over him, he looks pissed but I won't back down, I'm not worried about how he'll take my news because I couldn't care less. "If there's anything you need to share with me about her well-being, *that* I'm willing to talk about." The silence is filled with tension while I wait for him to spill. For the truth to escape him without warning. But he doesn't, and right when I'm about to push harder, the front door jingles open and Delaney comes rushing in, a flush on her cheeks but a smile gracing her face when she spots me.

I don't wait for Joaquín to say anything and I take the floor in four long strides and pull her into me, breathing easily for the first time today. I won't let anything hurt her, no matter what it takes, I'll protect her.

With everything I know about Guerrero, I have a feeling it'll come to a bloody ending.

TONIGHT, I'M HAVING Delaney come to family dinner. This has been a tradition since I was a teenager, and I started wanting to be with my friends every night. Since I'd been gone, it seems the tradition lived on and I'm grateful. I hate thinking of my family not living just because I was a selfish asshole and left them behind to deal with the shit I'd done.

Seeing my family happy, though, makes me damn glad I decided to come home. Seeing Jack with his fiancée and Mom and Dad laughing in the living room before dinner, it gives me a content feeling that I let settle deep in my chest.

The doorbell rings and I jump up to grab it, ignoring my brother's barbs at how fast I rush the door, when I get there I swing it open to reveal Delaney, dressed in a blue dress that hits just above her knees and a nervous smile gracing her face, a casserole dish clutched in her hands.

Before my family is witness, I lean down and give her a long kiss, trying to reassure her through the kiss that everything will be fine. Delaney has spent time in this house with me and my family, but tonight is different.

"Hi," I say when I pull back and pull her through the door.

"Hey," she says through a sigh and I see her take in another deep breath when she hears my family laughing in the other room.

Mom comes rushing in and grabs Delaney in a hug that seems to catch her off guard, I smile seeing Mom so genuinely happy to have Delaney here. "How are you, sweetheart?"

"I'm good, Mrs. Gentry, thank you."

Mom waves a hand in the air and scoffs good-naturedly. "Please, call me Melissa."

Delaney nods her head with a smile and gestures to the dish she brought. "I brought *elote*."

"Oh honey! You didn't have to do that, but I'm sure glad you did! I haven't had genuine *elote* in years." Mom opens the tin foil top and a smell hits me that makes me groan. The seasoned corn looks fucking delicious, as does the person who brought it. Suddenly, family dinner sounds excruciating.

"Well, my mama always said never come empty-handed, and I figured everyone likes corn."

We follow Mom into the living room where Laney waves at Michelle. I quirk a brow at Delaney. "I didn't know you knew each other."

Delaney gives me a soft smile and says, "She's come into the restaurant a few times."

We head into the dining room and take our seats. I look at my parents at the head of the table and look across to see my brother whisper into Michelle's ear. A spark of jealousy streaks through me, and I let my hand travel to rest on Delaney's thigh. This is a new thing for us both, but the feeling in my heart, the one that seems to call to her… I've never felt it before.

And I'm not ready to let it go.

23

DELANEY

IT'S BEEN AGES since I'd been in the Gentry's home. I remember it well and that was because his mom was the type who could make any space feel welcoming and comfortable, who made every corner of her house feel like a home.

Ford invited me here for their weekly family dinner. I remembered when Mrs. Gentry had decided to start that in order to get her family together for at least one meal. Back then, Bobby and I were not invited. It had nothing to do with anything other than these dinners were for family only. Which had me apprehensive in joining them tonight, but Ford insisted.

So, here I sat. In their family dining room, listening to the happy chatter around me and feeling so comfortable and yet almost overwhelmed by the love that their family shows one another. It makes me wonder how Ford went so long without this.

I would give anything to have my mother by my side again, to be able to have the father I once knew back and have my own little family intact once again. It makes a string of jealousy slither through me, but I push it away and take a look at Ford who's laughing at something his dad said, his right hand is firmly grasped in my left at his insistence. I wasn't about to make him eat left-handed, but he didn't give me a choice and I didn't want to push it.

Ford's mom engages me and Michelle in talks and Michelle starts talking about her wedding. They plan to marry next spring, right in the back yard with the barn as a backdrop. "That sounds beautiful."

Michelle looks at me in surprise and I flush, thinking I'd overstepped. "Thank you." She shakes her head with a smile and says, "All my friends think it's silly, but I just want something small and intimate, just for me and Jack and our families." She looks at Jack and he raises her hand and kisses the back of it, clearly hearing what she'd said. They look so in love that even I've got butterflies watching how they interact with each other.

I look to the man who's clasping my hand and find him already watching me with a similar look that makes me have to turn away, it's all happening so fast and unexpectedly that I'm having a hard time keeping up with the amount of emotions that keep evolving at a rapid speed.

I've spent so many years alone, just working and pushing myself to make everything work in my professional life that I never really took the time to do anything outside of it. I'd had a couple of men approach me about dating, but I wasn't ever interested. Then all of a sudden, here I am, taking another night off work, sitting at a house conversing about someone's wedding and actually finding myself enjoying myself.

"Wanna go for a walk?" Ford's voice hits my ear, making a slight shiver run down my spine and I turn to look up at him, he's got a gleam in his eye that I love. I nod and we stand to walk out the back door.

"Wait, I should help your mom cleanup." I stop and look over my shoulder to see her and Michelle standing to take the dishes.

"Nah, she wouldn't let you help the first time. You can help next time." He reaches over and slips his hand into mine, lacing our fingers together.

"Next time, huh?"

"You do know you're stuck with me, don't you?" A huff of laughter escapes me and I cover part of my face with my free hand, trying to hide the nervous flush that covers me. I can't for the life of me figure out why I'm acting like a love-struck teenager.

"Well…" I clear my throat and shrug my shoulders, unable to find words to say to him. The feelings that are in me are far too real, far too intense for how long we've been seeing each other.

I push the thought away as we walk into the barn, the cows munching on their dinners that Ford and his dad had come out to feed to them before we started dinner. They have the stalls opened to a pasture so that they can come and go as they pleased. Ford leads me to some stairs that are tucked in the back area of the barn, in a secluded little corner. "What's up here?"

"Come on up and see." Ford's smirk beckons me closer, and I ascend the stairs toward the closed door at the top. I feel him following behind me, sticking close enough that his body heat warms my backside.

I reach for the handle and twist the knob, pushing the door open. What I find inside is Joanna Gaines worthy. The small space has been completely redone to give it a farmhouse chic style that most people would die over. I walk in farther, inspecting the room. It's a studio-style room with the king-size bed in the middle. Cute bedside tables frame the bed and sheer curtains hang behind them, letting the soft moon glow spread across the room. There's a place for clothes, a dresser and a hanging rack and a small table that's meant for a woman to be able to do her makeup or hair. A door is to the left, leading to what I can tell from here is the bathroom.

I turn to Ford. "Wow. This place is beautiful."

He grins and steps toward the bed to turn on a lamp. The soft glow gives the room an even cozier feeling. He moves back toward me and stops just short of touching me. "I wish I could take the credit but… well, I had nothing to do with it." He laughs and I giggle, noticing some nerves that are slipping through Ford's carefully placed mask. His eyes flick over my face and his face sobers. "I'm really glad you're here."

"Really?" I ask on a grin.

"Really."

His hands find my hips and he pulls me closer to him until our fronts are fit so tight that you couldn't possibly fit anything between us. Ford takes his time looking over my face as if memorizing every crevice and slowly, he lowers his mouth to mine and I take his lips greedily. Kissing Ford has become one of my favorite things to do and I never want to pass up a chance to kiss this man. I feel my heartbeat in my chest, my blood pressure rising at the thought of what tonight could be and hope beyond hope that I'm not wrong.

He releases my hips and reaches behind me where my zipper rests, grabbing hold, he pulls it down, I can feel each tooth of the zipper separate and I wait for him to pull it off but he takes his lips from me and looks me in the eyes, asking for permission to do what he wants. I nod my head and lean back in to kiss him, my hands going to his buttons on the front of his shirt, undoing one at a time to reveal his toned chest to me. I've seen it before but somehow, knowing where we're headed, it's even more intense to feel it against my hands.

His rough fingertips run up my spine, making goose bumps rise and I shiver with a smile, I feel his own against my lips and his hands wander over my shoulder and peel the dress off of my shoulders. Gravity takes the rest of the dress down my skin and I'm left in just a lacy bra and panties, my shoes still on my feet while he's barely got his shirt off.

I finish the buttons and watch his green eyes take in my nearly naked flesh. He helps pull his own shirt off and undoes the belt on his jeans, letting them fall off, his shoes somehow disappearing with his pants and I take the opportunity to kick the flats I never get the chance to wear off my own feet.

With us both in our underwear, our breathing heats up and the fire lights his eyes when I look back up again. Without warning, he reaches around me and lifts me into his arms, my legs hook around his waist and I feel him turn us toward the bed, gently laying me on the soft plush without letting me go and I tremble with anticipation. It's been a long time since I've done this and I can't help the nerves, but for some reason, doing this with Ford, it's not as scary. It's comfortable, it's right.

His lips attach to mine and his hands explore, down my arms, over my bra and down my bare stomach, briefly hesitating at the top of my panties before he can't wait and he rips my panties down my legs and onto the floor. Before I can even blink, his hand replaces where they once were and his long fingers work over my mound before one enters me. It's tight, but he's gentle with me, distracting me with his mouth while continuing to pulse with his finger before adding another.

In an embarrassing amount of time, I've hit my peak and suddenly my puffs of air are briefly paused. "Ford." His name leaves my throat on a moan and he kisses down my neck, working me through my orgasm before he removes his hand. He lifts off of me and I open my eyes to see where he's going. He returns quickly with a condom in his hand and rips the package open before sliding the condom on with expert fingers.

A blush hits my cheeks and Ford looks down at me, his hand still on his shaft. "You okay, beautiful?"

I nod with a small giggle and gesture to him. "I haven't uh… I haven't done this in some time."

He leans over me, his eyes searching mine, probably trying to see if I'm going to back out now, and he kisses me softly on the lips. "I'll be gentle with you, always."

I nod again and grab his thick, muscular shoulders and brace myself. "Relax," he says and cups my cheek with a hand while his other holds his body weight over me. When I do what he says, he gently pushes inside of me. I can't help the gasp of air I let out at the feeling. It really has been forever, but more than that, it's *him*. He's the reason my breath is hitching, he's the reason that I'm feeling so much more than just the physical act of sex, but something that's been absent from my life for the longest time.

He starts to slowly shift his hips against mine, his pumps pushing farther and farther until I'm sure I'm going to burst open and I gasp just as his lips meet mine again. I revel in the kiss, letting myself relax and feel every single thing about this moment. I feel the orgasm rising and when I do, my eyes pop open and I can see the strain on his face and know he's holding back, I reach for his lips again and moan loudly, hoping that there's some soundproofing to this room and when it hits me, I gasp his name loudly.

"Laney." His moans vibrate against my ear and I collapse against the bed with him on top of me, he continues to move his hips until his orgasm has finished and then he lays gently onto his forearms, boxing me in and just stares at me. I smile as I think about what we just did, even knowing that it was where we were headed, I didn't think it'd ever feel that way.

I know now, if he left again, I'm not sure I would survive it a second time.

24

FORD

"WELL, OKAY, YOU must tell me what's got that permanent grin on your face." Laura sits in her usual spot, legs crossed on her oversized chair and a notebook in her lap, waiting for me to spill my guts once again. I know what has me grinning and admit that it's a much different me than how I've been in previous therapy sessions.

I think back to my night with Delaney a few nights ago, the night I've been dreaming of since I'd gotten my head back on straight. It was even better than I'd ever imagined, I knew how lucky I was that I got to be the one that made love to her, she was special, and I vowed to remember that.

She didn't leave that night, instead, we laid in bed talking about anything and everything, just basking in each other, enjoying the peace and quiet, the uninterrupted time together, finally together without an audience to do what we pleased.

It was the best fucking night of my life.

We've spent a couple nights the same way since, except last night when she insisted on going home. It was the first night I'd had nightmares since our first night together and I regretted letting her leave. Having her next to me quelled that demon and I was eager to keep it that way.

It was so close to perfection that I was afraid that I would blink and everything would change. Being with her was sweet and easy. She was a drama-free person. She absolutely hated it, she told me as much when I'd asked how she and Lizzie were friends. They were opposites and apparently, they attracted.

"Uh, well I've started to see someone." The grin on my lips is unintentional but just thinking of the woman who occupied ninety-five percent of my brain was enough to make me look like a lovesick fool that I didn't care to hide from anyone.

"Really?" Laura writes something in her notebook and looks up again, "Who is the lucky woman?"

"Her name is Delaney." She just stares, waiting patiently for me to say more. "She's a great girl, when I'm with her, I can get out of my head." I don't elaborate much more, I don't really care to share the intimacies of my love life with anyone, even my therapist.

"Ford," Laura sighs but in a way that makes it sound like she's pleased at what she's hearing. "That is so wonderful. You know, finding someone who you can spend time with, someone not involved in your work, it's such a stepping stone for you."

I shrug and nod along like I know what she's talking about. I hadn't really reached out to Delaney because I wanted someone outside of my professional life, hell, I hadn't even really worried about my professional life at all. I wasn't in the mindset to give a shit about what happened to me. I knew that the chances of me ever going dark again would be pretty unlikely, if I had anything to say about it. That part of my life was over and I was glad I never had to go back.

"Does she know of your past?"

"Some." I nod. I told Delaney some of what I could. Not everything was free rein on what I could or could not tell her. Some of the things that she probably deserved to know weren't things that I ever, ever wanted to share with anyone. Jack was probably the last soul on Earth I would ever tell, and in that moment, I'd been weighed down with memories and emotions I just couldn't hold on to anymore.

"And are you still writing things down for yourself?" She was referring to the journal that she had given me last session, I hadn't even touched the thing since I left last time and I didn't want to. Writing down my thoughts and feelings was more intimate than I was willing to be.

"Yeah," I lie, hoping I can find a way to write some sort of shit in there so she wouldn't hold it against me at the end of this torture.

I leave the office with a large sigh on my lips and make my way home. I plan to go to the restaurant later to help out, but for now, my bed is calling my name.

My restless night filled with nightmares was catching up to me. It was filled with red and dark, men and women and children screaming in my nightmares and I woke in a sweat that covered me head to toe.

I wonder if I'd ever sleep normally again after that horrific time of my life.

When I get home, I collapse on the bed without worrying about the clothes I'm wearing. My shoes slip off and before I know it, my exhaustion pulls me under.

—

I wake to the sound of vibrating and look out the window to see it's pitch black outside. "Shit," I say and jump off the bed, digging into my pants for my phone and see Delaney's name and smiling face looking back at me.

"Hey, baby," I answer and sigh. "I'm so sorry, I passed out."

"Hey, it's okay." She sounds weary and I furrow my brow when I ask her what's the matter. "Nothing." She giggles, "I'm being silly."

"What's going on?"

"Um, well. I'm actually outside…" She trails off and I walk to the door and open it, expecting to see her standing there waiting on me but there's no one there.

"Where, babe?"

"I'm out front, I don't want to disturb you though, should I just come by tomorrow?" I look at the clock on the small bedside table, it's just after one in the morning, she must have come straight from the restaurant. A warm feeling fills my chest and I grin.

"No, come up." I'm slipping my shoes on when she starts to second-guess herself and I jog down the stairs and out the door. She's still in her father's car and when she sees me, she hangs up the phone and opens the door.

"I'm sorry I woke—" I don't let her finish her sentence, I press my lips to hers, pinning her to the side of the car and holding her there, even when I stop kissing her, I don't unwind my arms and just breathe her in.

I grab her hand and start pulling her toward the barn, but she pulls back, "Hang on," She reaches into the back seat and produces an overnight bag. I shoot her a wink when she blushes and drag her back to my bed.

25

DELANEY

A PUFF OF air escapes me when Lizzie hits me from behind. "Sorry!" she yells as she rushes to the kitchen for another pickup. The place is packed again, and I swear, you'd think that I took out billboards or was offering topless servers for how busy we'd been lately.

The restaurant never struggled to get customers, we were one of the original restaurants in town that was still standing, we were nearly historic. Every business that operated when Mom and Dad started had closed their doors and, in their place, other businesses opened up. The hardware store coming in second to being the oldest place in town.

But the newest rush of people made me suspicious. Why all of a sudden were we slammed almost every day?

I couldn't complain though, we needed the extra income to keep up with our weekly payments to Rafael, who was due here tonight. I'd spent the morning counting out his weekly payment with a grimace on my face. I hated doing it, I hated that this man had control over things that I've worked literally my entire life for.

He came late at night, after we were closed, and he used that privacy to his advantage so he could box me in. It was his power move, to make me feel intimidated and try to get under my skin. I was pissed that it was working.

"Hey there." A chill slips down my back at the hot breath at my ear, I turn in the arms circling my waist and smile up at Ford.

"Hey," I reply on a sigh. We've spent damn near every night together since the first night and I found myself looking forward to closing down and crawling into his arms at the end of the night.

I'd only embarrassed myself once, and that was when Ford's dad caught me sneaking around the side of the house to the barn. He'd smiled at me and beckoned me to the back porch, handing me a beer and talking to me about mundane things that really didn't have anything to do with me or him.

It was his way, I think, to try to give me a hard time about sneaking around with his son. It did make me feel like a caught teenager and when Ford wandered up clearly looking for me, he'd joined us, just smiling at the sight of us and making an offhand comment about finding a more private residence for himself.

I didn't have the heart to ask if it was a temporary place to stay or not. Because I wanted him to stay, but I knew that wasn't an option. His life was elsewhere, it was all over the country doing things for us ordinary folks that no one could even know about and I wasn't about to be the one person who would take that away from him.

Ford's gaze roamed the room, taking in the surrounding chaos, and my eyes seemed to not be able to look away. He looks back down at me and raises a brow. "Babe?"

Babe.

"What?" I ask, not hearing him ask me anything.

He chuckles and says, "I said, you're keeping busy. It's packed again."

"Oh yeah, I have no idea what's going on." He gives a shrug in response and I scrunch my eyebrows together, suddenly suspicious. "Do you know what's going on?"

"Hm?"

"Ford?" I ask sternly and wait for him to answer my question, but he gets called away by Bobby who's sitting at the bar, he gives me a quick smack on the lips and makes his way over. He and Bobby have worked out some of their own things.

Bobby came in to talk it out with me. He didn't seem as enthusiastic that Ford was home as the rest of us, but he was slowly coming around. Losing his best friend had been hard on him. "I just worry about what will happen when he leaves again."

I'd paused my count, refilling the till at the cash register to raise a brow at Bobby and sighed. "Bobby, we can't constantly think he'll leave." Even if that thought was always in the back of my head.

He leaned his elbows on the bar, raising one hand to rub at his bottom lip, he eyed me uncertainly. "Lanes... I really don't want you to get hurt."

I knew what he was implying. Bobby was no dummy, I realized, he was around us when we were teens. Hiding my crush wasn't exactly easy. "I'm not going to get hurt."

"You did, though," he states, holding my eyes. "We both did. And if we—if you, let him in too fast, too deep, he's going to hurt you."

"Yeah well, I say he's not!" I snapped back. Instantly, I regretted it when I saw the crestfallen look on his face. Bobby and I had remained friends all these years, he'd been there for me through all of my struggles and I did the same for him.

He nodded. "Okay, Lanes. Whatever you say." I didn't reply or try to convince him. I didn't have to. Bobby knew me too well, he knew that outburst was one made out of fear.

WE'RE ABOUT TWO hours from closing when it happens, the restaurant, which has calmed down a considerable amount seems to go even quieter at the ringing of the bell on the door, when I turn to see the person who's entered my breath halts for a moment.

Rafael stands at the door, hands in his slacks and a glare in his eyes. He's wearing another impeccable suit that I'd find attractive if I didn't find him so damn scary and frankly, kind of the worst person ever. Rafael eyes the customers who look on in curiosity, Rafael isn't someone who would be recognized in this part of town. He's got his own empire where he's feared, but even knowing that, it seems everyone can tell that they don't want to mess with him.

I finally find my feet and quickly make my way over to him, ushering him to the back office. When we enter, I shut the door behind us, making sure to stand by it in case I need a quick getaway. He stands facing me, a smirk on his face at throwing me off with his arrival and I glare back.

"Why are you here this early?"

He sniffs and says, "Oh, I'm sorry. I didn't realize I was regulated to your schedule."

I shake my head. "You never show up before closing."

"What are you worried about? Your boyfriend getting jealous?"

My eyes widen a fraction, I'd completely forgotten about Ford being a witness to that, no doubt he was working on making his way back here. "That's not what I'm worried about. I don't want to be paying you during work hours. If we need to work something else out, then we'll do that."

Rafael smiles and I wonder if it's the first smile I've seen on him, a real, genuine smile that shows he's laughing at me. "Well, I think we could definitely work that out. Next week, you come to my house, I'll make dinner and we can discuss the precarious situation we find ourselves in."

"Precarious situation? This situation is because you won't leave me and my father alone."

"The situation is because your father made a deal that he could not follow through with." He strides toward me until he's nearly standing on top of me, but I hold my ground, practically holding my breath at his proximity. "None of this would have happened if your father hadn't fucked it up."

His accent gets thicker the more irritated he gets, and I cross my arms, hoping to make a barrier between us. "I won't be going to your house. You may come here to collect the money."

Rafael eyes me, seeming to decide how worth it I am, and says, "Fine. I will, when I want, and how I want."

I swallow at the threat. I've never been someone who hated anyone before, but if I was, it would be him. A knock on the door startles me and I turn, ready to open the door when Rafael stops me. "You forgot something."

The money. I spin back around and stride to the desk, opening the drawer and pulling out the envelope, when I slap it into his hand he winks at me. I grind my teeth when he says, "See you next week, *reina.*"

He turns and opens the door, revealing a concerned Ford, his stance is tall and intimidating, he's at least four inches taller than Rafael but I worry if it came down to it, Rafael wouldn't fight fair. He glares at Rafael as he walks past him but neither says a word.

When Rafael is finally out of sight, Ford turns to me and walks in, shutting the office door behind him, locking us away from the world and I breathe a real breath for the first time in ten minutes.

"What was that about?" Ford's stance is tense, his hands rest on his hips and his eyes glare at me accusingly.

I tilt my head and say, "Just some business I had to take care of."

Ford sighs and I can almost see him biting his tongue. "Who's that guy?"

"He's… a friend of my father's." The lie slips from my tongue too easily.

"Really? He seemed to be a little more friendly toward you than just a friend of your dad's."

His accusation is clear and I fold my arms over my chest, the defensive mode coming so easily. "What are you saying, Ford?"

He squeezes his eyes shut and sighs. "Nothing. Sorry."

"No, what is it?" I know what he wants to say and for some reason, I can't stop myself from pushing, from making him say it.

"It just seems like you guys have a bit of history or something."

We have history alright, history of me wanting to *kick his ass*, history of me wanting to throw caution to the wind and leave the restaurant behind, change my name and never, ever see Rafael Guerrero ever again.

"It's not really the kind of history that you think, he's just a business associate."

"Business associate?" His eyes drill me and it's then I see it, he knows that I'm lying. But I can't stop now, this problem is not his. It's mine. I have to fix this, and the last thing that I need is Ford trying to fix it all.

"Yes, Ford. Nothing to worry about." I already know he wants to argue but instead, he lets his hands fall to his sides and lets out a breath. Stepping toward me, he grabs my hips, his favorite place to grab me and pulls me close, my arms uncross at the sudden movement and I smile when he gives me his signature smirk.

"I don't know if I can ever not worry about you."

"Oh, really?" I tease, but I feel a warmth come into my chest.

"Really, babe."

Babe.

26

DELANEY

A SEMI-LONG-SUFFERING SIGH leaves my lips as I unlock the front door at home. It's been a few days since I've been here and I feel guilty not being around for my father. He knows that I've been with Ford but he's been almost suspiciously quiet about it. It's not a common thing for me to be staying anywhere else, this is the first time I've ever had a relationship that lasted long enough for overnighters.

I suppose he thought it was coming eventually, it's not like I'm a child anymore, I'm at an age most women would deem too old to not already be married or have children, but since neither of those things were ever on my radar anyway, I hadn't really ever thought about being behind.

Dumping my bag on my bed, my eyebrows scrunch when something comes fluttering out onto the bed. I snatch it up and then remember it's the photo I'd taken from my father's den weeks ago, but I totally forgot that I had it to begin with. Curiosity has me making my way down the hall to his den where he sits watching some news station, but when I get close enough, I see he's not watching the TV. His eyes are glazed over and his hand clutches a glass with an amber liquid resting inside, condensation lines its walls telling me it's been in his hands for some time.

"Papá?" I question and sink down onto the ottoman, I wait for him to acknowledge me, but it takes a minute for him to focus.

"Laney-girl." His rough voice strangles out of him and he adjusts his position in the chair, grimacing slightly at his stiff joints. "What are you doing here?"

"Ah, well." I give him a smile and rest a hand on his knee. "I still live here, don't I?"

He chuckles. "Well, it's been a bit hard to tell."

I blush at Dad's obvious teasing, it's funny that he's doing this for the first time when I'm in my mid-thirties, the opportunity had never made an appearance before now. It shows me Dad's not as old as he acts sometimes.

I watch his face sober slightly. "Are you sure you're making a good choice with Ford?"

The question surprises me. He's never said anything but nice things about the Gentrys, our families have never had any problems with the other. Every time Dad's around the restaurant on a Thursday, he's made a point to talk to Ford's parents, laughing and joking with them. "What do you mean, Papá?"

His eyes look almost weary now like he doesn't want to talk about it now that he brought it up, but I wait patiently for his answer. "It's nothing, don't worry about it. If you're happy, I'm happy."

I smile, but shift my attention to the photo that crinkles in my hand, reminding me why I came down in the first place, I push the photo at him. "I was wondering what this was from? I haven't seen it before, I was going through some things a couple weeks ago and found it."

He takes the photo with a blank expression, but when he sees what I'm holding he pauses, I hear him take in a sharp breath and his eyes glaze back over, I watch in surprise when tears form in his eyes. The number of times I've seen him cry are few, mostly after Mom died, but even then, he tried to never let me see them.

I give him a minute to pull himself together, wondering if just the sight of seeing Mom in the photo is what set him off. "Who's in the picture with you and Mom, Papá?"

He swallows and his gaze returns to mine, when it does I steel myself, ready for anything.

"This is Xavier Guerrero." His answer shocks me and I stare at him wide-eyed.

"What?"

With another sigh he continues, his eyes on the photo in

his left hand while his drink rests in his other, seemingly long forgotten. "A long time ago—before you were born—we were actually friends with the Guerreros. My family and theirs were very close, we were basically family." His eyes lose focus and I can tell he's in another world, recounting the past in his head. "I was meant to marry Xavier's sister, but I left for university in America first. I was to get a degree and then find a good job in Mexico City, and I was prepared to do just that. Xavier's sister was a good person, I could have had a fine life there.

"But I met someone else. My Annie." A tear breaks free from his eye and I feel myself getting misty-eyed. "Annie was so beautiful. She wasn't only beautiful on the outside but, your mother, she had a heart of gold. She was ambitious and smart. And the miracle of it all was, she wanted me too. She wanted the whole thing, the family, the restaurant... and the love."

His eyes wander back over to the photo, his hand starts to shake slightly and he pulls his gaze away. "I wanted to be the one to give her all of it. So, I told my parents that I was marrying her. I didn't ask, I didn't tell Francesca, Xavier's sister, I just followed my gut and married your mother. I was totally in love; I didn't care what anyone thought and neither did she. And then we took over the restaurant, your mother learned everything she could about Mexican cuisine and she perfected it, too." I smiled, remembering my mother in the kitchen. She was the best cook in town, people loved inviting her to potlucks because her dishes were always different and unique. I learned everything I knew from her, I wasn't bad myself, but I rarely found myself in the kitchen because it reminded me too much of her.

"We went back to Mexico once the restaurant was up and running. I wanted to introduce the love of my life to the people most important to me. Your mother was nervous." He smiles fondly as the memory flitters through his mind. "I teased her about it on the way, but she just said, 'I have to make sure that the family of the man I love approves. How will they treat our children if they don't love me?' It wasn't the first time we'd talked about children, but it was the first time I felt it could be real." I smile at the thought of their first conversation about me. It must have felt so far away at that time, but now we were thirty-some years down the road. "We arrived to a party thrown in our honor. I was surprised because when I'd told my parents, well, they were none too happy about it. The family plan was ruined because I'd gone and fallen in love. But it seemed that everyone had swept it under the rug. The Torrezs and the Guerreros were once again united and happy.

"It wasn't until later when the alcohol had taken control that we were pulled aside by Xavier. He talked to your mom and me and had us completely charmed until the real subject was approached."

I wait for him to continue but he pauses for some time, gathering his thoughts I think, until it's been five minutes and I'm still waiting on the edge of my seat. "What happened, Papá? What did he say to you?"

He finally sets his now warm drink on the side table and rubs a hand over his aged forehead. "He wanted us to be a part of the Guerrero business. Using the restaurant to take care of some income that they came into every month."

I hear myself suck in a breath. "Launder money?"

"Yes. Your mother was furious. She outright refused, before I could tell her that wasn't the best idea; to flat out shut down Xavier. But he just smiled at her and said, 'okay'. Like it was no big deal that she just turned down the only way they'd actually accept us."

"But wait, that's it? Then it was over?" I don't believe that for a second, Rafael was dangerous, I knew this, hell, anyone who'd even glanced at the man knew. He has a presence that would make even the fiercest dog cower too.

He gets a far-off look on his face and I wonder which number drink he's really on; he's been telling the story to me but it's almost as if he's not even really here. Like he's just murmuring the words out loud to himself.

"Papá? What happened after that?"

"It was over." He stands then, leaving the photo behind and disappearing down the hall to his room, his door shuts and the conversation is officially over. But nothing sits right with me. If Mom had shut him down so harshly, how could he go back to them for money? And why were they willing to loan us something when my parents had disrespected him, so to speak.

I had more questions than answers after that little conversation and a lot of those questions I wondered if I'd be able to get out of

Rafael himself. I just didn't know if it was a conversation I was willing to have with him.

27

FORD

THE LINE JUST keeps ringing, no one on the other end to pick it up and I clutch the phone tightly in frustration. I hate that I'm being ghosted by Gemma right now, every time I've tried to get in touch with her, she sends me straight to voicemail.

I need connections. I need to figure out what the hell Guerrero has on Delaney and her father, if I can figure that out, I can fix it and she won't have to have him sniffing around her.

I tend to rely on my gut for most situations, it's led me straight more times than not and I can't not follow it here. With Gemma not answering, however, and my clearance being temporarily suspended, I'm left with very few options. And one is an option that I don't really want to follow through on.

"Ford." Laura looks up, surprised. "We don't have an appointment today."

"I know." I rub my chin and sigh, looking for the words that will get her on my side. "I need a favor."

She scrutinizes me for a moment before nodding her head toward her couch. I take my seat and wait until she's comfortable. "I need you to tell my boss I'm ready to work." The blurted-out words don't seem to surprise her very much and I feel like holding my breath, waiting for her to shut me down.

"Ford," she starts. "Why?"

"I just need to get back to work."

"Getting back to work means leaving town, right?"

"Not necessarily," I hedge. I don't want to leave town, in fact, I'm planning on never leaving town again. Not permanently anyway.

"Well, getting you back to work takes time. And I can't suddenly throw you back in."

"It's not suddenly," I argue, my temper rising. "We've been doing these sessions for weeks."

"Let me ask you a question," she starts, her eyebrow raising and a look on her face that makes me regret coming in here. "Have you written in that journal yet?"

I sigh and try desperately to not roll my eyes. "Sure," I lie, knowing she'll see through it anyway but not even caring.

"Okay," she replies but her tone tells me she's not buying my bullshit. "How about Delaney? Have you talked with her about everything?"

A shrug hits my shoulders. "Define everything."

"Your past. Your sudden urge to jump back into the FBI. Have you discussed it with her?"

"Well, it's not exactly her problem, is it?" The anger in my voice surprises even me. I haven't had a moment where I felt like lashing out since I officially started dating Delaney. And I hate what I've said, of course, when I actually get back to work, it will concern her.

"Ford, I'm going to slap a little reality in your face right now." She squares her tiny shoulders and points a finger in my face. "You hurt her. On two occasions. From being blindingly drunk and out of your mind with the demons in your head. Not telling her why, not explaining why it is that you behaved in such an aggressive manner, is not going to end well."

My anger is back and boiling and I stand to leave, only stopping to hear her last blow. "I'm not reinstating you until you get this out of your head."

I don't look back at her when I practically stomp out of her office and down the street to my car, fury blinds me, and I jam my key in the ignition, but I don't get to start it before a roar leaves my chest. I scream until I can't anymore. Everything starts coming to a head. My behavior toward Delaney when I first came to town, hurting her and then her just accepting my apology, her letting me off with nothing more than pretty words. I'm pissed.

I'm pissed at my therapist for not doing the one thing I need right now. For not giving me the tools I need to protect Delaney, all she did was remind me how I was a danger to her myself. My phone breaks through my inner turmoil and with my chest heaving from exertion, I let hope hit me when I think it could be Gemma finally returning my call but it falls slightly when I see Delaney's name on the screen.

I take a deep breath before answering, "Hey, babe."

"Hey." Her voice has a lilt in it that indicates she's smiling and for a moment I let myself breathe that in. "Are we still on for tonight?"

Our date. We were supposed to have a night to ourselves, no restaurant, no family; just us. And I can't do it. I can't bring myself to go and smile and be happy after just being drug through the coals by my fucking therapist.

"I, uh." A sigh hits me. "Sorry, hon, my parents need my help with something tonight." The lie tastes like acid as it rolls off my tongue.

"Oh." Disappointment is clear in her voice and I hit my head against the steering wheel. "Okay, well, tell them I say hi?"

Her sentence trails off into a question and I clear my throat before I accidentally invite her to the fake family night. "I will, babe." I don't wait for an answer when I hang up. I feel like screaming all over again. I hate that I not only blew off my girl but lied about it because of some internal bullshit that won't let me be.

I wish I could just forget every moment I spent undercover. I wish I could go back and make different choices. But I can't. And I'll never be able to forget it.

28

DELANEY

IT'S BEEN A little over a week since I've seen Ford. The only communication we've had is via text message and I've initiated every conversation. I don't pry, mostly because I know if I do, it'll be the fastest way to push him even further away. I think over that last week we were together and wonder if there was something that triggered his sudden disappearing act but come up blank.

I even went as far as tracking down Bobby and asking if he had seen or heard from him and I realized far too late what a mistake that was. With him already doubting his once-best friend, this just added fuel to his 'don't trust him' fire.

Meanwhile, I've been dealing with the town rumor mill running rampant over the mysterious man who's been frequenting the bar often. And not just to pick up money and run, oh no. Rafael has made it his mission to make me uncomfortable, to push my every button and because he does it during the busiest hours, he knows I'm not the type that would kick him out and make a scene.

I stare at him in the booth he's occupying, annoyed he requested a four-person table at this hour. He's never come in with any companions. Always just him and eighty percent of the time he sits there staring and analyzing the place like he's preparing it for demolition. Maybe he thinks he is.

My teeth will have zero ridges by the time this debt is paid off because of the grinding his presence causes, Dad hovers behind me, always waiting for the other shoe to drop just as I am and never once saying a word to Rafael. Mostly because, Rafael has decided all business he wants to have with us will go through me and not my father.

I sigh and make my way to his table with his plate of food, it's the same thing every single time. Enchiladas de Chile Ajo, which is just a fancy way of saying red chile enchiladas. I don't know why, it's not necessarily popular around here but it is a classic dish.

I set the plate down and make to leave when his voice has my feet hesitating. "Sit." His demand has me narrowing my eyes and I turn to give them to him, no longer wanting to hide a single ounce of the hatred that oozes out of my pores for this man. He is the devil. Seeing my face, he sighs and gathers his fork before saying,

"Please."

I concede but keep my legs out to the side, ready to bolt at the first chance I get. "What can I do for you, Mr. Guerrero?" Though my tone may sound polite, he raises a brow humorously toward me like my answer humors him.

"Call me Rafael." He pauses his eating to look me in the eyes. "I like how you say it."

"With a hefty dose of disgust?" I know mocking can only get me so far, but I can't seem to help it. Even in the face—literally—of danger.

He smirks and shakes his head. "No. I would say I detect more... fear."

A shiver rakes down my back and I cross my arms defensively. He's not wrong, I am scared. I do fear him, I fear that he's going to take this further than it needs to go, I fear he'll never let my father and I go and we'll have to deal with Rafael Guerrero my entire life. "I'd prefer if we keep this professional."

"Oh, I'm aware of what you prefer. But you seem to be forgetting who's actually in charge here."

"You're a bank. Nothing more."

My bitter reply makes his anger rise and I wait for the threat that's coming. Instead, he leans forward, and my spine stiffens at the proximity, somehow even with a table between us, I still feel like he's too damn close. "Someday. Someday very soon, this place will be more than just a restaurant. You are an asset to the Guerreros, and I'll stop at nothing to have it."

"Then I will just say to you exactly what my mother did." I level my gaze. "No." My firm tone makes me proud; I was sure I was going to tremble, standing up to people has never been my strong suit but I don't want to let him know I'm bluffing.

He sits back, a lick of surprise slithers across his face before he carefully puts a mask back on. "You know about that?"

"Of course, I do."

"And you'd still say no? Even after what happened to her?" His eyes blaze and suddenly I'm confused.

"What?" It slips out as a whisper before I hear Lizzie calling my name.

"Your presence is requested." My eyes are still trained on his, but I stand anyway, knowing that even if I don't want to, I need to question him further and I rush to Lizzie to help with whatever problem she needs.

But by the time I'm done, Rafael's seat is empty. The questions I need answers to burning in my throat.

"HEY, IT'S ME, uh, I just got done with work so... I don't know." I clear my throat midway through leaving another voicemail on Ford's phone. "I haven't seen you in a while, I hope everything's alright." I stop myself from saying more and press the red button on the screen of my phone, strapping myself into the car and heading home.

Today was a stressful day and the conversation with Rafael is making me crazy. What did he mean by what he said? *Even after what happened to her?* What *did* happen to her? I think about taking my questions to my father, but I hesitate.

He's been hiding this from me all along, every secret he's told no doubt feels like he's protecting me, but instead it's making me crazy and quite possibly putting me in a dangerous situation. Every time I think I'm in the loop, that I know what is happening in my business and my parent's past, something else comes up and I just know if I question him, if I push for answers, he'll lie.

The only person I feel would actually be honest right now, believe it or not, is Rafael. He seemed so surprised by my knowing that I feel if I hadn't been interrupted he would have told me everything I wanted to know.

Which was why I was once again trying to get a hold of Ford, even his family hadn't been coming in on their normal night and I was worried he was telling them not to.

Was he ghosting me? After all the things he said, about wanting to be with me and protect me. About not knowing what it was between us but needing to find out. Or did he find out it wasn't all that great and now was done trying?

Another scenario, one I didn't want to believe was that he was gone. That his boss was letting him come back and he'd just left without a word.

I knew I needed an answer, but being that it was two in the morning and my body was aching in places I didn't know it could, it would have to wait. But tomorrow. Tomorrow I was getting answers.

29

DELANEY

AFTER MAKING SURE the restaurant was covered for a good portion of the morning, I make my way over to Ford's parents' house. I didn't know what I was going to encounter or if he was going to be here, but I steeled myself in preparation for the fallout I felt in my gut that was coming.

I was upset that I hadn't heard from him, but mostly I was worried that something had happened, something to set him back. We spent a lot of our time talking about our wants for the future, or our time in high school, but we rarely touched on the subject of his career or why he was here and I feel that it's partially my fault.

I didn't ever want to push him to open up because I was afraid I would make him recoil into a shell I wouldn't be able to penetrate again.

Stepping out of the car, a brief breeze stops me and the smells of the early stages of fall hit me. I can't wait for the time where Texas isn't a blistering hot mess and the cooler weather finally hits, even the few degrees that it declined in the fall would make all the difference. The fall sweeping in and introducing the holidays was my favorite time.

I take in a breath and push the distracting thoughts out of my head. Ford's family home is one that has been here for ages and is a favorite of mine. I admire the flowers on the porch and take them all in, hesitating in my ascent up the front steps.

I contemplate going around back to the barn, but not knowing if he was going to be there has me biting my lip. I decide that it's not worth seeing the empty building and wander up the front steps to the front door, I rap on it gently, almost not hard enough to hear.

But of course, Melissa does and when she opens the door, her eyes light up. "Delaney, dear! Come on in!"

I step in after her. "Sorry for coming unannounced."

"Nonsense! We love having you, you're welcome whenever you want. Tea?" She heads to the fridge without waiting for a response and grabs the pitcher of iced tea out of the fridge before grabbing two glasses and clunking them down on the worn farm table to the side of the kitchen.

"How have you been, Mrs. Gentry?"

She levels me with a look, and I correct myself by saying her name. "So, dear, we haven't seen you around! Where have you been?"

"Oh you know," I hedge, not sure how to say, 'Well, your son hasn't been speaking to me and I'm pretty sure he's not planning on it anytime soon so I doubt I'll be seeing you a lot in the future.' Without sounding crazy. "The restaurant has been really busy lately, it keeps me on my toes."

"Of course, Ford has said how hard you work."

I briefly close my eyes and sigh, "Melissa, is Ford here?"

She squints and takes a sip of her tea. "What do you mean, honey?"

"Well, he and I... we haven't talked in a while and I didn't know if he went back to work or..."

Melissa eyes me and I can tell her mom-radar is firing. "I see. No, he hasn't gone back to work, he's just outside now."

My eyes look out the back window, somehow thinking I'll suddenly see him standing there. "Oh," is my brilliant reply.

We're quiet for a few long seconds and I think of what to say, nothing immediately comes to mind, so I stand, wanting to get out of there, wanting to save myself from embarrassing myself any further. "Well, thank you for the tea Melissa, I hope to see you guys in the restaurant sometime."

She stands and hugs me tight. "And here," she says sternly.

I give a polite nod and make my way out the front door, but

instead of heading to the car, I hustle around the side of the house. As much as I don't want the confrontation, as much as I hate the fact that leaving here, I might leave brokenhearted, I can't not know any longer.

The barn door opens on a creak, alerting anyone around that someone's here and I wince, I guess it's better he knows I'm coming. I don't waste any time climbing the stairs to the door and I knock briskly, wanting to get it over quick. When no one answers I knock again and the door opens slightly. I take my chances of invading his privacy and push it open, looking around for any sign of him and breathe out a rough breath when I see the room is completely empty. The blankets are thrown around the bed, half spilling on the floor. There are clothes everywhere and a mess of papers and other things litter the small desk.

I sigh and move to leave when I see a notebook on the side table. It looks well-used and my curiosity has been itching inside the room. Maybe this will have a few answers for me. Picking up the book, I notice it's nearly half-full with messy scribble and there are torn out pages as well. I flip to the first page and read a few sentences to see what it is.

My therapist wants me to write in this stupid book, saying it will help confront fears that are following me but it won't fucking help me. The demons that follow, always will. Writing it down makes it no different, it doesn't make it real because the horror was always real. But if I want to get reinstated, I have to do this.

So here I am.

I turn the page, knowing it's an invasion but desperate for some clue to where his head is at and pause when I read my name.

Everything in me wants to protect those I love, even Laney. I can't help myself when it comes to that. Even if protecting her means I have to leave and make it right elsewhere before I can make it right here.

I scoff. Great, so he loves me and he's leaving. I start to close the journal, not wanting to read anymore and so angry that he didn't just talk to me about these thoughts. I could help him, despite how new we are, it doesn't mean my feelings aren't completely valid here. We've been telling each other things that I would have never told another soul before and yet he's over here planning his escape.

Before I can close the journal, the worth *death* catches my attention.

Everything that happened in that house haunts me so badly that living is sometimes worse than the thought of death. Wouldn't that have been easier? Just dying right along with those people, those innocent people who had no idea what was going to become of them. I knew. I knew because I came into the situation to save them, and I failed.

Oh, Ford. This time I snap the book closed and leave the room. Ready to search for the man who's fighting demons that none of us could even come close to comprehending. This isn't something he should be dealing with on his own and yet here he is, hiding himself away from me, cutting me off, and hating on himself in a notebook.

I stomp down the stairs and search around the barn. Melissa said he was here, but I haven't seen a sign of anyone. His car is here but there's no trace of him around. Defeated, I head back to the car and wonder what I should do. Laying my head against the headrest, I contemplate telling him that I read his journal, then I decide it doesn't matter if he's not talking to me.

I shake my head, pulling out my phone and putting it to my ear, hearing the ringing continue until a generic voicemail picks it up. Hanging up, I start the car and head for the restaurant. I'm exhausted. I hate not knowing where he is or where his head is at but if he doesn't want to talk to me, what am I supposed to do?

A new kind of tired takes over, making my body ache in places I didn't know it could. Is this the result of loving someone? To feel pain all the time, in every bone?

I start the car, pulling out onto the road and heading to work. At least at work, there are things I can control. I put the thought of Ford out of my mind for the time being, if he wants to talk, I'll be here. The chasing on my part is done.

30

FORD

I PUT THE phone back in my pocket with a sigh, Delaney hasn't stopped calling for a week and I can't bring myself to answer the phone. I feel my dad's eyes on me, no doubt he saw who was calling. "How are things with that girl of yours?"

Subtle as a bomb. "Fine," I answer, clipped. We're in his truck heading home from the hardware store, the very one that's across the street from her restaurant, but I couldn't go in there. Not until I can get myself straight.

"Haven't seen her around much lately."

I sigh and lean back in my seat. No, he hasn't. It's not her fault, she's been consistently trying to get in touch with me and I've ghosted her, I'm surprised she hasn't left some sort of nasty voicemail saying how over me she is. But that's not Delaney. She's sweet, she's sure of herself, and she's not going to let someone like me ruin her. "I've been busy, so has she." Is my answer to Dad's non-question.

"Hmm." He hums and I wait for the inquisition. It doesn't take long. "I'd never seen Delaney so relaxed as at that dinner we had her over for." He pauses but I wait, knowing there's more to come. "Mom and I have always kept an eye on her, you know. After her mama died, well, her daddy didn't take that well of course and she was suddenly thrown into adulthood. You shouldn't have to lose your parents that young, but you also shouldn't have to be responsible for a parent either." He pauses, referring to her dad and I know it's all true. I know she was thrown into it and yet, she handled it better than most would.

"We'd go over there, every week, same time, and she always smiled. However, there was a light missing in her eyes. It was subtle, you wouldn't realize it unless you knew her, but it wasn't there." He pauses. "Then she came to the house and was glowing. The light wasn't only there it was fire. That was because of you."

I don't answer, mostly because I'm worried if I did, I might actually choke up. I didn't know the effect I had on her, I only worried about the one she had on me and I'd bet money that mine held that same fire he was talking about.

We make it home and I'm still thinking over his words when

the front door slams open, my mom stands there, hands on her hips, looking like she's ready to fight and I pause my steps. There's been few times I've seen Mom so riled up and with one sentence I know why. "What did you do to that girl, Ford Michael?"

I wince, middle names were never good. I may have been through the military, but it was nothing compared to a mom's middle-name-thrashing. "Nothin' Mama," I answer, trying for calm and innocent.

"Nothin', my behind."

I pause at the bottom step and look up at her, she's not just mad, she's upset. "What happened, Mama?"

"That poor girl showed up here just a bit ago looking for you, she had no idea where you were or where you've been."

I rub the back of my neck and pinch my eyes closed. "I've been dealing with some stuff, Mom."

"I know that, Ford. I know." She sighs and her hands fall, somehow Dad disappeared to let Mom handle this talk all on her own. "But the fact is, she does too. I've never seen you like this with a woman. Ever. Don't shut her out, honey."

I nod, knowing she's right. Knowing that if I let Laney into my head, into the demons and the hurt, she'd accept me completely. It didn't matter what I'd done, she cared enough about me to love all parts. "I'll go see her." The promise sounds weak, I don't know if I have it in me to actually follow through.

"Good." She pauses and raises a hand for me to come up to her level. Reaching around me she gives me a hug that I didn't know I needed, a hug from a mom is a luxury that I haven't had in ages. "But first, help your daddy with that fence."

I smile and nod my head, pulling away from her and heading back toward the barn to help Dad. All the while, Delaney's face fills my mind, much like it has been for the last two weeks and I make the decision to force myself to go see her tonight. I can't predict how it will go or what she'll say. All I can do is hope she can forgive me.

THE RESTAURANT IS bustling and I smile. I wonder if Delaney has figured out yet that I've been leaving flyers and posting online about the restaurant anonymously. It was something I thought would help, I know they make ends meet but I also know it's barely that way, that they have to try really hard to make that happen. But this place is good enough that people should be lining up outside the door to get the amazing food they serve.

When I step inside, I immediately look toward the bar where she normally stands, instead I see her father talking on the phone, his expression pinched in worry and my gut tightens. He sees me enter and hustles into the back before I can get to him.

I glance around the room, looking for the gorgeous brunette who's changed everything for me, and come up empty, I make my way toward the bar before I spot Lizzie rushing around. I get her attention and she narrows her eyes. I don't know what Delaney has told her, but I doubt it's anything good.

"What are you doing here?" she asks in a rush when she comes to stand in front of me.

"I'm looking for Laney, you know where she is?"

"She's home. I figured you'd be with her."

I narrow my gaze. "No, why is she home?" It's unlike her to be home on a busy night like tonight.

"She's got the flu. Just started throwing up in the back and had a crazy high fever." She whispers the last sentence not wanting patrons to hear. "I rushed her home and her dad came in to cover."

"She's sick? And alone?" I ask urgently, already heading to the door.

"Well, she said she'd call you and see if you'd keep her company." She narrows her eyes. "Did she not call?"

I shake my head and sigh, of course she didn't call, I haven't answered in weeks. "I'll go take care of her."

She sighs with relief and briefly puts her hand on my arm. "Thanks!" Before anything else is said, she gets back to work and I make my way out the door.

THE HOUSE IS as dark as it can be with the sun still in the sky, every curtain is closed when I let myself in, the front door being unlocked which I planned on pointing out as soon as Delaney was better.

I'd made a short pitstop at the local grocery for soup, some sports drinks, and medicine. If she was feeling like crap, I knew she wouldn't want to really eat but she would need fluids and I didn't plan on leaving until that's what she got.

I make my way upstairs, like muscle memory I find her door at the end of the hall to the right. Her comforter is pulled up over her head, the white bedding with lilacs covering it clean and matches her perfectly, but it's the moaning body underneath that has me sitting on the edge of the bed and pulling the blanket down.

She groans and clenches her eyes tight.

"Baby," I console, reaching forward and putting my hand on her forehead. It's on fire and I pull my hand back when she tries to weakly wave me off. "Laney," I try again.

I move around the bed so I can fully face her and try to get her to open her eyes. "Laney, have you taken anything?" I don't want to give her too much and make this worse but since I have no idea what she's done for herself, I don't have a good place to start.

Thankfully her answer is a shake of her head and I know. "Okay, babe, hang tight."

I leave her room and rush to the kitchen where I'd set the bag of supplies and grab what I need, with the Sprite and medicine in hand, I head back to her room. This isn't how I imagined apologizing, and I know the only reason she's not shoved me out the door is her literal inability to get out of bed. But at least it's a start.

I make her swallow the medicine with a swig of Sprite to follow and she lays back down, the whole time she doesn't open her eyes or say a word, so I know this sickness has really knocked it out of her. I take a seat in the chair in the corner, knowing that I can't do much for her but not really willing to leave right now.

Thinking over the last couple of weeks, I want to go back in time and take it all back. I can't believe I was so selfish and pushed her away. After my therapist basically slapped reality in my face, I had to do some serious soul searching and it wasn't easy. I had to face some shit that I wasn't wanting to. But I did it, if not for myself, then for Laney. I needed her to understand that I had some issues, not that she didn't know that, but I had to find a way to tell her that I wasn't completely *right*, right now. I wanted to be, and according to Laura, that was a step in the right direction.

I didn't know how to do this. To be the man that she would need, and with the shit she was dealing with, she needed a strong one. Delaney wasn't the type to want to need anyone, but if she let her shield down, if she let me in, then I'd have to be ready for that. Everything between the two of us had escalated so fast that I didn't even realize how far gone I was for her, but in that same breath, I wasn't sure if I was all that ready for these feelings to have taken hold of me. I knew it before I pursued her but I didn't want to face that.

Now I was sitting here, staring at the woman I cared about more than anything and seeing her in pain and knew that I didn't want to be anywhere else.

I stand to stretch after an hour of sitting around and start to look around the room, she's been in it since high school and the decorations still show a touch of that. A corkboard with old pictures from high school, her and Lizzie at a pep rally, smiling big with arms around each other. A photo of her, me, and Bobby, her in the middle of us after one of our games. Our smiles are all huge, Bobby and I are covered in dirt and sweat and Delaney has her head faced slightly down and away, looking like she's laughing at something. I vaguely remember this, her mom took the photo after we'd won a big game, not that I can remember who it was against. Delaney though, she was there for every single one, cheering us on.

A photo of her and her parents at what looks to be a birthday party is next. Her smile lights up each picture, she looks like she's the happiest person on the planet.

And then there are no other photos that seem to be after high school, like after her mom passed, she stopped taking them. I peek around some more, finding budgeting books and materials that look like everything from the restaurant, she obviously has a hard time leaving work at work. But something else catches my eye and I see an old photo under the edge of one of her books. Not giving a crap about privacy, I pick it up and look at the worn edges. It's her parents, from the looks of it, but instead of Annie Torrez's smiling face, the same one I see on her daughter, her expression is solemn and reserved.

Her father isn't much better, even from the picture I can tell that his body-language is tense, and he's not thrilled with wherever they are. The old man they're standing with looks well off, his suit is fancy—expensive. And it matched the expensive shoes that adorn his feet. But he's the only one smiling in the picture.

I'm still holding it when I hear someone come in downstairs, assuming it's her father, I stuff the photo in my pocket before I can think better of it and turn to wait for the discovery of me being in her room with her.

When he comes around the corner, his eyes flash to mine but not with surprise, more like resignation. He nods his head at me and I follow him out the door, giving Delaney's sleeping form a last glance and slowly close the door.

When we reach the kitchen, I point to the bag on the counter. "I brought her some soup too, but she didn't seem up for eating." I feel silly saying that, like we've had normal conversations before. I'm not a fan of Mr. Torrez, not after finding out about his affiliation with Guerrero.

"Thank you." I blink in surprise at the thanks and nod my head at him, just as I'm about to leave, he speaks up again. "I never meant for this to happen."

Not wanting to get into it, I pretend to not understand. "It's the flu. Can't really predict that."

He shakes his head. "No, you can't. But you can control choices and I'm not happy about how mine have affected her."

I pause with a sigh on my lips, I don't want to have bad blood with her father, but at the same time, I want to lay into him for how he's treated her. "Sir, I don't know what's been going on... but whatever it is, I don't want it affecting her either. I can help." I wave my hand. "All you have to do is ask."

He nods and I take that as my cue to leave, just before I can close the door, I say, "Please let me know if she gets worse." I don't wait for confirmation because I fully plan on being here bright and early tomorrow before he'd be able to even give me a call.

If I've learned anything, it's that I can't disappear on her. No matter my personal issues. She needs me, and fuck, I need her.

31

DELANEY

I WAKE WITH a start. I don't remember getting home last night, all I remember was suddenly feeling like puking at work and practically being shoved out the door by Lizzie, after that it was a blur. I slept last night, I know, but I had a fever the whole time, everything hurts still and when I turn my head, the room spins.

"Hold up, not too fast." The voice surprises me and I look to where he's standing above my bed.

"Ford?" My voice sounds like I smoke ten packs a day and clearing it feels like swallowing razors. My throat has somehow become unusable.

"Hey, hon." He gives me his signature smirk and I let my body melt back into the bed. I'm mad at him, right? I shouldn't let him be in here. "I'm sorry you're not feeling well, but you need some more medicine."

I oblige, knowing that it will help get rid of this achiness that is killing me. I haven't felt this bad in years, I'm lucky enough that I don't tend to get sick all that often but when I do, it's rough. Every time.

After I've swallowed—painfully—the medicine down and taken a sip of cold Sprite. I lay back against the stacked pillows he placed there and look up at him. I haven't seen him in weeks, but my body remembers and I know that I missed him. I missed him the whole time.

"What are you doing here?" Even having the raspy voice, he pauses, knowing why I'm asking.

"After I saw you yesterday, I couldn't stop myself from coming back."

I squint. "You were here yesterday?"

He nods and gives me a soft smile. "Yeah, when I heard you were sick I had to come. Your dad is at the restaurant, taking over for ya." His tone is casual but not his stance, he has his hands tucked in his back pockets, like he's not sure what to do with them.

"I can take care of myself; you don't have to stay." I lean my head back, eyes closing and wait to hear the sound of him retreating, when I don't, I see him standing there, seemingly at war with himself.

"I want to stay, if that's okay?"

I sigh but don't reply. Because what do I say? *Oh, you only ghosted me for weeks, making me think we were done and then suddenly you're back to take care of me while I'm sick.*

Or worse, *Yes, please stay. I need you.*

Yeah, I can't say that one.

"Laney," he starts and takes a tentative seat on the edge of the bed. "I can't say how sorry I am for the last couple of weeks."

"It's fine, Ford, I get it. We went too fast and you needed to stop."

"No, that's not it." He shakes his head and grasps my hand in his, I look down at his big, calloused hands around my small ones. "I needed to work out some of my shit in my head and I couldn't do that and be what you needed."

What I needed was you, I think. But I stay quiet to let him get out whatever he needs to.

"There are things…" He breathes a deep sigh. "That I've been through, things I've seen. It haunts me. It's why I'm here at all. Everything that happened really fucked me up." He winces at his curse, I'm not sure if that's because of the curse, or because of the memories that he seems to be having flashing in his mind. "I haven't had a real way of working through it."

"You could have talked to me." My voice, as raspy as it is, comes out strong. I hate that he didn't feel comfortable coming to me.

"I know that," He squeezes my hand, his eyes on mine. "It wasn't you that was the problem, it was my own issue. It was me trying to sweep everything under the rug instead of dealing with it. It's why I'm not already back at work."

I wince and sigh. "Do you want to go back?"

"I do. It's a part of me. It's what I've done my entire adult life, I can't imagine doing anything else."

I shouldn't feel sorry for myself when he's baring himself to me, I shouldn't be thinking how I don't want him to leave, to go back to his old life. It's selfish, and it's not me. So, instead of making my fear known, telling him I don't want him to go, I squeeze his hand in return, trying to muster up a smile and say, "Then you'll get there. Just don't rush yourself." I don't know if I say that last part for him or me but it seems to appease him either way.

"Are you hungry?" He's standing now and I see the subject change, I know this isn't the end of the talk we're going to need to have but for now, feeling as awful as I do, I let him change it and nod my head. Ford hustles out of the room before I can say anything and I lean back, resting my eyes against the headache that is threatening to break open my skull. It's serious pain.

Ford comes back with a bowl of soup and spends the next half hour slowly spooning me mouthfuls until I'm too full for much else. "I bought a store brand kind, but when I told my mom you were sick, she insisted on making you some. It's her cure-all soup that she always fed us when we were young."

After I've eaten, sleep threatens to pull me under and Ford

takes his leave, but this time, I know he'll be back.

I STEP INSIDE the bustling restaurant a few days later. The second I do; I want to step back out. The place is nuts, as it has been for the past few weeks, I have no idea why the place has suddenly decided to take off, but I don't have the energy to complain. I may be over the flu, but it still has left me weaker than I like.

Lizzie comes rushing up to me, her face lit with excitement as she wraps her arms around me. "You're back!" her voice sings in my ear and I wrap my arms lightly around her waist, a little chuckle leaving me.

"I am."

"Thank God," she exclaims. "It's not the same without you. I can't remember the last time I've gone that long without seeing you," her rambling keeps my attention except for when I catch a glimpse of Ford working the bar, chatting with Bobby. "It was totally weird, and I almost came to check on you, but Ford said he had it handled." She leans in close to whisper. "Which I'm sure he totally did." With a wiggle of her eyebrows, I scoff at her.

"That was not at all what happened. I didn't leave bed hardly at all."

"Well, whatever happened, I'm glad you're better, your dad is not nearly as much fun as you are."

I contemplate that for a minute, I don't necessarily think that I'm any fun, as a matter of fact, in the last ten years or so, I haven't let myself step out of the serious roll that I took when everything fell on my shoulders. But when Ford started acting like his old self again, I felt lighter when I was with him.

"Oh, and that guy came while you were out." She looks like she wants to question me but she hesitates.

"Right. I uh, forgot about that." I rub my forehead. I hadn't thought of Rafael in days, why couldn't I just forget him altogether?

"Well, your dad talked with him but he didn't seem too happy. He stormed out of here. Hasn't been by since." I know Lizzie wants more information, I know she's seen him around and doesn't have a clue why he's here, but I can't tell her. I can't put her at risk and give her any details.

"Don't worry, I'll get in touch with him this week." Though I won't even have to.

Making my way toward the bar, I contemplate running up and wrapping my arms around Ford, but we're not totally over our little... argument? If that's the right way to look at it. He has some things that he's working through, and as much as I want to jump in headfirst, I can't hinder his recovery.

"Hey," I say when he comes near, pausing his conversation with Bobby.

"Hey, there, what are you doing here?" he answers and I pause to give him a confused look.

"Well, I think the better question is what are you doing here?"

He shrugs and looks around, grabbing a towel to fiddle with in his hands. I can sense he's trying to hold back a little and I can't figure out how I feel about that. "I wanted to help out. I knew you guys were a hand short and as much as I'd love to hang out in your room all day, I didn't think you'd appreciate being watched."

I laugh a little. "Yeah, you're probably right about that. That might have been a little weird."

Ford nods and grabs a random glass to wipe down. "So, you're feeling better then?"

"I am." I give a nod and a grin, then gesture to the back. "I'd better go see how things are going. I'll see you later?" I don't know why it comes out as a question but a relieved breath leaves me when he nods his head in agreement.

I head toward the office, wondering how much I have to get caught up on since I've been gone for a few days, it's amazing how backed up things can get and I know Dad can handle it, but I also know how long it's been since he's been the only one taking care of the books.

But when I step into the office, I can't stop the gasp that leaves me when I see the disarray. Dad sits in the middle of it, a bruise marring his face and papers scattered everywhere. "Papá, what happened?" The voice that comes out is low and shocked.

"*Mija*. What are you doing here?" He pauses what seems to be his attempt to cleaning the mess.

"I'm better, Papá. I was coming in to catch up. What happened here?"

He sighs and slumps down into the desk chair, I can tell he's exhausted, from whatever happened here. But I have one guess and it's confirmed when Dad lifts his hands helplessly. "Rafael."

My fists curl involuntarily, and I throw my purse onto the small couch in the corner. "He did this? And hurt you?"

"It's okay, *mija*. He was upset."

"Upset about what?"

He looks at me then. "He was upset it wasn't you here, dear. Apparently." He pauses. "he wants more each week, and I didn't have it. So, when he asked for you and I said you weren't in. He was unhappy."

"What the…" I trail off and run a hand over my head. Who the hell does this guy think he is? Ordering me around and making me his personal delivery lady? "That's it. I'm going to the bank and getting a loan. Then we'll pay him and be done with it."

I gather my purse but before I can leave he stops me. "Honey, I don't think it's that simple. I think he wants more than that." His eyes tell me something that makes panic want to seize me but I can't let it.

"I have to try." I don't wait for another response before I'm out the door. Ford gives me a questioning glance but I just wave goodbye and head to the door. I'm sick and tired of being pushed around. I'm tired of Rafael being in my life period. I want him out, I want this situation dealt with and I want to be able to move on with my freaking life.

MY HEAD BANGS against the steering wheel when I sit in my car hours later. I don't know if it's leftover exhaustion from the flu or the angst I felt when I was trying to secure that loan but whatever it is, it makes me want to hide away in my room for the foreseeable future.

The bank tried, they did. They ran my credit and made a real go of getting me the loan, they even expedited it so I could get an answer today. But it wasn't going to work. The amount I needed was too high for the poor credit I'd been issued due to student loans.

I was out of luck. I didn't know another way to get Rafael off my back. The only thing I could do was talk to him, make some new deal to get him off my back. I didn't know if it would work or if the deal would be worth it. But I had to try.

I make my way back to the restaurant and see that it's slowed down significantly since I went charging out of here earlier. Ford is still here doing the closing now, due to the fact that most everyone had already left. I walk straight to Ford, I don't think before I do. I'm sick of thinking, of overthinking everything.

I grab his shoulders when he turns toward me and grab a hold of him, pulling him to me and hugging him tightly. He responds without hesitation, grabbing me around the waist and squeezing me to him. Maybe he expected me to kiss him, but hugging feels almost more intimate. He's always been able to keep my worries at bay with just a hug.

"You wanna talk tonight?" he says in a low, husky voice.

I nod against him and pull back, giving him a soft smile before I start helping him close down. We've had a rough few weeks but I'm done fighting it. I want to help Ford, and mostly, I want to be able to confide in him what is bothering me.

So, with the decision made, I finish the nightly close up, and follow behind him on the way to his place.

Ready or not, we're happening.

32

FORD

TO SAY I was surprised that Delaney agreed to come home with me was an understatement. I was sure I was going to be blocked by one of her walls when I'd asked and when she so willingly agreed I buried that surprise and led her to her car. I hadn't been able to look away from the headlights indicating her following me the entire drive home and I didn't know if that was nerves for the conversation that was to come or if I was just waiting for her to bail.

When I pull into the drive and she parks on the street, I hustle out of the car and to her door before she could open it herself and the shy smile that graces her face makes it difficult to restrain from kissing her. However, not knowing exactly where we stood has me holding back.

Being with her was so easy, but I know these last few weeks I hadn't given her much hope in the way of this being a relationship that would continue. It hadn't been my intention, it was the opposite, actually, which was why I took that extra time to work on my issues.

I wanted to be better for her. It was that simple.

When we enter my living space, I gesture toward the bed and she bounces on the end of it, waiting for whatever I'm going to do. When I grab the desk chair and sit, she gives me a sideways look. "What are you doing, Ford?"

I shrug, acting like everything is normal. "What?"

"Why are you over there?"

I scratch the back of my neck and say, "I think we should talk…" I trail off because I'd wanted to say, 'first', like I was expecting something after our conversation. Which I was, absolutely, but I wasn't about to make her run from me by admitting to it.

"Right." She smacks her lips and looks at me, her face a mask of resignation and I know whatever's been going on with her, the things she's tried to lock down, away from me, are about to slip out. Or so I thought. "You first?"

I sigh but don't argue. She deserves to know why I've been acting strange around her, she deserves the truth of it all.

So, I tell her everything. "It was a mission that was supposed to be a sting. It wasn't supposed to be an extraction, but I couldn't help it. Seeing the helpless people there held against their will made me lose my fucking mind. I couldn't stand it. It hurt that they thought I was a part of it, but what could I say, 'Oh don't worry, I'm an undercover agent, but shh, you can't tell anyone'?" I sigh and rub my brow, Delaney sits there cross-legged on the bed, a frown marring her face as she listens to the horrors that have been taunting me for a year. I don't want her to have to know this, that there's real shit out there like this, that there is horrific people in the world, but I can't hide it from her anymore if I want this to be more, if I want a real future with her, she has to know that I come with these images that will haunt me forever. "So, I went against orders. I'd made up my mind that I couldn't do it anymore." My hands clench into fists and I look down at them, unable to maintain eye contact with her. "I couldn't let that scum walk the earth after what they'd done. I couldn't allow those innocent kids to get beaten and assaulted every fucking day and continue to live with myself." A shaky breath leaves me. I hear a sniffle from the bed but don't dare look, if I do, I won't finish the story and I won't be able to let her in. It's now or never. "I was going to end them, it wasn't even an elaborate plan, I went at them with my gun, but they somehow saw me coming, like they knew my plans and just as I went to put a bullet in their heads, their triggers were pulled too and the kids I was trying to protect..." My voice cracks and I can't bring myself to say it out loud. I clear my throat roughly. "Then I turned the gun on myself."

I'm stuck in this memory. I can hear how it's affecting her, but I power through it. "I didn't get my chance, though. Gemma knew what I was doing, long before I did, her team rushed in there and tackled me to the ground before I could pull the trigger." I wipe at my face that has become a broken mask and go to look at Delaney when her body lands on top of mine, she's straddling me in the desk chair, her face buried in my neck and her arms wrapped around my shoulders and neck so tight I shouldn't have been able to breathe.

"I'm so, so sorry that you had to deal with that."

"It's my job, Laney," I murmur.

"It's the hardest fucking job in the world." She leans back slightly but I tighten my grip, not wanting her to leave, she doesn't, just holds my head in her hands so that I can see her eyes. "You never had to do that job, but if you didn't, who would? I know you didn't get to save those kids and God; I can't imagine what that feels like. But at least you tried, you didn't let them die with no hope, they had you there with them. Someone who cared. Someone who loved them."

"They shouldn't have had to die." I clear my throat when my voice cracks. The emotion clogging it, their faces… I'll never forget them.

"No, they shouldn't have. You're right." She looks down and I wait patiently for her to get her thoughts together. "But sometimes things don't go to plan. My mom shouldn't have died either, but it happened. Because that's life, and people are assholes."

I smirk slightly at her statement. "You're right."

"I know." Her smile is small. "I'm so glad Gemma's team was there for you. I can't imagine…" She trails off but I nudge her chin, getting her eyes back on me. I make a gesture for 'continue'. "I can't imagine my life without you in it now." She sighs and my heart is about to burst out of my chest. "These last few weeks, you not answering and me not seeing or talking to you, it was so off. I was off. I didn't realize what was wrong with me until now, it was you. I needed—no, I *need* you."

I push my mouth to hers before she can say another word, I don't have the right ones to tell her how I feel, because blurting out 'I love you' isn't going to be something I say when our emotions are high, but it's something I can show her. I can show her with my kiss, with my body, with every bit of me that she'll take.

She moans against my mouth and I stand, walking us toward the bed before lightly dropping her onto it, only detaching my lips for a second before I climb back over her, I take it nice and slow, not because we've had time apart but because I don't ever want to rush the way I love this woman. I want her to be able to feel it in every touch I give her because it's what she deserves.

When her hands reach for my shirt I help her rip it off and she copies the motion with her own, both flying in different directions. Before I know it, we're both naked and moving together as one unit. It's effortless with her, as is everything we do together and I couldn't be happier for it. She's been the woman I've needed in my life this whole time.

Something resolute settles in my soul, something that almost feels peaceful. I know now with one-hundred-percent certainty that I can't leave her. I can't leave behind this woman who owns my mind, body, and soul. I have to find another way. So, with each caress of her skin, each kiss of her lips against mine, I say it. *I love you.*

IT'S THE MIDDLE of the night, though it's the most normal thing in the world for humans to do, sleep still alludes me. It's not nightmares keeping me up this time. It's thoughts of Laney and me, it's thoughts of our future together and what that means. I know I have to have a talk with Gemma about what I want in the future. About where I want to work and be and something tells me she won't be all that surprised.

Delaney stirs next to me and looks into my eyes the minute hers open. "Hi." A shy word slips from her and I turn to face her more fully, I kiss her full-on the mouth and sigh in contentment. "Why are you up?"

I smooth the crease between her eyebrows with my finger and smile. "Just thinking."

"Oh yeah? What are you thinking about?"

"Us."

Her grin widens. "What about us?"

"Our future. What it will look like. Where we'll live, work, be. All of those good things." I smile but her eyes darken a little, instead of joy, there's worry and concern there. "Laney."

"I need to talk to you about something."

33

DELANEY

I SITUATE MYSELF sitting cross-legged on the bed facing Ford, what I'm about to say, how I'm going to explain my situation, I have no idea. But Ford has been through enough, he doesn't need this shit too. I have to give him a chance to decide if he's willing to possibly put up with it in his life.

"I've been dealing with some things at the restaurant," I pause and tuck the sheets under my arms more securely. I definitely never thought I'd be having this conversation while we were naked. "There's this guy, and he um, well he and my dad made some sort of deal. It was years ago, I guess. But we were having some trouble

and Dad got a loan to help us out. I never thought anything of it."
I continue to tell Ford about Rafael and not surprisingly, Ford sits
and takes in every detail, in a way that I can tell he's formulating
a plan and response.

"So, it's every week now and more than before. I have to talk
to him this week to get it worked out to a lower sum, but he's
not backing down." I don't mention all the shit with my family,
knowing that just adds confusion. There's no real need for it
anyway, if it was that important, I would have known about it in
the beginning.

Ford is rubbing his top lip, I can see his thoughts churning
from here. "Alright," he says finally but I wait for him to add
something to that.

"Alright?"

"Yeah, alright. We'll work something out. I'll help you."

I shake my head and a puff of air slips out; I don't know if it's
exasperation or relief. "What… um, how will you help me?"

"I'll get you the money to cover. That way you don't have to
deal with this guy anymore." He nods his head, almost to himself,
like it's a done deal already.

"Ford, no."

He looks up at me with surprise. "What?"

"I didn't tell you so you could handle it, or whatever. I told
you because this guy, he's kind of dangerous. And I don't want
to subject you to that unless you're really willing. But I can't take
your money."

He leans forward and looks me in the eye. "This problem; it's *ours* now. Everything you're going through, so am I. No more 'my problems' and 'your problems' bullshit. I have the money to cover this right now, let me help. If it makes you feel better, you can make payments on that. But I won't let you be in danger. Period."

I wipe a tear that somehow escaped me during his little speech and nod my head, I don't want to take his money. I wasn't planning on him even offering, but a peaceful feeling settles over me and I realize how much I've been stressing about it. Maybe it's because I've been fighting all my life. I've been holding up my family's business by the skin of my teeth, desperate to keep it afloat and not let Dad and Mom down. Maybe I'm just tired of dealing with it all on my own.

"Okay," I whisper. "But I'm paying back every single cent."

"Sure." His agreeable response leaves me with a smidge of doubt but I don't have a chance to question him before he seals his statement with a kiss.

AS MUCH AS I hated it; I took his money.

I lied to my dad about the money, telling him that a bank had graciously given me the loan and we could finally get out from under it. He hadn't been as relieved as I thought he would be and

I thought he might call me out on my lie. But he didn't, he just nodded his head and then left the restaurant.

I held an envelope with the cash inside, it was heavy, and I felt its weight on my shoulders. Rafael wouldn't bother us after this, was the thought I kept in my head as I waited for his untimely arrival.

Ford wasn't far from me today, he was manning the bar while I waited for the arrival of the devil himself. I'd wanted to do this day on my own, to handle this last piece with Rafael and be done with it, but Ford refused. He knew more than he let on, I know he did. So for the sake of argument, I said he could be here as long as he didn't come back into the office. To which he gave me a look I know he's used on others before to get his way, and after some persuasion on my part, I got him to agree.

After our conversations the other day, I'd felt somehow lighter than I was before, like there was a wall between us that wouldn't come down but now that I knew what he'd been through, I could finally see the real Ford.

The things that he went through before showing up here, the reason he had to come here, it was so clear to me why he'd struggled so hard. I couldn't even imagine going through that and coming out the other side of it even remotely normal.

I still had so many questions. I didn't understand why he woke scared, so much so that whatever was coursing through his veins caused him to react so violently to whoever was waking him up. I had my suspicions, but I wasn't ready to voice them just yet. We'd already gotten so much out in the open that I wasn't sure how ready we were for more of it.

My thoughts are interrupted by the bell chiming on the door, I look over but already know who stands there. Rafael is a powerful guy and just by looking at him, you can tell that. But what most don't sense, others who aren't privy to the power he wields, is that he just might be the most dangerous one around.

I nod my head at him and lead the way to the office. I can't just hand over a giant envelope of cash in front of everyone out there, if I did I wouldn't hear the end of it from Lizzie and the last thing her scatterbrain needed to know was anything I was dealing with behind the scenes.

The office always feels twice as small as it is when Rafael enters but I stand tall and face him. I take the envelope and hand it to him, my spine stiff and chin held high.

He takes it and his face gives away his confusion, something I don't often see with him. Opening the envelope, he stands a little taller when he realizes what it is. "I see." He clears his throat and I would swear he was disappointed. "Unfortunately, even with the loan now paid, that doesn't mean we're done."

My throat constricts. "What are you talking about?"

"Your father's deal with us is quite extensive. We have some things we have to nail down, but I'm not done with you yet." Without another word, he moves around me, closer to me than I'd like and I stand stock still. When the door clicks shut behind him, I breathe my first breath in the five-minute span.

I clutch my head with my hands and think. I can't believe we're not done with this. It was the entire reason I'd let Ford lend me the money in the first place. I hadn't wanted to lay eyes on Rafael ever again, and he was telling me he had more business with my dad.

I was livid, no wonder Dad wasn't relieved when I'd told him we were done with Rafael, because he knew that we weren't. Would we ever be? I knew I'd have to confront Dad; again, but I wasn't sure I wanted to know what he'd gotten us into.

34

FORD

THAT WEIGHT THAT had been on Laney's shoulders wasn't lifted the way it should have been. When Guerrero walked out of the office, he shot me a smirk that made my teeth clench. I'd waited tensely for him to leave the restaurant before heading to the office to find out what had happened.

She was sitting behind the desk, her head leaned into one hand and her eyes closed. "What happened?"

She opens her eyes; there's an anguish in them that I wasn't expecting. Giving him the money was supposed to make her life easier, better. Was supposed to give us a chance to finally move on and have a life without something hanging over our heads. I know I was putting myself into this, I was inserting myself into her problems because I couldn't bear the thought of her having to deal with this on her own and Lord knows, her father isn't any help.

"It seems," Delaney puffs a breath. "That the deal was much more than the loan."

I take the seat in front of the desk and lean my forearms on the edge. "What does that mean? What did he say?"

Her eyes are on my arms as I wait patiently. "Your arms are sexy," she mutters, I can tell she's trying to distract herself from this conversation, but I huff a laugh and tell her to focus for a minute. "We can get to my sexiness in a minute, what did he say?"

"Nothing specific. Just that he's not done with me. That my father and him had a deal that went beyond the payment of the loan." Her posture relaxes, she slouches down and her eyes glaze over. I can see her ready to admit defeat.

"We need to talk to your father."

"Yeah? Well, I have. He doesn't seem too keen on giving me the information that I need, he prefers just waiting for things to unfold before saying, 'oh yeah, by the way, I made a deal with a drug lord.'" Her eyes widen but she doesn't correct herself. I forget that she doesn't know how much I already know; but it doesn't seem like something that would actually help so I continue to keep my mouth shut for now.

"Your father knows more than you and given that he's thrown you to the wolves and lets you handle the deal with Rafael now, he needs to tell you every single thing he knows."

"How do I get him to do that?"

"Don't give him a chance to say no." I see when she starts to agree and with a nod of her head, we make a plan.

DESPITE US MAKING a plan to confront her father, I can't stop myself from digging into this situation myself. This was my damn job, getting information on subjects who weren't keen on being found.

Digging into people's personal lives was like riding a bike for me, finding out their contacts, their family, their habits, places they came and went to on a regular basis, finding the right people to talk to when the contacts of the FBI only helped you so much.

We didn't always have the resources we needed which meant that I had to improvise often, it was a good thing now that I had because I had people who knew me, who were on my side who could have an idea on Rafael's big moves, on his plans for the future or why he wanted to use *El Abrevadero* for his business ventures.

Miles was a guy that knew a lot of people in Mexico, he's been somewhat undercover for his entire career, no one knew exactly what it was that he did, but he had contacts that the FBI would froth over. I never told my superiors about him, knowing he'd have a field day if he was ever contacted by them. I guess you could say he was a vigilante of sorts. He liked to infiltrate trafficking houses and free people from them. People trusted him; he was a go-to guy for not only information but on where to find anything you needed. I wasn't sure where he got money to live but all he'd say was people paid him in gratitude. I never pushed him on what that meant.

So, I wasn't surprised when he answered his phone already knowing who was on the other end. "Beck, what a surprise." I, of course, never told him my name either. Knowing I could easily be traced if he ever decided to switch sides on me. I wasn't betting on him ever doing that, but you could never be too careful when it came to the lone wolf types like him.

"I wish I was calling to catch up."

I hear him shuffling on the other end of the line and hear the keys of a computer tapping away. "Yeah, that's not typically why people call me." He laughs and says, "So what is it you need?"

"I need some information on someone."

"Name?"

"Rafael Guerrero."

From his quick inhale I can tell the name has struck a chord, but the keys type anyway. "What are you doing digging into that asshole?"

"It's not something I wanted to do, but I haven't much choice. He's messing with my woman and I need to find a way to get him to stop."

"What could he possibly want with her?"

"I'm not sure his final motivation, but it has to do with her family. Something about a history with her parents and grandparents."

He hums on the other end and I can tell he's thinking it over. "What's her family's name?"

"Torrez."

"Ah, the family of Towers," he muses, I can tell he's reading something on his computer, probably personalized profiles he's made of people he's come across. I'm shocked to learn that her family has reason to be in his files. It sets my teeth on edge.

"What does that mean?" I ask, staring out the front windshield of the car.

"Well, legend is that the family of Towers was supposed to guard the warriors of the village and you know what the meaning of Guerrero is?"

"Let me guess, it means warrior?" I curse. Letting my head fall back against my seat. This was more than I could have predicted.

"You're not a stupid one. So, the Guerreros have always believed that specific families in their village would have a certain duty to them, depending on their names. The Towers protected them. Other family's names would mean things like 'provide' or 'heal.' And the Guerreros are old-fashioned. I'm guessing that Rafael is trying to do the one thing that his father never could and that would be getting them to fall in line. Sound about right?"

"Yup." I want to let another curse fly but refrain. I can't believe her father kept this from her. It would have been helpful to know. If she wasn't a Torrez, she wouldn't have to be thrown into this bullshit, and that's exactly what it was, bullshit.

"So I'm guessing that he's trying to get her to cover his ass in some way… are you guys in Mexico?"

I furrow my brow. "No, Texas."

"Texas, no shit? So he did expand. I'd heard he was finally venturing into the States, but didn't realize he'd already done it. Rafael is a serious businessman, he's already made more money than his father could dream of. What's he after her for?"

"At first it was paying off a loan her father had, now we don't know what he wants but he's not done fucking with her."

"I have a pretty good idea what. Torrez…" He sounds like he's thinking something over so I wait him out. "Is her father Joaquín? Mother was Annie?"

"Yeah, how the fuck do you know that?"

"It's my job, profiling anyone who can be dangerous. So her mother was the one they took out when she refused, huh?"

I shake my head. "Wait, back up. What?"

"Annie Torrez was the first person in the family to refuse the Guerrero's, she had balls. But it didn't last, the rumor was that they sent people to kill her, to show Joaquín that they weren't taking no for an answer."

My blood runs cold. I can't even fucking breathe. Delaney was sure it was a random robbery and that her mother had just been unlucky, but that wasn't it at all, she was murdered, intentionally by the Guerreros.

"You'd better stick by her, man. If she's putting up a fight, there's no telling what he'll do."

"Thanks, Miles." I hang up after saying goodbye and close my eyes. This is so much fucking worse than I'd realized, than Delaney realizes. And her fucking father knows everything. He's purposefully putting his daughter's life at risk because he's a coward and I suddenly want nothing more than to put a bullet in his head myself.

I grip my steering wheel and force myself to calm down. I can't get emotional now, it'll only lead to more problems, and with all the shit we have coming our way the last thing I need is a fucked-up head.

Good fucking luck.

35

DELANEY

UNDER THE PRETENSE of a family dinner, Ford, my dad, and myself, sit down at my small kitchen table and dig into food that sits like concrete in my stomach, my eyes have barely left the faded plate that used to be part of my mother's favorite set of plates. I imagine they used to be bright blue, that they used to have a shine to them that gave you a feeling of comfort whenever you saw them.

Now the blue had faded and the yellow flowers that used to adorn them are barely visible anymore. I used to think that I would paint them again or take them to be restored so something of my mother's could grace a table of my own someday. I could use the plates to feed my own husband and children. But this feeling inside, this dread that courses through my blood has me holding back on wanting to even think about a future right now.

I know that it's only a matter of time before Rafael is back and demanding more of me, I just don't know what he's going to be demanding. I don't know what's to come from him now that I have finally paid the loan. I almost wish I hadn't done that, then I'd at least know what was coming. I'd know all I had to do was pay a little every week, nothing else. But I'd gotten greedy with the thought that I could somehow escape him.

I look over to where Ford sits, he's been tense since showing up, I'd expected him to be the one trying to encourage me, to comfort me when I was about to pry information out of my father. But he's been silent.

We couldn't catch a freaking break, the two of us.

Finally, when I realize I can't even eat the food that sits on my mother's plate in front of me, I give up on the thought of pretending I wasn't really begging for information from my father and just ask. "What is your deal with Rafael Guerrero?"

My father looks up, startled, from his plate of food and pauses, the fork in his right hand stilling just above his plate. "I don't know what you mean, *mija*."

I use a face I only would normally give Rafael, one that's stern and unforgiving. I don't want to hate, but right now, the situation my own father has put me in makes it very difficult to just forget the fact that he's done this to me.

"Rafael," I repeat. "He says there's more to the deal than the loan. What is the deal?" I enunciate every word to make myself clear. That I'm done being a pawn in some game between him and this man who thinks he has me in the palm of his hand. I hear Ford clear his throat, but I can't give him my attention right now.

"Honey, maybe we should talk about this another time." At that, I toss my napkin on the table and stand. I glare and lean into the table, resting my hands on either side of my discarded plate.

"I'm done being the only one in the dark. *Done*," I huff. "Tell me *everything*. Right now."

I've never talked to my father this way before and I know he's pushing down the instinct to correct me, to put me in my place. But I can see on his face that he knows he can't keep it a secret any longer.

"The deal." His voice cracks and he takes a moment to clear it. "The deal was for the restaurant to help with a venture."

"What does that mean?"

"You don't need—"

"No! I'm so done being a pawn in your little games. That restaurant is just as much mine as it is yours. And if you're using it for anything other than what it's truly for, I need to know, now."

He sighs and I see him struggling to get his words together, I want to yell at him. I want to scream at him to just spit it out, but I hold myself back. "We would store some of his products."

"Products?"

"His drugs." It's Ford who answers and I spare him a glance. I can tell he's throwing out a guess but he's keeping his eyes; his glare, on my father.

"Drugs? In my restaurant? In *Mama's* restaurant?" My voice breaks but I push on, I feel my chest getting heavy and I stand up straight again, crossing my arms over my chest to try and get the pressure to ease off.

"I didn't want to. But when your mother refused…"

"What?"

"They—" A sob escapes him, I pause in my pacing.

"They what?" I can feel myself losing my cool, my control is slipping, and I don't know if I want to know what he has to say. But it's not him who answers.

Ford looks at me, a look of pure torture on his face, his voice is soft when he says, "They killed her, Laney."

I flinch. Somehow, I knew it was going to be bad. But I had no clue how bad it really was. How bad it was truly going to be. "No," I refuse. "No, it was a robbery."

My father is shaking his head. "No, *mija*, when she refused, they took drastic measures." His accent thickens so much it's almost hard to understand him, but I do. "Si no estuviera de acuerdo en ayudarlos... Te llevarían a continuación".

If I didn't agree to help them... They were going to take you next.

His words make me stumble back a step and I see Ford's head snap to my father. "What the fuck did you say?"

Without thinking, I take the plate I'd been admiring before

and throw it against the wall. A cry tears through my throat, both because the news is breaking my fucking heart and because I just broke a piece of my mother that I never wanted to lose.

I can't believe this. I can't understand, how are there people in the world who think they can just control others this way? How dare he! How dare Rafael think that he can just bulldoze his way to success, to getting his way.

I pause my thinking and look at Ford then, "You knew."

He looks back over at me and anguish covers his face. "Laney..."

"You knew about my mother? How could you not tell me that?" I'm full-on yelling now, but I can't seem to care. My trust in him starts to crack right before my eyes and I look to the both of them.

"Laney." Ford stands and reaches for my arms.

"Don't touch me!"

He flinches at my words and his eyes glass over, but I can't care. Not after the shit I've heard. Not after he's kept things from me that he shouldn't have.

I leave the kitchen, blocking out my father's cries and Ford's protests at me leaving. Grabbing my purse off the bench beside the door, I wrench it open and head for my father's car, the keys fall and I hear Ford behind me when I go to pick them up but I don't look back. When I'm almost there he grabs my arm and turns me around, but I rip it out of his hold. "Just stop, Ford."

He blanches but keeps protesting. "Laney, you can't leave in this state. Please." His begging falls on deaf ears as I slam my door shut and forcefully start the engine. I don't know exactly where I'm going, but I don't look back as I speed down the street.

Away from the hurt, away from the pain, away from the lies.

36

DELANEY

IT'S BEEN A few days since the altercation at my father's house, a couple of days since I found out that my mother was murdered by the one person who is making my life a living hell. I want to give up. I want to surrender to him, to tell him to just end the pain that is coursing through my body.

It won't leave me. It won't relent.

It took me this long to find what I needed. I'd spent day and night driving around town, looking for the blacked-out car that seemed to belong to the devil himself and when I finally found it, I followed him. I had to wait all night in the parking lot of a hotel where it seemed him and his men, or whoever was with him, were calling home for the time they were in town torturing innocent people, or maybe it was just me he was tormenting.

The next morning, he finally drove somewhere where I planned to confront him. I had all of this anger inside of me. All of these pent-up emotions that I needed to get out and even though I'd spent a half hour yelling at Ford and my father, it didn't seem to release all I needed to.

So I decided to go to the source. The man who was responsible for the murder of the most important person in my life, he was responsible for the way my life took a drastic turn all those years ago. He was the reason that I felt hate.

And not surprisingly, I hated it.

After ten missed calls from Ford I'd finally turned my phone off, I didn't know much about the FBI but I knew they could easily track my phone for him if he asked them to and I knew it wouldn't be a good idea if he showed up when I was in the middle of confronting someone.

I needed time away from him and my father. I knew I'd go back, eventually. But I couldn't stand that he knew, this whole time, he knew that my mother was killed by the very man who came to see me every week.

Thinking about that made me realize it was probably a good thing that I didn't know he was her killer because I probably would have done something reckless like shoot him or something. We kept a gun in the office, ever since Mom, for safety. But I'd only ever shot it at a range. I'd never dreamed I'd actually have to—or want to—use it on someone.

I didn't have it now, and I really didn't care. Though I know that Rafael could kill me with his bare hands, I wasn't here to kill the man. I was here to get some answers.

My father hadn't given me enough to make sense. I didn't understand what my family had done to get themselves into this situation in the first place. My mother wasn't the type who would do anything illegal, she would have never agreed to the terms that Guerrero wanted her to and I understood that. Because I wouldn't either.

I step out of my car, eyeing the warehouse that lies beyond a high fence, I don't know how I'm going to get inside, but I figure there's probably about a dozen cameras on me right now and if Rafael doesn't want to see me, they won't open.

Right as the thought crosses my mind, the buzzing sound of a motor starts and the gates slowly slide open. I step through them and steel myself when they close behind me immediately after I'm through. *No going back now.*

I walk to the main entrance and brace myself for someone to come running out with a gun pointed at me, but that's not what happens. Rafael himself walks through the smaller side door and grins when he sees me walking his way. "I knew someday you'd find your way to me."

I bristle at his words. It's not the first time he's insinuated that he wanted something more with me, I've never really corrected him out of fear but today, after everything, I feel no real fear. That anger that sparked me to find him in the first place comes raring back and I glare at him. "I'm not here for you. I'm here for answers."

He doesn't lose the grin on his face. If anything, it gets wider. "I love a woman who knows what she wants."

"You killed my mother." The words leave me before I can stop myself and I watch as his head rears back and shock replaces his grin.

"I—" he stutters and chuckles. I've never seen him at a loss for words, always so in control. "I didn't."

"Don't lie to me. I've had enough lies."

"Who's been lying to you, *reina?*"

I ignore him. "I know that you killed my mother because she wouldn't do your bidding. I know I'm next on the list, too."

His face transforms into a mask of anger, but not toward me. "I would never let anyone kill you."

I pause and watch his face. I can tell he's serious, I just don't know why. "Why not? I won't do your bidding any more than my mother would."

This time, he ignores my question. "Then we'll find another way to work that out."

"And the drugs? I won't store them for you. I refuse to do anything illegal."

He shakes his head and sighs. "I'm afraid that's already been arranged by your father. We can't change that now."

"Sure we can."

He chuckles and takes a step toward me, his hand lifting to touch my cheek and I don't move to stop him. "Well, I suppose I could take you instead."

"What?" The word comes out as a whisper, the fear I refused to feel coming back up. Bubbling inside of me like it wants to explode.

"I won't make you store the drugs, but I get to keep you instead."

"That's absurd," I refute, taking a step back. "You can't just take me."

He looks frustrated for a moment but then tries to cover it up. "Then I suppose you'll be storing my product."

I don't answer. There is no right answer. I either become his personal slut, or I break the law? This can't possibly be happening. I feel like I'm going to be sick and before I can answer, he leaves me with, "You have forty-eight hours to choose." He turns and disappears back into the building he came from.

And I'm left there with not a clue what to do.

37

FORD

IT'S BEEN DAYS since our argument, and I haven't heard a word from Delaney in all that time. Not only that, she hasn't been in the restaurant, and even though Lizzie and Delaney's other employees have no idea what's going on, they know something serious is up. She would never just leave without a word. Hell, it seems like she never leaves the place unless she's fallen ill.

I go back and forth between my place and the restaurant, I don't hold out much hope that she would just show up at my parents, but after the state she left in, it's hard to say where her head is at. I know she's probably not feeling like going to her dad's right now, so I don't bother trying there.

I recall the last thing he and I talked about, after watching Delaney tear out of the driveway, I resisted the urge to jump in my car and go after her, thinking she just needed a little time. Had I known she was going to disappear the way she had, I wouldn't have hesitated.

Instead, I forced myself to go back in the house and have a real conversation with her father. They know what I do for a living and sitting on this information could potentially get Joaquín in some serious trouble, not only that, not giving the information to Gemma could get me fired for good. He hadn't moved from the seat where he broke down, the dish that Delaney threw was still in pieces all over the kitchen, the scene replayed in my head and a sick feeling gathered in my gut.

I leaned against the wall, not wanting to get comfortable, all I wanted was to get out of here, but I had to get some things straight with him before I could move on.

"Tell me everything, Joaquín."

He has the balls to look up and glare at me, the hate for me is clear on his face, but I have a way of concealing how I feel and just watch him with a passive look. "What makes you think I'd do that, huh? All of this… it could have been avoided."

I huff and shrug my shoulders. "You're right. It could have been. If you'd just told your daughter what was going on from the start."

"She didn't need to know."

"Except she did. She had every right to know, it's her life at stake."

He shakes his head. "I wouldn't have let anything happen to her."

I scoff, thinking about what happened to her mother. It's not his fault, not really, but he wasn't able to stop them from murdering his wife, so why does he think he would be able to stop them with his daughter? Rafael takes what he wants, regardless of the consequences.

"Our family, we have a history," he starts. I don't tell him I know about the history he's talking about, maybe his version is more accurate than Miles' version, maybe there're more clues to the puzzle. "I became aware of Rafael's motivation long ago. When he took over for his father, I was sure I'd be dead within the year. But he was motivated by more than money, more than the drugs. It was the way he looked at her, the way that whenever she was around, even though she never once looked his way, he would pause what he was doing to watch her."

My mind reels at the new information, my gut clenches uncomfortably, what he's insinuating is not what I was prepared for. Knowing she was out there alone and distraught makes the anxiety I didn't even know I had rear its ugly head. "You're telling me he's in love with her?" I can hear the disdain in my voice.

Joaquín shrugs like it doesn't bother him that much, like it's not a dangerous criminal who's not only in love with his daughter, but knows things about her, where she works, what she drives; and she's out there all alone. "It's always been one-sided, but definitely there for a long time."

I shake my head. "Alright, cut the shit." My voice raises, I'm done with the off-topic subjects, the diversions. "What does he have on you?"

"It's a family thing. You won't understand."

I stand up straighter. "Try me."

"The Guerreros own the town we came from, which means, in that culture, they own the people; the families. It's not a custom that is familiar here, obviously, which is why we never went back. Annie learned about it when we started dating, and she told me then she would never subject her children to that sort of life."

I shake my head at the bullshit, I knew I liked Mrs. Torrez more.

"But of course, that wasn't how they worked. For years after we married, they left us alone. I thought we somehow were getting by with something, I didn't know why they let us be but I was grateful. Happy that I could raise my daughter in a safe town, have our business and grow as a family without the stress of working for them.

"It ended quickly though, or at least, it felt that way. When Delaney was around fifteen, they started showing up again, started badgering us to help them with their things, wanting us to store drugs, money, even guns for them." He pauses, seeming startled that I was standing there still. He just admitted all of this to a federal agent. I can't do anything without proof but it's a fact he probably doesn't really know.

"Well, you know the rest. Somehow." He narrows his gaze, but I don't give him anything. He doesn't need to know a single thing about how I know his family's history, how I know any of it.

"So what does he want now?"

"Truthfully? I think he really just wants her."

My fists clench and I close my eyes. *That fucker.* I knew it was going to be something like that but I wasn't prepared for it to be said so plainly. Her father doesn't even seem to care. "And you're okay with that? That he wants to take your daughter against her will."

"It wouldn't be like that. She would have a choice. And she would be treated like a queen if she was his woman."

The anger builds so swiftly that I don't even realize it when the punch gets thrown, his head jolts back and a grunt leaves him. I didn't give it everything I could, I didn't want to kill the man. Well, maybe I did. But I didn't.

Without another word, I'd left the house, more determined than ever to find Laney and protect her from this bullshit her father allowed them to get involved in.

It was time to finally put all this shit to rest.

PACING MY ROOM didn't do much good, I'd used my computer to try and track Delaney's cell phone, but it didn't work.

Which either meant she turned it off, or it was turned off for her. I prayed it wasn't the latter.

No one had heard from her in the last three days and I was starting to get desperate, to think of outside sources that could help me track her down. I didn't think Gemma would help, not because she doesn't care but because she knows that I've been trying to look into Rafael this whole time, and she doesn't want to encourage my working right now.

Thinking over all the people I could contact, anyone who would help me, I thought of one person; well, two. I hadn't spoken to them in years, the last I'd seen them we were being shot at and I was gunned down by some Russian motherfuckers. So reaching out to them, out of the blue, would probably raise some red flags. But desperation was gripping me tight. I reach for my phone as there's a knock on my door.

I sigh, knowing it's my mom on the other side, checking on me once again. She doesn't know the details, but she knows I haven't seen Delaney in some time and now she's worried about it. "Mom, I'm fine," I lie as I swing open the door.

What I'm not expecting is Delaney standing on the other side of the door. Her hair is damp, and she looks like she could fall over if a light breeze blew by. "Laney." My voice is a whisper, obvious relief fills the air between us. Without permission, I reach for her and when she doesn't stop me, doesn't even try, I pull her to my chest and hold her tightly.

We stand there for several minutes, her gripping me just as

tight, breathing each other in. I feel a weight lift off my chest at knowing she's safe, not knowing where she'd gone has been killing me slowly.

"I'm sorry." Are her first words and I freeze.

Pulling back, I frown at her. "You have nothing to apologize for."

"I do, though. How I acted and treated you was uncalled for."

I shake my head, still holding on to her shoulders and looking her over, grateful that I'm able to see her in her light blue shirt and jean shorts. "It's over, if anything I should be the one who's sorry."

She bites her lip and I can see her eyes get glassy. Before I can ask what's wrong, her lips are pressed to mine tightly and she's pushing us back into the room. I reach behind her to shut the door and grab her hips. I don't question the kiss; instead I revel in it.

It's been too fucking long since I've had this woman, since I've held her and had any sort of peace and as much as I want to ask what happened, where she went, I let her take the lead and push me onto the bed after discarding my shirt.

I grasp her shirt and pull it over her head, holding her eyes, I undo her bra and the button on her pants quickly as she does the same to mine. Her eyes spark and I lean up on one elbow to grab her neck and pull her down to my lips, trying as smoothly as possible to flip us so she's under me. When I see the acceptance, the willingness in her eyes, I push into her.

My eyes close involuntarily at the motion, at the love that suddenly fills my chest, it's enough to make me want to burst. I continue the quick movements, holding her to me and trying to tell her with my movements what she means to me, how much I truly care for her, how much I love her.

With each thrust I want the three words to burst out of me but I hold back, not wanting it to be said in a moment of passion, when her cry of release leaves her I let my own follow and slow my movements, holding myself above her.

When I look back at her, I see her mouth opening and closing, and finally she says, "I'm so happy I'm here."

I can see more, more words floating around in her head, more emotions—that probably match mine—floating around in our hearts and heads, but for now, I let it go, and hold her as we fall asleep.

HOURS LATER, I awake to a dark room, the silence in the room tells me all I need to know and without looking I know that Delaney is no longer here. I close my eyes and breathe through the pain lacing through my heart.

I don't know why she left but I can't deny that it hurts that she did. I just hope she doesn't disappear like last time. I shift and grab my phone off the nightstand when I see there's a text from Gemma on the screen.

We need to talk.

That's all it says. I decide I can't wait to find out what she wants, so while I get dressed and the morning sun shines through the barn window, I listen and wait to see what fate awaits me.

38

DELANEY

I DON'T KNOW why I left. I regretted it almost immediately, I almost went back but once I'd already locked the door and closed it, I was embarrassed to think about walking back up the stairs and knocking on the door.

Last night was unexpected, I hadn't meant to just fall into Ford the way I had but something inside of me needed him more than I wanted to admit. I hated needing anyone, of course, I wasn't really someone who relied on people for anything, let alone comfort. But Ford makes me feel like I can and last night, I needed him.

The restaurant was just opening and everyone is busy getting their sections ready and tidy for the customers that are sure to arrive soon, I count out money for the day and look at the schedule of incoming shipments from our vendors. David, our cook has been hounding me about trying to go completely grass-fed beef and as much as I want to, it's hard to get the budget together with all the money I've been giving Rafael.

Though I suspect that I won't really have to worry about that soon. I have a choice to make, and despite the fact that one of the options is to hand myself over to a dangerous man who could kill me without a second thought, the choice wasn't that easy.

My mother would have never wanted this. It's why my parents got into trouble in the first place. They wouldn't have wanted to have their family-friendly restaurant be part of an illegal operation. My mom wouldn't have wanted to have me involved in any of that. But what was I going to do?

Really, I didn't have a choice. It was clear to me that my father wasn't going to stand up to Rafael, he had before, with my mother at his side and look what happened to her. He made a deal that he thought he could get out of or work with. One that kept me safe, kept our restaurant intact but one that also sacrificed a lot of what I thought he stood for.

It was why I was unable to stay with Ford, I wanted to, but a part of me knew I was going to have to let him go. I couldn't have him involved in this shit. I was pissed that my father had even put me in this position. Ford deserved more than what I could now give him. I thought I could be that person for him, the one who could maybe stand by him and be the strong counterpart. But all the crap unraveling was making that seem like a far-fetched dream.

I expected my father to be here at the restaurant, ready to grovel and beg for forgiveness but I hadn't seen him and according to Lizzie, she hadn't either. "I'm surprised the restaurant didn't burn down."

"Wait, he didn't show up at all?"

She shakes her head, worry in her eyes for me. "When you didn't answer the phone I went and checked the house but no one answered the door." Her eyes look at me accusingly, in the history of the restaurant, it was a rare day that not a single Torrez was running the place. But I had a feeling her glare was more about being left out of the loop. She was my best friend, and she didn't have a clue what was coming.

"I-I'm so sorry." I rub a hand over my forehead, my stress palpable, and try to breathe through it for a moment. "We had a little… fight. So we're not really on great terms at the moment." Anyone else in the world I would have given an excuse to, but Lizzie was my constant, I swear she stayed at this restaurant for me alone, not because she wanted to be a thirty-year-old waitress, but because she loved my family like she loves her own.

"Are you okay?" The news that Dad and I fought is foreign as well, my dad and I, while we're not the best of friends, we've never taken anything so seriously that we would fight over it.

"I'm okay."

She regards me carefully and leans against the bar, propping her hands on the edge behind her. "Have you seen Ford?"

I nod my head and give her a fake smile. "Yeah, saw him last night." Though I'm sure she would be delighted, I keep the part about it being an overnighter to myself. Last night isn't something that I want to share with anyone, it felt too sacred. Too emotional and real. I know Ford felt it too, it was the way he held me, his eyes held emotions in them that I'd never seen reflected back at me and I knew if I'd stayed this morning, we would have had a conversation I wouldn't survive. Regardless of what we were, I knew it couldn't last.

For one thing, he was leaving. I saw the text from Gemma, his boss, I knew what she had to say, don't ask me how, I just knew that it was telling him he was reinstated. And I was happy about it. Not only because it meant he could get back to the job he was meant for, but it meant he'd be far, far away from the shit I'd gotten myself into.

I don't know what I would do if he got hurt because of me. It would kill that last part of me that held hope.

And while it was ripping me apart inside, because I'd finally found someone I could see a future with, after all these years alone wishing that I would get to this point, where I could let myself fall for someone, love someone, build something, I had to let him go.

I blink my eyes against the tears that suddenly build but Lizzie sees them before I can fully hide them. "Honey, what is going on?"

I shake my head. "Nothing, don't worry about it. I'm just, I don't know, hormonal or something." I let out a forced chuckle and wipe my eyes.

"Laney…" I can tell she doesn't believe a word I'm saying but before she can say anything more, customers enter the room, lunch is approaching and we're about to be busy. I thank my stars that I can push this conversation off for as long as possible and I throw myself into work, all the while thinking of the way the hours are quickly dwindling down to my deadline.

HOURS LATER I'M bussing tables, it's not normally something I have to do but our busboy called out sick and I have to pitch in so the waiters don't have to add more to their workload. I'm clearing a table when the door chimes again and I get myself in hostess mode.

I head to the front but instead of customers, it's Ford. He looks devastatingly handsome in a light blue shirt and dark blue jeans. His hair is perfectly tousled, his eyes blaze into mine with almost a look of desperation. I know it's something more than that, with that look alone tears threaten to come back but I turn around and head to the back.

Already knowing he's going to follow me; I clear up the tears before he can have a reason to ask me about them. I don't know how I'm going to do this. I don't know how to break up with someone, let alone someone I… *holy shit.*

Before my thoughts can run off with that thought, he's behind me in the office and shutting us off from the world. "Laney," he says and his voice is so full of love and confusion that it damn near rips my heart out of my chest.

I turn and steel my spine, *I have to do this for him,* is what I keep reminding myself. If I was trying to be selfish, if I was doing this for myself alone, I wouldn't be having so much trouble. But I'm doing this for him.

Because I do love him.

"Laney, why did you leave?" His voice almost breaks on my name, but he has a better resolve than I do and catches himself.

"I had to work." I give him the bullshit answer.

"Laney." He shakes his head. Ford's hand reaches for me but at the last minute, he shoves one in his pocket and rubs his jaw with the other and leans his body back against the door. "What happened, babe?"

Babe. Just hearing the endearment makes me want to crumble. "What do you mean?"

"I hadn't seen you in days. Where'd you go? What happened?" he asks and then his eyes shutter. "And don't give me some story. I deserve the truth."

I shrug my shoulders, ready to do exactly what he's accusing me of but I don't know if I can. So I think of some sort of version that would be safe. "I went to deal with Rafael."

His face loses all the color it normally favors and he stutters for a minute before replying, "You're not serious."

Nodding my head, he steps toward me. "What did he do to you?"

Here's where I could lie. I could say he persuaded me, that I think there's something there I want to explore. But as much as that would definitely push Ford away, as much as it would definitely put the end to this that I desperately need, I can't use that reason. It's too much, and I don't want to hurt Ford. Ever.

"Nothing. Actually, he and I came to an understanding," I start, my thoughts scrambling for something to say. "He has good reason to use my family's restaurant and it's not illegal." What that is, I don't know.

"Wh—" Ford stops himself and looks at me like I've lost my mind. "Laney. You cannot be in business with him. He's a criminal."

"Ford, you know just as much as I do how much my restaurant has been struggling. He's willing to help. I just have to handle some things for him."

"Some things? What things?"

This is the part where Ford will start to hate me. "I don't see how that's any of your business."

I was right. The way he reacts, it's as if I've just slapped him across the face. I wait for his reply but realize he doesn't have one. I wouldn't either if I was in his shoes, after everything we've shared and talked about, I'm here throwing it in his face.

"Ford, we need to talk about something else." He pauses his movements and waits, not looking me in the eyes. This is going to hurt. "I think we should maybe take a break."

Ford stares at me and slowly, there's a devastation that crosses his face that breaks my heart, it's followed quickly by panic and then his eyes glass up and I nearly break. *No. Don't do this now. You can't.* I scold myself. I can't let myself show him the emotion that is brimming over every edge of my heart.

"You don't mean that." He scoffs, shaking his head and his eyes narrow.

"I do." And another thought hits me. "And I talked to Rafael, with the new deal, I'll be able to pay you back right away."

He doesn't say anything. I don't know if it's because he can't believe me or if anger is starting to take root inside him. I wouldn't blame the man for hating me. It would hurt, forever. But after the love we'd shared, even before my revelation, he's going to remember me and curse my name.

Ford opens his mouth several times. Seemingly trying to figure out what he could possibly say and then without a word, he turns and storms out of the office. I count to sixty and then I lose it. I *break.*

The tears are so overwhelming that I sink to the floor, I can't even hold myself up with the sobs that are wracking my body. *This is not my life.* I tell myself. I found the only man I'll ever love, and I just had to rip his heart out, because another man is making me do things that I just can't live with, and I can't make Ford live with them either.

I stay there for so long I wouldn't be surprised if Lizzie comes looking for me soon. I shake my head as my phone rings and I move to answer it, I don't really want to deal with him right now but I don't have a choice so I pick up the phone, "Hello?"

"Hello, Delaney." The voice on the other end jars me and I flinch at the sound of Rafael's voice.

"Why do you have my father's phone?"

"Well, *reina*, you see. Your father and I have been having a titillating conversation about your choices."

I shake my head in refusal and say, "No, I still have time."

"Not anymore. I'll send an address and if you're a good girl like I think you very well could be, you'll show up. Maybe your papá will be fine, but then again, maybe not." The phone clicks and goes dead and a chill runs down my spine.

A second later my phone vibrates with a message, the address clear but my head muddled with horrified thoughts. I look around the office that has been like my second home for my entire life and let another tear escape me.

"I'm sorry, Mama." I wipe the tears under my eyes and take a breath. I know what I have to do, and it's going to hurt, maybe even more than what I've already had to do today, but I refuse to let my mother's legacy turn into a place that is used by a drug cartel.

Leaving the office, I find Lizzie and wave her over. "Hey, what's up?" she asks, her eyes are still clouded with worry, no doubt she saw Ford storm out of here but she doesn't ask.

"I have to run out, I'm not sure I'll be back tonight. I hate to ask—"

"I've got you, girl," she cuts me off and I'm surprised when she grabs me in a crushing hug. I feel my eyes start to well again, but I blink, trying to keep them at bay and I hug her back just as tight.

When we pull apart, I look at her and then the restaurant once more, I may never see it again, the thought catches me off guard but I brush it away. "Bye, Liz."

She waves and gives me an encouraging smile and I try my best to force one for her and rush out before I can change my mind. I run to my father's car and speed down the street, I don't know what waits for me, but no matter where my father and I stand, I can't let Rafael hurt him.

39

FORD

THE CAR IDLES outside of the restaurant where the woman I love just tore my heart from my chest, to be honest though, she'd already had it to begin with; she just crushed it in the palm of her hand. I couldn't understand why she was pushing me away, after everything we'd done, everything we'd shared.

None of it made any sense.

I knew I wasn't an easy person to live with, to *be* with. But I was trying damn hard. I wasn't perfect, I had some fucked-up shit in this head of mine but I would never do anything to purposefully hurt her.

And yes, I'd been reinstated. Gemma had let me know I was cleared to return whenever I was ready, and I'd told a small fib about not being sure I'd ever be fit to return to the field. It had her hesitating, making me think that maybe she wasn't totally believing me. I'd explained what I really wanted to do and after a lengthy conversation, she told me she would get in touch with the information I'd need for my new job.

I was looking forward to it, I was excited at the prospect of settling in an office somewhere and having a normal life for once. I almost couldn't believe these were my thoughts, but it was Delaney who'd changed everything for me. I wanted to do this for her, for us. I wanted to give her all of her dreams and then some and I was looking forward to getting our life moving forward.

And after last night, I thought everything was set in stone. I know she was having a hard time with everything that had happened and especially after her encounter with Guerrero. I wanted to kill that man. Men like him needed to be done on this earth, they didn't deserve to be here in the first place.

Plus, what her dad had revealed? That shit would fuck anyone up. To find out that her mother was murdered intentionally. There's something about it that changes you.

My thoughts are on a rampage and I know it's because my heart is hurting in a way I've never known before, when I lean my head back against the headrest, I see something across the street and refocus.

Delaney rushes out, keeping her head down as she digs her

keys out of her purse and rushes for her car, she jumps in barely pausing as she peels out of the spot she was in and down the street. I stare for about two seconds before putting the car in drive and following at a distance.

—

DELANEY

THE DARK STREET sends another rack of shivers down my spine. Even though it's holding steady at a solid sixty degrees, the rain that's come out of nowhere gives me a chill that tends to be perfect for this situation.

The address I'd received from Rafael isn't one I'm familiar with and the further out of town I drive, the more idiotic I feel. I know I was about to hand myself over to the man, but I can't help the fear that easily enters into every joint of my body.

How is it that just a few short months ago, my biggest concern was getting bills paid, and now I was making a deal with the literal devil?

I don't want to do this; I think to myself. And it was the truth. But if I admit it out loud, if I let myself really think the words, really let my brain believe it, I wouldn't be able to save my family. And that included my dad, Lizzie, any of the employees, Mom's legacy, and Ford.

I knew I'd never see the man again and I would eventually let myself be okay with that, I'd mourn him as if he'd died and eventually, day by day, maybe it would not hurt so bad. Maybe it will be okay someday.

I reach the destination according to my GPS but I don't see anything, of course, it's pretty hard to see much with the rain that's coming down. Where I'm at must have been a thriving town at one point, but now everything has been closed down and abandoned. *So many places for him to hide*, I think. There's barely any light save for an old barn light on the side of the road, one that's not really meant to do much and it's not helping. I slow my car and pull off the side of the road and wait.

It's not long before another car pulls up opposite me and flashes their lights, I get out against the rain and I make my way to the halfway point, I have the gun tucked into the back of my jeans and feel my fingers itch to grab it, to feel its supported weight in my hands but I refrain, knowing it'll only cause more problems.

Rafael gets out, an umbrella above his head before even a drop can touch his perfectly done hair and he steps forward, I hold my ground and he comes close enough that the umbrella covers us both.

"*Reina*," he greets me with a smirk on his lips.

"Where's my father?" The question comes out with a chatter to my teeth and I grind my teeth down to hold it steady.

"Oh, he's fine. I'll be happy to let him go."

I raise a brow and let out a scoff. "Really? Then why all of this?"

He licks his lips and shrugs. "Well, I wanted an answer."

"I was going to give you one," I say and shake my head. "You didn't even give me the full amount of time you promised."

"One thing." He leans closer, trying to intimidate me. "One thing that you'll learn about me, is that I am not a very patient man."

I let a breath out. "You don't say."

His lips quirk in amusement and his eyes crinkle at the edges. It'd be endearing if he wasn't such a horrible person. "I love that about you."

"What's that?"

"You're not afraid of me."

I cross my arms and roll my shoulders back. "I—"

"I told you, no company."

I don't follow his comment and look at him in confusion when he raises a gun to something behind me and pulls the trigger. I turn quickly, right as I see my worst nightmare come true, right as Ford crashes to the ground. "No!" A guttural response leaves me, and I go to run to him when my arm is grasped. I spin to face Rafael head-on and glare through the tears. "You bastard!"

He gets in my face then. "You don't follow my rules, then I have to take drastic measures. You bring a federal agent in here, then I'm sorry but I have to cover my ass."

"Just give me my father and let me go!" I'm a little hysterical right now, but after my day I think I deserve to be.

"I can't do that. I need you to pick, Delaney." I hesitate. I don't want to go with the man who might have just killed the only man I've ever loved, a sob wracks through my body at the thought of him lying there helpless on the ground and when I look toward him, he hasn't moved.

Ford. I will with my head, praying he'll move, praying that he's just knocked out and not what I fear the worst. "Let me go to him," I plead, my voice cracking.

He regards me for a moment, thinking over my request before letting my arm go, I don't ask again, and I run to where Ford's fallen to the ground. He still hasn't moved. The rain coats us both until we're soaking wet, I fall to my knees beside him and touch his face, he was hit in his right shoulder but must have hit his head when he went down. "Ford." My voice cracks again and I let out a sob at the sight of him.

I lean over and kiss his cold lips. "I'm so sorry, Ford." I feel under his jaw for a pulse and breathe a silent prayer of thanks when I feel it beating. I take off the small jacket I'm wearing and make a half-assed wrap for where he's been hit. Next, I reach into his pocket, leaning over him and hoping that Rafael can't see what I'm doing, I find Ford's phone and quickly press one more kiss to his lips and whisper the address to the first responder before hanging up the phone and shoving it back in his pocket.

It's all I can do before I feel Rafael coming for me.

"I love you," I whisper, for the first and last time.

When I finally look away from him, I see my father has been pulled out of one of the vehicles and is walking toward me. He hugs me and I hold him for a minute. "It's time to pick, *reina*." I cringe and I look at my father one last time. "I love you, Papá." Tears can't escape me fast enough and I lean forward. "Please make sure he's okay."

Dad looks to where Ford is and back to me with confusion swimming in his eyes. "*Mija?*"

I just shake my head and turn back to Rafael. I steel my spine and I swear there's a glint of respect in his eyes, but I could give a shit less what Rafael thinks of me. "I'll go."

He accepts my answer with a nod, and before I can utter another word, I'm ushered into the back seat of a car.

"*Mija!*" my father yells and I give him and Ford one last look before I'm closed off from view. They pull away quickly, and just as fast as I arrived, I'm taken away.

40

FORD

A SMELL I'M all too familiar with sends memories flashing through my brain so fast I can't place one before the next. I know I'm in the hospital, the sterile stink and the humming of the machine that's to my left indicate that much.

But I can't remember *why*.

The last thing I can remember was following Delaney to the darkest part of Texas I'd ever seen. Working off of a gut feeling, I knew who she was meeting and suddenly wished I'd had a gun with me. But I didn't, because I didn't technically own my own and my issued ones had gone back to the agency during my break.

When I saw Rafael get out of the car, I knew shit was about to turn bad and I couldn't wait long before I was coming up behind them. Surely, he saw my car pull up but I didn't care, I didn't give a shit what he thought or if he wondered why I was there. All I cared about was getting to Delaney, protecting her.

Fuck. Where is she?

I can't remember anything past making my way behind her and— shit. That's right. That's what that pain is in my shoulder. The fucker shot me.

Before I can even push a button to find out what the hell has happened, Gemma James herself walks through the door, her hair in her pristine bun without a hair out of place and her suit tailored to perfection.

"You just couldn't help yourself, huh, bud?" Her sarcasm catches me off guard. I've never known her as the sarcastic type and she was my partner for years before we went our separate ways.

"Trouble finds me, it's not my fault." I grimace when I try to sit up. It's not the worst injury I've ever had but it sure as hell still hurts.

"Sure," she says like she's not convinced. "So what the hell happened?"

I squint. "You didn't debrief Delaney?"

"Delaney? What's she got to do with this?"

Something tight twists my gut when the question leaves her mouth. "What do you mean? She was there. She was with me."

Gemma sees the panic and lifts a hand to calm me down. Regarding me for a moment, she sighs before finally saying, "Ford, some paramedics brought you in here, but their report was you were by yourself in the middle of the road. No sign of anyone else, just you."

I close my eyes and think. I can't remember exactly what happened, but she couldn't have possibly gone with him... could she?

"Delaney was there," I say again stubbornly.

"Who else? Who shot you?"

"Guerrero."

Her expression tells me she was waiting for me to say that but she still clicks her tongue in disappointment. "Damn it, Ford! Do you know how many people are after him? I told you not to engage!"

Her rage doesn't faze me. "He went after Delaney! I don't give a fuck if he's the motherfucking Pope! I would have done anything for her." The crack on my last word betrays my hard tone, but I continue giving Gemma a hard stare. "You have to help me find her."

Gemma shakes her head. "I can't do that Ford, I'm way out of my jurisdiction right now. If I infringe on their investigation I could be fired."

I glare at her with rage pulsing through my veins. "He has Delaney."

"I know, Ford... I just don't think there's anything we can do."

She looks defeated but it's not enough. She opens her mouth to say more but her phone interrupts her and she leaves the room to answer it.

I sit there for about five seconds before I decide what I've gotta do. I have to get to Delaney, no matter what it takes.

IT DIDN'T TAKE much to leave the hospital because Gemma got pulled away before I had to make up an excuse to leave. She did leave me with a warning to not go after Delaney, but there was something in her eyes, something that told me that she already knew I wasn't going to listen, so when I boarded the plane, I didn't feel a lick of guilt.

I wasn't sure what to expect when I got to my destination. We hadn't necessarily left on bad terms, it had just been another job and time to move on. It'd been so long since I'd seen them that I wasn't sure what the reception would be like.

In my line of work, it wasn't prudent to keep tabs on friends, that could backfire at a moment's notice and I couldn't let that happen to anyone, which was also another reason I'd hidden from my parents for so long.

The plane ride is only a couple of hours and thankfully Colorado's weather holds up enough for us to land without any delay. I catch a taxi and give them the address that I'd stolen from Gemma some time ago. I didn't actually think I'd use it, but I'd retained it the second I saw it on Liam's file and committed it to memory.

Liam Stokes was my best friend for years; he and I have been through a lot in this life. We met in the army and immediately hit it off with all our similarities. We'd both been running from something when joining and found our family in the unit we were stationed in. After we both had done our stint in the military, the FBI approached us both and we decided to go for it together.

The rest is history. We rarely got to work together in the FBI but we always tried. We were both undercover agents working on our own missions so we would go years at a time not speaking but it was like no time had passed at all when we met up again.

I was hoping that would be the case this time as well.

It was really his wife that I was mostly concerned about. Margaret Davis was a stubborn woman who didn't give a lick what anyone thought of her, and yet, she was the most selfless person I'd ever met. She was tough and when she and Liam had first met, she'd gone through hell and back with him and didn't miss a beat.

She loved him fiercely and I saw that he felt the same toward her, it had made me jealous that he'd found someone that would stick by him. I thought, at one point, that maybe I had feelings for her too. But I realized I'd just really wanted to someday find for myself what Liam had found.

I did with Delaney.

I have no idea where she could be right now, but I know wherever it is, it isn't good. Her father must be with them too if no one was there when the paramedics reached me. I only got to see her for maybe thirty seconds before Rafael had the gun up and fired at me. I should have been more fucking prepared for it, I should have, but I wasn't and now she was in the wind.

I push her out of my head when the taxi stops outside of a nice apartment complex in some suburban part of Denver. I toss him some cash before exiting the car. Before entering the lobby I take in a much-needed breath of fresh air, shouldering my bag on my uninjured side, I head inside.

From the looks of the lobby, it would seem they were doing really well for themselves. I head to the elevator and wait for it to take me to the floor I need, when I exit I take another breath and picture Delaney.

If anyone can help me find her, *will* help me find her, it'll be Liam. With his skills he could probably find her easily and I'm praying to God he still dabbles every now and then and has kept up with them.

I knock on the door and take a couple of steps to the side, hoping they'll hear me out and open the door, that they'll give me a chance to explain my absence, my dilemma and hopefully help me out. Finally, someone opens the door and I wait a few seconds before I step into view. Margaret's eyes widen and her mouth opens in shock. She still looks as beautiful as ever.

"Uh, Liam, you might want to come here," she says over her shoulder and I give her a smirk, hoping my charm will somehow still work its magic on her the way it has in the past.

"Ford?" Liam asks with surprise in his voice when he sees me, I see relief flash through his eyes before he runs his eyes over me, noting anything that might be amiss.

"Hey guys," I reply, shifting my feet.

"What are you doing here?"

"I, uh… I need some help."

41

FORD

EXPLAINING EVERYTHING THAT has happened takes more time than I want but the both of them want every detail that they can get. I go through everything I know from the moment I saw Rafael to the moment he shot me and left me for dead, to the last moment I saw Delaney's face.

Margaret and Liam both listen intently, I didn't know what either of them were doing with their lives, I didn't know if they'd even help me. I was counting on their kindness for all of this, but they'd been through shit before and I knew after explaining what Delaney meant to me, when they'd looked at each other, they got it.

When I'm finished retelling my nightmare, they both seem to be thinking everything over and I roll my shoulder, wincing and letting out a breath of air. Margaret gets up, muttering something about aspirin and walking down their hallway.

I look back at Liam and he's still looking in the direction that she went. "I think I have some contacts that can help."

I let out a relieved sigh and I nod my head. "I appreciate it, man. I'm sorry to barge in here like this."

Liam shakes his head and waves his hand. "We'd always help you man; you've helped us more than you know. We know what it's like." He's quiet for a moment and seems to be trying to find the right words to say and then finally, "She missed you."

I sit back and frown, I know we'd formed a bond and I felt bad about the way that things were left. "I'm sorry. I haven't kept in touch with anyone. I've been... completely off the grid."

"Yeah." He nods, I know he gets that but it's not always easy for people on the outside to get it. "You know she became a cop?"

I'm sure my expression gives away my disbelief because he chuckles. "No shit?"

"No shit." He looks away for a moment with a fond smile on his face. "She's damn good too, studying for the detective's exam."

"Damn." I think about the time I got to spend with Margaret and then say, "It shouldn't be at all surprising."

"Right?" he agrees and just then Margaret comes back with a bottle and hands it to me before going into the kitchen, she returns with a bottle of water and then takes a seat beside Liam across from me and Liam announces he's going to call in some favors before leaving the room.

"How are you?" I ask Margaret when he's gone, and I see her sigh and stiffen her shoulders.

"I've been fine." She gives a forced smile and I grimace. "How are you?" She quickly realizes she already knows and says, "Sorry, I know you're shitty. I shouldn't have asked that."

I chuckle. "It's okay. I'm okay, I just need… I need to get her back and safe."

"Well, Liam's the best PI in Denver, he'll help you and I'll do whatever I can."

"Liam's a PI now?" I ask with what sounds like relief in my voice and I shake my head.

"Yeah, he started right after leaving the feds, well, kind of while he was in still… that's a long story though. He's great at it. My department uses him all the time."

I nod my head. "He told me you're a cop, that's incredible Margaret."

"Thank you."

We sit in silence for a moment and I'm trying to figure out why she's so pissed at me, but it's not exactly coming to me. "Are you okay?" I finally just ask.

She looks at her clasped hands and then out the window beside the couch, then at the coffee table that separates us before finally answering me. "Yes. I just… it's so weird to see you after all this time. I—" I want to tell her to spit it out but I hold it in. "I tried calling you. About, oh, three—four, years ago? I think."

I rub my face at this because I know exactly what happened when she did. My phone had been turned off for a while at that point because I was undercover already and there's no way I could have had any contact with her at that point. "I'm sorry."

"Yeah," she replies. I know there's not much she can say because she knows how my life goes. "I just thought you meant what you said, about if I needed you? And, I don't know, Liam was gone, ya know? He was gone and I was alone and I didn't know where the hell anyone was and… you were my last chance."

Shame burns inside of me because I had said that. I'd promised to be there for my friend if she needed me and I wasn't. I was a total jackass and there wasn't shit that I could do to make it up to her.

"It turned out alright, obviously." She gives a tiny smile and I take it for everything I can. "I am happy now, you know. I just, I wish you would have kept in touch."

"Margaret, I—I'm so sorry." I hold eye contact with her while I deliver my speech. "My life these last few years has been hell, literally. And I would have been a terrible friend, but that doesn't excuse anything I did to hurt you."

She holds my eyes and I can see the changes in her. The old Margaret would have blushed and looked away but she doesn't, she holds her gaze and tries to see if I'm full of shit. After another minute she nods. "Well, you better not do it again."

I give her another smile and nod my head.

Liam returns a few minutes later and gives me some information from his friend. "He ran the number you gave me and says it's still in Texas, at some abandoned warehouse just outside of Huntsville."

I shake my head, she's in fucking Huntsville? "That's only about an hour away from home," I reply and curse.

"Well, the phone is there anyway. I also called around, this Guerrero guy? He's bad fucking news, Ford." Leave it to Liam to give it to me straight, the guy never skirted around an issue when having a conversation with me.

"I know he is, that's why I need to find her." I shake my head.

"Well, if what her father said was true, that he thinks he loves her—" Margaret ignores the look I send her way and stands. "Then he won't hurt her. But he might leave the country with her which means we need to get our asses in gear, and fast."

"Wait, we?" I look at Margaret incredulously and also somehow hopeful at the same time.

"Of course, Agent Dimples, you think we're going to let you do this alone?" I look at her with a slight chuckle and try to hide the emotion suddenly hitting me.

Then something hits me, "Shit, I can't fly back."

"Why not?" Margaret asks.

"Gemma," Liam says at the same time as me and I shake my head again. "It's okay, we can drive. If we get pulled over, well, we have an officer with us." He gives Margaret a cheeky grin.

"Gee, thanks," she mutters.

Minutes later we're all leaving their apartment and heading for their truck, them silent and on task and me with my head running through scenarios I don't want to think about.

I just have to get to Laney before it's too fucking late.

42

DELANEY

I FEEL LIKE some kind of prisoner of war or something. Not that it's that extreme, the room I'm in isn't actually that bad, it's more like surreal that I'm actually here, that this is actually happening to me.

We arrived at the warehouse shortly after our altercation and I was immediately brought to this room, it's so weird because I know where we are, but the room feels like I'm in somebody's house. When I came in, the first thing I saw was the bed and I shivered at the thought of why I'd need a bed in the first place. Rafael had come up behind me then, so close I could feel his breath on the back of my neck and said, "Not to worry, *reina*, when I do have you, it will be in a much nicer place than this. We still have time."

And that was what I was worried about. I hadn't ever told anyone about the warehouse because right after I'd left here things spiraled out of control so fast I didn't have the time. So no one knew where I was.

I think back to the night on the road and pray that Ford made it out of there in one piece, pray that my father helped him and that they're both safe and sound somewhere far away from this danger that now surrounds me.

I can't even begin to imagine what horrors await me. No one is coming to my rescue now, this is how it's going to be from here on out and I don't know if I have it in me to keep myself alive until then. The thoughts of what lies ahead in my future has a whimpered sob escaping my throat. "Oh God."

The door opens and a man comes in with another tray, never making eye contact and setting down the food on the small desk that occupies the space across from me. They come in every few hours with food. I can only tell that it's night when they go several hours in between meals. The food is always spectacular looking and by the third meal, I couldn't stop myself from eating it.

I wanted to fight it, I wanted to make it clear that I wanted nothing from him, that I wouldn't cooperate with him so easily. And then it hit me when I thought of escaping, I couldn't do so if I was weak, if I didn't have any energy, I wouldn't have any strength.

So, I ate, I prayed and I waited to make my move.

MY MOVE WAS coming faster than I thought. Rafael himself had come to get me and had his men wrap my hands with what felt and sounded like duct tape. "I thought I wasn't your prisoner." I sneer at Rafael.

He strokes my cheek in a loving way and I try my best to not recoil, it'll only make it worse. "No, my dear. Just a precaution," he says, his eyes darken but his words stay soft, throwing off my reaction.

"Where are we going?"

But he never answers me, he makes a gesture to the man behind me and then I'm pushed forward, never rough but always sure and I'm moving toward the door to the outside. *I wish I still had my gun,* I think. They, of course, took it from me when I'd been shoved into the SUV the night of the accident and I was cursing myself for not hiding it better, but where exactly was I supposed to hide it? My bra? I'm not exactly packing a punch in boob size.

I move my feet so I don't get shoved again and think of a way to get myself out of this, but I have nothing. I know zero self-defense; I don't know what you are supposed to do in a situation like this and I feel like an idiot because of it.

But when two more men come and grab each arm, I know any fighting I do is futile. The only way I can get myself out of this is with help, or trying to catch them off guard. But I'm not sure how much good it will do. With no weapon, no idea where we're going and no help, I'm not sure how I'm getting out of this.

43

FORD

THE DRIVE TO Texas didn't take nearly as long as it normally would have and I have Liam to thank for it, his lead foot got us home in record time. We didn't make a single stop except for gas but now that we're in town, the first stop we make is to the restaurant. I first need to know what Torrezs, if any, have been around. They can't just take them both and not leave someone here in charge.

We all rush in and Margaret makes her way to the restroom, claiming an imminent eruption and I shake my head, I'd missed her sense of humor. She hadn't said a word, but I knew she had to of needed to use it long before now and was trying to hold it in until we got to town.

I track down Lizzie now and she seems startled to see me here.

"Ford! You're back!" She smiles at me and then it falls when she sees my scowl.

"Who's here?" I ask.

"What?"

I shake my head, knowing I'm not being clear. "Is Laney here? Or her father?"

She squints at me and shakes her head. "I was told Laney was with you. Mr. Torrez is in the back, Ford—what is going on?"

I don't take the time to answer her. Liam and I both head toward the back and I march directly into the office, he seems startled at first but settles down at my presence, a resigned look on his face.

"Ford," he says and then eyes Liam, but I don't give a damn about introductions.

"What. Happened?" I ask, my teeth grinding so hard I'm worried I'll crack a molar.

"What do you mean?" He plays innocent.

"I mean, where the fuck is Delaney?"

His face stutters and he pales slightly. "She's with Rafael now."

I slam my hand on the desk. "Where?"

"Ford." He appears to be trying to calm me and it just makes my blood boil that much more. "What's done, is done. We can't fix it this time."

I stare at the father of the woman I love with disbelief on my face, I stand at full height and then turn a little, letting out a scoff. "What the hell is wrong with you? She's your daughter!" I yell, knowing it'll do no good, but I can't help myself. This is all wrong.

"I know. And I'll still see her. But you don't understand the Guerreros, this is their way of life and unfortunately, Torrezs are a part of it."

I let out another disbelieving sigh and say, "Not anymore." I didn't even realize Margaret was in the room with us until I turn to go and hear her say, "Disgusting bastard." Truer words have never been spoken.

IT'S FAIRLY EASY, with Liam's help, to track down the warehouse. The phone's tracking went offline, which was why we'd made the stop at the restaurant first, some hopeful part of me had wanted her to be there. I'm a little concerned when I don't see any cars. And to top it off, the gate isn't even locked. A place like this, regardless of what they could be manufacturing or storing inside, would be heavily guarded no matter what. We all pile out of the car, scanning the area, looking for any trace of human life or activity but we all come up empty. I rub my head in frustration, this is not what I wanted, not what I expected.

Coming home has left an impact on me that I can't forget, it's brought me here to this place, to a job that is unlike any other.

Because the objective is one I've never had before. One where someone I love is at risk, and while risks are something that doesn't usually bother me, it's a different story when Laney is involved.

"Maybe they left in a hurry," Liam supplies. I know the both of them are trying not to point out the obvious. That she's gone. That I'm unlikely to find her. But that can't be the end of this story.

I think of where they could be going and only one place comes to mind; Mexico. It makes sense that they would go there. He probably has more resources there than anywhere in the world, more people to back him. Miles had told me as much when I'd spoken with him.

Miles might even know.

As the idea hits, I grab for my phone but pause when it's already ringing. Gemma.

"Busted," Liam says when he sees the caller ID himself. I roll my eyes and contemplate not answering the phone, but at this rate, I'm already in the dog house— and maybe on my way to the big house as well. We all pile back into the vehicle before I answer the phone.

"James," I say.

"Ford, what the hell are you doing? Why are you in Denver?" She sounds even more irritated than usual.

"Just a little vacation," I answer nonchalantly. I know I have to get off this phone but until I know what she's calling for, I can't give away my position.

"Listen, I know I told you to back off but I have some news." I sit up straight and turn the phone to speaker. "The feds that are working on the Guerrero case are trying to raid his warehouse tonight, which means they'll probably be finding your girl there."

"The warehouse is empty," I murmur before I can think better of it, I bite my lip and squeeze my eyes shut.

"What? How would you know that?" she asks suspiciously.

"Just… a guess."

"Ford. Where are you?"

"Never mind that, what's their next best guess on where Guerrero would be?"

"Well, they were going to have two units set up, one at the warehouse and one at the airstrip."

I smirk. "Thanks for the info." Before hanging up the phone, I vaguely catch a curse through the line before it goes dead.

"To the airstrip," Liam says. "But which one?"

"There's only one in this county," I reply and start to guide him there. I just pray we get there in time to stop them. I can't let her leave the country.

THE RIDE TO the airstrip is quiet and I appreciate the fact

that they know small talk is not in the cards right now. I think of Laney, of how she is right now and how brave she's been through this whole fucking mess. Just thinking of her father pisses me off and has me envisioning hanging him by the literal balls when I see him again.

I can't even imagine it.

And maybe that's because my parents are badass. That they would do everything in their power to protect me and my brother at all costs. But to even think of sacrificing your kid to save your own hide? That's fucking spineless.

That's exactly what Joaquín Torrez is. A spineless fucking coward.

If I have any say in the matter, he won't have a thing— positive or negative— to say to Delaney once this is all said and done.

If I find her.

I push the voice to the back of my mind. The voice that has always been there, taunting me like the demons they come from. I can't think like that. Like I'll never see Delaney again.

"Can't you go any faster?" I grunt out to Liam who, by all accounts, is speeding his way to the airstrip like there's a tornado chasing us.

It doesn't faze him. "Chill, princess. We'll get her."

It's almost calming that he thinks so. Once upon a time, there was a chance that he'd never see the love of his life again. And now he's about to marry the chick.

Finally, after what seems like days, we make it to the airstrip, we pull up to the main entrance, the area deserted for the most part. There are no people I can see from where we're standing and that panic that's been settling down in my belly starts to roar to life.

"Fuck," I snap. "Where is she?" I jump out of the car and spin around, the others follow my lead when I hop the fence that's keeping me out. The main building is large and that's when I hear the dull hum from somewhere in the distance.

"Gentry." Margaret signals in the other direction, clearly hearing what I am and we all take off at a dead sprint, at the same moment, a roar of vehicles come from behind us and a quick glance tells me the feds are here. Good. The more people, the better.

I round the building and the sight in front of me almost has me pausing, the sight of Rafael with his hands on Laney makes a sheet of red filter my vision.

I'm going to kill him.

44

DELANEY

"STUPID, STUPID, STUPID," I mutter to myself when the SUV makes its turns. Left and right all over the place like they're purposefully trying to make it hard to remember, but I'm not blindfolded so it doesn't make a bit of difference.

It's only really hitting me now how idiotic I'd been to try and fix all of this myself, but I couldn't seem to help it. I'd wanted to make this all go away for myself, my father, our restaurant. I wanted to desperately keep my mother's legacy intact and now, looking back, she would have probably lost her mind at what I'd done to keep everything good the way it was.

I really missed Ford. But it wasn't fair to miss him, I'd broken his heart and mine in the process. I'd nearly gotten him killed and it was my fault entirely that he'd been there at all. I could have easily been the reason that he died that day. *God, please don't let him be dead.* I send the silent prayer just as we take another turn and I suck in a breath when I see what's before me.

Planes all over the airfield. So we're going somewhere far enough away that we need a plane which means I'll probably never step foot in Texas ever again. The thought hurts my heart. I will myself to keep the tears at bay.

This isn't supposed to be my life.

I let a tear fall but wipe it away quickly with my shoulder before anyone can see me, the last thing I need is anyone in this car to see me being weak. I haven't let Rafael see one tear since I left with him and I wasn't about to now.

When the car comes to a stop, Rafael steps out and talks with someone who was waiting by the plane and I just sit in the car, I don't move knowing that when I do, it'll be to get on a plane to leave the only home I've ever known and I'm not ready to do that. I don't know if I'll ever be ready.

Suddenly, a flurry of activity is happening outside of the car, I see panic line Rafael's face and I sit up again to survey the area and there are multiple black vehicles speeding onto the tarmac, Rafael rips open the door and grabs my arm, yanking me out roughly and I let out a cry of pain as it wrenches my shoulder. He rushes me to the plane all the while spitting out expletives in

Spanish, I can tell his panic mode has engaged and it unnerves me to see him like that.

I look around the tarmac to the people who've rushed out, but I'm suddenly dragged up the stairs to the plane and I can hear the engine already running and ready to go. I'm desperate to see who it is though, that little piece of hope that still resides inside is strong. My hair whips in front of my face and I shake my head, trying to see, all the while Rafael hasn't let go.

I turn, making glaring eye contact with him. "You will never win!"

His eyes, that are dark already, turn midnight. "I will have you! You belong to me! You've always belonged to me!" The manic pitch to his voice sends a violent shiver down my spine and I pull against his hold again. People are jumping out of vehicles, FBI graces their bulletproof vests.

My breath catches in my throat at the sight of guns being aimed at us and I let out a gasp, fearing that they think I'm here willingly. Then out of the corner of my eye, I see a group who don't match the rest but are also there with guns trained on me. I twist out of Rafael's hold and take a step forward toward a figure I'd recognize anywhere when I realize the stairs are retracting. "No!" I say and Rafael grabs me again, something butting up against my back and I freeze, looking to the man I love who hasn't lowered his gun. He mouths something to me before Rafael is jerked back and falls into the plane.

I don't waste time looking back at him and I don't waste time thinking about how bad it's going to hurt when I hurl myself off the stairs that are halfway closed. I hit the asphalt with a sharp pain as I hear my name being yelled. But my body shuts down, a trauma to my brain and the pain that's slicing through that same shoulder that Rafael wrenched earlier has me holding still, unable to move. I close my eyes and wait for relief.

FORD

RAFAEL PULLS A gun on Delaney and it's in that moment that I knew I'd have to go against what I knew the FBI wanted and take the shot, they were about to let him escape with her in his clutches and I couldn't fucking let that happen.

When she dove off the stairs, I held my breath and fear replaced rational thought. I didn't heed the orders of whoever was yelling. I ran into the chaos, not caring whose investigation I was ruining, not caring if I was about to be shot by either side of the firefight. My only thought had been *her*. When I reached her and heard a little moan escape her, relief hit me with a mighty punch as I pulled her into my arms.

The agents are all screaming out demands at each other and I see Liam and Margaret attempting to help and also diffuse the anger that's being shouted in my direction, but I don't care. Delaney's body gives up on her, her limbs hang, her bound hands useless. I take my time lifting her up and making my way to one of the many vehicles on the tarmac, she doesn't speak and when I finally get a good look at her, her face is wet with silent tears, her eyes closed and body heaving with sobs.

I whip my knife out and carefully cut through the tape that holds her hands together, silently cursing the man who did this to her and vowing to tell him exactly how I feel about it when I get the chance. It's then I notice that the plane is barreling down the runway and lifting off. "Fuck," I curse and watch as Rafael escapes, a gaggle of agents either watching from the ground or taking care of those he left behind.

Laney hasn't paid any attention to her surroundings, but I know she's awake and aware, her mind is just not in the moment and I pray that he didn't do anything to her that could mess with her brain later on down the road.

With her wrists free, I slowly help her move her hands to her lap and help her sit back, I let my stare glance over every part of her and give her a moment to breathe before asking, "Are you okay?" I want to say so much more than that. I want to yell and scream at her for making me worry, for pushing me away and trying to handle this herself.

But my mom taught me enough to know that won't help anything, so I just wait for her to compose herself. With her eyes closed, she nods her head and lets out a sigh. "I—" she starts but then she shakes her head and turns it to me, her eyes open and the despair in them makes me want to cry. "I'm sorry."

My eyebrows furrow and I grab her hand. "You don't have anything to be sorry for."

A scoff leaves her. "Are you serious? You were almost killed because of me, I pushed you away to help you escape my fucked-up life," I raise a brow at her curse, but she ignores me. "And it didn't even work."

I grab her knees and turn her until she's facing me and I hold on to her hands, and she hisses out a breath. I see where the ground tore through her shirt and look around. Margaret is close and I ask her to find someone to help. "Look at me," I say to Laney, my focus solely on her now. Slowly she lifts her head to meet my gaze. "I'm pissed at you." I rush on at the note of surprise in her eyes. "I'm pissed because you pushed me away. Getting shot was not your fault, that was that fucker, Guerrero's. But you and me? Yeah, I'm pissed about that."

"Ford—"

"No," I cut her off. "Laney, you don't understand the worry that's been eating away at me for the last week. I've been in a full-blown panic, wondering where you were and worried about what was happening to you. But." I pause to calm myself down, then I admit. "I'm just fucking glad you're safe."

"Ford, this isn't the life you deserve. You deserve so much better than me."

"You obviously don't know me as well as I thought. Because

us going our separate ways isn't an option anymore. You leaving me isn't. An. Option. We've been fighting a war, yes, but you better fucking believe we'll always do it together. Side by side." Even I could hear the desperation that was leaking through my voice, but for the first time in my life I didn't care that I was giving away my position. I didn't fucking care. And that spoke volumes for me.

Before she can reply, Gemma calls my name, I know I'm in for it right now and I have to deal with the shit I just interrupted but I don't want to leave Delaney after what she's been through, Margaret approaches and after an awkward but quick introduction, I excuse myself to handle it.

"Gem," I start but pause at her raised hand. She looks irritated, her eyebrows furrowed in frustration as she looks me over.

"I know why you did what you did, and it was the right thing for you," she says but I can tell the lashing is coming. "You'll have to come in and get debriefed, Delaney too. They'll want to question her, make sure she's legit and not a part of his dealings."

Anger invades my senses and I clench my fists at my sides. "She has nothing to do with his drug shit."

"I know, I know," she placates. "But they don't know that. All she is right now is a suspect. There's not a lot I can do for her, but I can help you. You infiltrated an active FBI investigation. Not only that, you invaded their raid."

I huff and look away. "He was taking her God knows where, I wasn't about to just let him fucking do that."

Gemma nods and looks me over. "Despite all of this." She

waves a hand around. "You look good, Gentry."

I don't reply as I look over to where Delaney sits in the back of the truck talking with Margaret and Liam, Margaret says something to make her laugh a little and I feel my chest lighten.

"Listen, I trust you. So as soon as she gets looked at, follow behind us and we'll get everything straightened out."

"What about them?" I say, gesturing to the pissed-off looking agents behind her.

"I'll handle it," she says and then pauses as she turns. "Oh, and bring them too." She points to Liam and Margaret with a pointed look, she has as much history with them as I do and I'm surprised that Margaret hasn't come over to her. But then again, after the anger she directed toward me when I first saw her, I'm not sure she doesn't have some sort of ill-feeling toward Gemma as well.

I head back to the truck, a real gulp of air finally making it into my lungs for the first time in days and I send out a silent prayer of thanks. I don't know what I would have done if he'd succeeded in getting her wherever the hell he was going. I do know, I wouldn't have stopped looking for her.

Because Delaney Torrez is mine.

45

DELANEY

THE FBI OFFICES are nothing like what I had expected. I was preparing myself for a blaring spotlight over my head, someone with a no-bullshit attitude to interrogate me and give me the fifth degree, someone who was ready to lock me up just for my connection to Rafael. Instead, I got the nice lady who apparently ran this particular office and she wasn't razzing me nearly as much as I expected.

"I understand there's been some bad dealings with your father and Guerrero," she says as she flips through some sort of report.

"Yeah, um, it's actually a lot to explain," I start but pause when she raises a hand.

"Oh, I have the full report."

My eyebrows crinkle. "You do?"

"Yes, your father, Joaquín, came in just before you all arrived and told us every bit of it. It's not great for him, but he's taking full responsibility for knowing about Rafael."

I rub my brow and think over that. "Is he in trouble?"

She sighs and sets down her papers before looking at me. "No. Technically, there is no agreement other than verbal. As long as there are no drugs found on the premises, that is, his house or the restaurant that you two run, he won't be charged. Though, I have a feeling he'll be feeling the guilt for a while."

"The guilt? But he didn't hold any drugs for Rafael."

"I'm not talking about that, rather, the guilt over you being involved in this deal. He expressed his concern over and over again about your well-being. But I was assured Agent Gentry had a handle on the situation."

He definitely did. I hadn't expected to ever see him again and when he'd shown up, help in tow. I could have kissed him. The relief I'd felt was overwhelming and I wasn't sure if it was just from seeing him, or if it was more about the fact that I was being rescued from being abducted by a very dangerous man.

"What about Rafael?" I ask. "He got away, right? What does that mean?"

"Well, unfortunately, he's in the wind, for now. Somehow that plane had no radar, and I'm assuming they didn't make it far before switching transportation." She rubs her forehead. "He's smart. Probably because he grew up a criminal and knows tricks that no others know. So, we'll continue to try to find him and put him behind bars."

"You got some of his guys though."

"We did." She nods. "And that will help with charges against him, when we find him." After that, she dismisses me, and I leave the room feeling lighter and more exhausted than I've ever felt. I rub my shoulder gently. A paramedic came to take my vitals, nothing was wrong except for a muscle sprain and some serious road rash, so he'd given me a sling and covered the parts that were bleeding. It sure as hell felt like something much worse than that. I head to the front of the building, hoping to see Ford but only finding Margaret on the phone. When she sees me, she quickly ends her phone call and heads toward me.

She's maybe the nicest person I've ever met. I immediately took a liking to her and her husband, Liam, and thanked them profusely when they explained they were here to help Ford. "Everything okay?" she asks me.

"I guess so. They're letting me go."

She shrugs. "Well, of course. You didn't do anything."

I point at her phone. "How about you? Everything okay for you?"

"Oh yeah, just telling my partner to cool it. I used some sick days and they were panicking." She laughs.

"It's really cool that you're a cop. How'd you get into that?"

We take a seat and Margaret tells me her history, which involves how she met Ford and how she knew she had to make a change with her life. "I didn't want to be stuck in a job I wasn't passionate about anymore." She shrugs. I think she undervalues how hard that probably was, but maybe she's worked through that part of her life. Maybe she's forgotten how hard it probably was to take that plunge in her life. Change is scary.

We wait a while longer, talking about life and common interests when both Ford and Liam walk out of the door I'd come from, both scowling, Gemma brings up the rear, staring at something on a tablet.

I frown at Ford's tense expression. "What's going on?"

Ford comes to stand beside me and wraps his arm around my waist. Gemma is the one who answers me. "We've got word that the plane landed in a field only an hour away. The man who owns the field called the cops and our agents got wind, headed over and confirmed the plane. We have a strong suspicion that Mr. Guerrero isn't happy and will want to take it out on someone."

She lets that sentence hang heavily in the air between us. I have a bad feeling that the 'someone' is me. Gemma nods at me like she can read my mind. "I'm afraid you're still not quite in the clear."

Ford's arm tenses around me, and I instinctively lean into his side. "So what do we do?"

"You do nothing," he states emphatically. "You go to a safe house while the rest of us take care of the situation."

His statement that so quickly dismisses me makes me bristle. I couldn't just sit in some house somewhere and wait for word. I can't let people who shouldn't have been part of this in the first place take the fall… not that it's my fault, per se. But Rafael wants me, so why would I sit around and wait to see if people I care about—new friends or not—get hurt.

"No," I state. I look to Gemma, trying not to step on any toes, but also knowing that she happens to be my boyfriend's boss and will have the most say. "I want to help."

She starts to nod before Ford stops her. "Not a chance in hell is that happening." Suddenly he's pushing me, taking us away from the group and into a private-ish corner. "Laney, you are not going to be put in more danger. I won't allow it."

I narrow my eyes slightly. "Allow?"

His jaw clenches, I see in his eyes that he's desperately trying to find the right words to say, but he's a guy. There's a good chance his foot is about to go into his mouth.

"Laney… look. I'm trained for this. You're not. You have no idea what this guy is capable of and if anyone—*anyone*, is getting hurt. It will be me."

See? Foot enter mouth. "I have no idea? Really? Was I not basically abducted by the man and held in a warehouse for days? Threatened? Did I not jump out of an airplane?" I know *technically* that's pushing it, but I did jump out of a plane.

He sighs, steps back, rubs a hand over his face. It's then I see the fatigue that's plaguing him. The worry over me has been eating him alive for days. While I was being held captive by the enemy he was mobilizing his help, tracking me down, fighting for me. I doubt he slept a wink. With his other added stress, this has the potential to kill him.

Without another word, I step into him, hugging him to me tightly. I know I've caught him off guard, his arms take a few seconds before they finally fall around me, squeezing me back and holding on like he's afraid I'll be taken away with the next breeze.

When I step away again, he keeps his arms around me but looks down when he feels my gaze. "I want to help. I want to put this behind us." I purposefully say *us,* knowing that putting that thought in his head, the thoughts of our future, he'll think about something other than the immediate danger we face.

Finally, he nods. "But, under my authority. Which means no matter what happens, you do as I say, when I say." Agent Gentry just gave me that order, I can see how serious he is and immediately nod, holding back the *Aye, aye, captain* that's sarcastically floating around in my head.

We head back to the group where Ford informs them that I will be helping in a safe and monitored capacity, I can't refrain from rolling my eyes then. Liam volunteers to stay and help but Margaret informs us she has to get back home. After a hug from her and a be safe, Liam takes her so they can get her on a flight back home.

After they leave, I turn back to Ford and Gemma. "So, what now?"

44

FORD

BEING BACK IN the field is like second nature to me now. I'm reissued my gun and badge, both of which feel like having limbs reattached to my body. We head into a room filled with monitors, probably twenty or so people are spread around the room, on various phone calls, pulling up maps, talking to their superiors.

I'm introduced to the special agent in charge who greets me with a rough handshake. "If I knew nothing about you, I'd have you fined for the shit you pulled." He sighs. "But given what you've done for us, well, I can forgive it."

Before I can reply or thank him he cuts in, "*If* you can get

Rafael Guerrero's ass in cuffs."

"I won't stop until I do, sir." That's the fucking truth too. With him on the loose, there's no guarantee that Delaney will be safe and that's not something I can deal with.

Delaney looks like she's about to pass out standing, she must have been awake for close to thirty-six hours and with all the stress and drama her exhaustion is finally catching up to her. There's a small couch in the main office, tucked away in a corner and I settle her down there.

"I should stay awake, Ford. I want to help."

I shake my head at her and move her hair off her shoulder. "There's nothing you can do right now. I'll wake you when we have something." I give her forehead a kiss and watch as she falls asleep before I can even walk away.

I'm tense over the next few hours. The stress of the situation would normally be heightened but this is something else altogether. The added factor of this being about Delaney, about the danger she's in, it adds a new level of vulnerability that I've never felt.

"We'll find him," Liam supplies. He's been staring at his own computer for the better part of three hours, combing through anything he can find that would help us. Truthfully, anything he can do is likely already being done. I know him though and there's no way he can sit back and let others do all the hard work.

"I know," I reply just as Gemma and another group of people come back into the room. She nods at me. "We've got a hit."

This perks me up. I didn't think it would happen that fast.

"He had his pilot land at a private airstrip outside of Falfurrias."

"How in the hell did you find that out?"

"The owner called the cops the second the plane touched down. It's not exactly normal for a private jet to randomly land in a private field."

It's not, but just automatically calling the cops? "It's not his first time dealing with trouble."

"He alive?" It wouldn't surprise me if Guerrero didn't want to have witnesses to his whereabouts.

"He is. Didn't confront the matter directly but there was a car there not two minutes after the plane landed. Guerrero planned it all."

"Fuck." Which means he's already on the move. "We gotta go."

"Hold on, we need to figure out where he's headed or else we'll be on a wild goose chase."

"I've got it," an agent says, pulling up a map on the large screen on the far wall. On the screen is a map of south Texas, from Falfurrias to Mexico.

I point to it. "We have to stop him before he's over the border." Otherwise we'll be shit out of luck.

"Border patrol will stop him," Gemma says.

Shaking my head, I stop and think. If he was planning this the entire time, which I'm not entirely convinced of, then he would have had an alternative route planned already. "He has another plane."

Gemma shakes her head as another agent whose name I

haven't learned speaks, "We don't have any indication of that."

"Well, we had no indication of him landing on someone else's airstrip either."

Gemma moves quickly, snapping her fingers at someone. "Add to the APB." Meaning, we're looking for someone at any airport, airfield, or anywhere that has a noted plane.

"We've gotta move."

WE'VE BEEN COMBING over every single piece of data that we can find but nothing points us in the direction we need. No planes were jacked, no crossing over the border—that we know of—it's like he's disappeared into thin air.

It's almost six in the morning when Delaney comes out into the main room, her eyes are heavy but clear. I make my way to her and wrap her in my arms. For a moment, we both just hold on to each other, breathing the other one in. Like me, she was scared of how yesterday was going to turn out. Being able to hold on to her, to love her and know that we're in this together is a powerful thing.

"Anything yet?" She breaks our silence.

"Not yet, babe," I say, leaving one arm over her shoulders and looking to where everyone is still working, staying awake and alert on coffee and junk food. Not a single person has gone home.

They've taken turns with breaks, giving each other small periods of rest before they're back in the thick of things. This office is a well-oiled machine. And the one that I'm supposed to start working at soon. Something I've yet to share with anyone yet.

Gemma approaches with a fresh coffee in hand, her blazer missing and sleeves rolled up. Her normally very put-together bun is disheveled, she's not one who likes to be 'casual', this look is one she only dons when things have gotten intense. She hands the coffee to Delaney who smiles back. "Thank you."

She nods at her. "Of course." She fidgets uneasily and I can tell she's got something that she doesn't want to share.

"Spit it out, James."

With a sigh and nod, she looks at Delaney and says, "I think we have an idea on how to get Guerrero to come forward."

"Okay," she replies with a nervous chuckle. "How's that?"

"We use you as bait."

47

DELANEY

BESIDE ME, FORD explodes.

"That's not fucking happening." His growl is aimed at Gemma but I feel his wrath all the same. "Are you out of your fucking mind, Gemma?"

She raises a placating hand to him. "Calm down."

"Calm down?! You want me to calm down." Ford starts to pace the room and I sip the coffee in my hand. It's so early and after the past few days and the coma-like sleep I just had, I'm not sure I'm awake enough for so much drama.

"Gentry, you have to look at this logically." This comes from

Liam who's joined our little party.

"Fuck off, man."

Liam looks amused at this. "You know of all people we would never let anything happen to her."

"Really?" he says, his look is pained. "Like I *didn't* protect Margaret?"

He sighs. "This isn't the same thing at all. You guys got fucking taken. This time, we control the narrative."

"Um," I start to interrupt when Ford continues. "We cannot risk it."

"We have to get Guerrero somehow, we can't let him just escape."

I sigh, sip another bit of coffee, then I say, "I'll do whatever you need, Gemma."

Ford spins around, his eyes are like daggers. "Like hell!"

I walk, very calmly because getting mad or emotional right now won't do any of us any good anyway, and I grab his hand. "Let's go over here." He starts to resist but eventually relents.

We find an empty conference room and I set the coffee on the table while Ford shuts the door behind him. I look him over and see the stress and exhaustion all over his face, in his stance and demeanor. He's used to these kind of hours, to staying up for hours on end while trying to solve something.

"What's going on?"

He shakes his head. "I can't do it." His declaration is a whisper.

"Do what?" I ask, coming to stand in front of him and looking into his eyes.

"A few years ago… I was Gemma's partner. And we had a mission." He sighs and rubs his face. "The mission was Liam."

I scrunch my face in confusion. "Liam?"

"It's a long story, but basically, he was on the other side. He was the bad guy and it was my job to take care of it. Which is how Margaret came to be and… Damn. It's a long story, as I said, and I'd love to tell you one day, but the bottom line is I fucked-up. And it almost got Margaret killed."

I hesitate, not wanting to dispute something I don't understand and let him finish his thought. "I can't do that with you." He emphasizes every word, his eyes holding mine and trying to push this point into my brain to make me see where he's coming from.

I rub my lip and think about it. "You know what I want?"

He shakes his head. "What?"

I take his hands and place them around my waist where he immediately tightens them. "I want to go to sleep with you by my side, I want to wake up and have coffee with you in our own kitchen. I want to go on dates when I'm not working, I want family dinners with you and your family. I want to have a life filled with love and fun and *you*." I press a kiss to his lips, he moves one hand and grabs the back of my neck and holds me to him. When we pull away, he rests his forehead against mine. "But we can't."

Ford's head jerks back, his eyes gazing into my own. "What?"

"We can't do any of that *until* Rafael is out of our lives."

He sighs, part relief and part—hopefully—resignation. After

scrubbing his hands over his face, he grabs my hand and I follow behind him as he exits the room, heading back to where everyone is waiting. "Okay." He addresses Gemma. "But I'm not leaving her side."

Gemma nods her head, her expression says she was expecting that. "We have a plan."

THE 'PLAN' SO to speak, was to dangle me in plain sight for all to see. Including, hopefully, Rafael. Ford was not in on this plan and hated being left out of it altogether. But we started making habits. A pattern of sorts for him to follow. The thought, and I suppose most logical explanation for what has happened is Rafael is, for the lack of a better word, obsessed with me. The legend that I had no clue about was, the village my father's family comes from had a tradition of sorts and the idea of arranged marriages was normal. So much so that it was just how things were done. I'd learned that my papá was actually expected to marry Rafael's aunt years and years ago and defied everyone to marry my mother. And from there, though the Guerreros had pretended everything was fine, started the spiral that led us to today. It was why Mom died, it was why Dad was in massive debt and tried— very unsuccessfully—to keep me out of the business and why Rafael was obsessed. According to my father, Rafael was under the assumption that I was his to have. His father had alluded to it, and my father had half-heartedly agreed. For years he had been able to keep me out of it, so busy, as Rafael very impatiently waited. Until finally, he couldn't take it anymore and everything imploded.

So that was the plan. I was bait for an unhinged man in hopes of him foolishly coming out of hiding to get me alone.

The FBI was watching our every move with hopes that somewhere out there Rafael was too. So every day, I went to work 'business as usual' and every day, except Tuesdays, Ford came along. Tuesday was our trick day. We were hoping that if he was watching, he would notice that I was alone on Tuesday nights, giving him an opportunity to get me alone.

This was where Ford damn near had a heart attack. The thought of Rafael anywhere near me made his head spin. But to get it to work, we had to dangle the bait.

So, today was the third Tuesday in a row that I've worked at the restaurant, with Ford out in a car or van or wherever the FBI was keeping tabs, and I was waiting to see if today would be the day. We've been on edge these last few weeks, it was stressful waiting for someone to kidnap me. Believe it or not, there's no guide available called "How to Prepare for a Kidnapping." I checked *Amazon* and everything.

As the sun starts its descent, the shadows play across the booths on the far wall and an uneasy feeling begins to fill my insides, churning my gut.

Feeling suddenly naked without a weapon or any way to communicate, I check to make sure no one else needs anything before making my way to the back office. I'll just call in to Ford for a moment, let him calm me down, then I'll head back out and await my doom.

I make my way into the office and shut the door behind me, I'm about to step around the desk when a hand clamps down on my wrist and spins me around.

Anger.

That's my first thought when I see Rafael's large figure looming over mine. His eyes are on fire and his expression is furious, he clamps his hand over my mouth when I open it, even though I had no intention of screaming.

"You break my heart, *reina.*"

"I was trying to survive."

His eyes glow like molten lava, but a hurt look flashes across his face. "Why would you need to survive *me?*"

I furrow my brows, watching him, you would think that we were lovers who broke up, who were in the midst of a quarrel. Not a psycho who was literally trying to force me into a relationship.

He shakes his head. "I love you, *reina.* How can you not see?" His grip tightens on my arms, surely leaving bruises. "I can make you happy."

At a loss for words, I just shake my head, not understanding where any of this has come from but knowing this guy has had it in his head that somehow, I was meant to be his.

"I *will* make you happy." Eyes that no longer connect with mine stare absently around the room before he nods his head and pulls. "Come."

"No!"

It's instinctive to resist him, even knowing that there must be someone outside who knows he's in here. Hell, they may even be making their way inside right now. I just have to wait them out.

Though I pull back, Rafael manhandles me in front of him and makes me walk out the door first where I'm half expecting to see Ford standing there, but no one is in the back hallway.

I allow Rafael to push me toward the back door and force deep breaths. Something like PTSD is causing flashbacks of being on the plane and I want so badly to stop him. To get away from him and never stop running.

This is the plan though. Get him *here* and the FBI will do the rest. Except… when we make our way through the back door, no one is there either and my pulse skyrockets.

Where are they?

There's an oversized SUV about twenty feet away and we're headed in a rush right toward it. When we get close enough that he's about to open the door, I'm suddenly thrown into the SUV's side, my head slamming into the passenger side window and momentarily disorienting me.

I turn when I've finally got my bearings again and see Rafael groaning, gritting his teeth. "*Mierda.*"

"What—" But the pain he was once feeling takes a back seat when he pins me to his front and swings me away from the car, I barely catch myself and he hauls me up.

That's when I see him.

Ford is standing there, a mask of fury on his face, pointing a gun at Rafael. Rafael shoves something against the side of my head and with my hair flying around my face I can't tell what it is by sight, but any dummy would know that I've got a gun to my head right now.

I can't help the tears that silently track down my face.

"Put it down, Guerrero!" A strong female voice echoes out, I recognize Gemma coming to Ford's side and another agent along with Liam come rushing up. It's now four against one.

But that one has an advantage; me.

48

FORD

I TRY WITH everything in me to calm my breathing but my heart is pumping so wildly in my chest that I can feel it in my throat. The sight of that motherfucker holding a gun to my woman makes me want to do things to him that I've only had the pleasure of doing to few.

Right now, it's not about me. My demons. My regrets.

It's about her.

Protecting her.

Beating the ever-loving shit out of this fucker in front of me and making him regret the very moment he set his sights on

Delaney Torrez. If he knew what was good for him, he would give up right this second and walk away.

"Let her go." The growl that rips from my throat surprises even me.

"No. She is not yours, she is mine."

Instinct rushes me, wanting to refute his statement, to give in to the bait he's dangling. "You don't have shit, man. The only way you're getting out of this is in a body bag."

Gemma makes a small noise in her throat, warning me I'm not allowed to kill him but fuck that. I'll do whatever it takes.

"Let us leave… or I will do it." He lifts his hand and presses it into Delaney's head farther, a small noise of protest escaping her lips.

Our eyes lock and I shake my head so small that only she can tell I did it. She nods her head back, just slightly, and I steady myself. She won't stay still, she can't.

It all happens at once. Delaney drops herself to the ground, making him lose his shot and taking Rafael partially down with her as he tries to tighten his grip on her and I take the shot, hitting him in the shoulder that's holding her, I successfully get him to drop his hold and Delaney crawls toward us on her hands and knees. I meet her halfway while the agents surrounding us make for Rafael.

I grasp Delaney under the armpits and pull her up into my arms, wrapping them around her and holding her tight. Her breathing is erratic and her heart is pounding against mine, she pulls her head back and looks up at me then, she opens her mouth to say something but stops. "I'm so glad you're here."

I smirk at her and shake my head, looking over to the bastard on the ground. "Sneaky fuck managed to get past us."

Gemma makes her way to us with Liam on her tail, we all watch her agents cuff Rafael and drag him away. He looks at Delaney and my arm instinctively pulls her tighter to me. "This is not over, *reina*."

"Like hell, it's not," I mutter.

"I'm sorry it went that far, Delaney," Gemma apologizes. "We were trying to be discreet, but in doing so, he managed to make his way around without detection. It's our fault."

"No fault," Delany says and sways a bit. "Though my head's poundin' a bit."

"Yeah, you got a nice little goose egg forming there," Liam notes. I look for myself before seeing the damage done from me shooting that bastard in the back of his shoulder.

"I'm sorry, babe." I lightly run my hand over the sore spot.

"Nothin' a little rest can't help." She smiles up at me. I kiss her on the head, eyes closed, I thank my stars that this nightmare is finally behind us. No more drug lords coming after her, no more added stress at the restaurant.

Just her, me, and a good life to get living.

I turn to her then and before she can say anything, I grab each side of her face and press my lips to hers. I kiss her nice and slow, letting my lips tell her everything she needs to know. I'm here for her, I'm not leaving. She reciprocates willingly and only pulls away when she needs to take a breath.

I look her in the eyes and in them, I see the love I have for her shining right back at me. "So," she starts. "What now?"

"Now?" I ask, taking one of her hands and squeezing it before letting out a happy sigh. "Now, we live happily ever after."

She laughs outright, and I stare in amused wonder. "That… was really, *really* cheesy."

49

DELANEY

LIFE GOES ON somewhat normally in the months that follow the incident. I don't talk about it much except to the therapist that I'd started seeing, Laura, she was the same one who helped Ford with his problems and I'd decided I needed a way to work through my feelings about my parents, the drama with the cartel and the life I was desperately trying to just enjoy.

It wasn't easy, but then again, what was?

Ford and I rented a small house outside of town. As much as I loved the barn, it wasn't a very good place for us to both live and I was ready to move on with life, to have my own home for once, and it was a step in our relationship that felt right.

Ford started working with the local FBI group here in Texas and I was extremely glad with how taken he was with it. It was really hard work and he didn't enjoy every day, as is with every job, not every one of them can end happily and he has his really bad days. But as far as his nightmares went, he didn't have them nearly as much as he did before. It was when he'd committed to putting away alcohol for good that we noticed the nightmares stayed at bay.

He still went to therapy, which I thought was great for his mind and anxiety. His mental health needed that little extra boost. As much as I wanted to be the one he confided in, I knew it was hard. *It's hard for me to be weak in front of you*, is what he would say. I'd never thought of him that way and I don't think I ever would, but I guess everyone measures weaknesses differently.

I think the fact that he stuck with the FBI, that he continues to fight for the good of mankind, he shows an unbelievable strength every single day. It was in that strength that he showed me love. I'd truly never been happier in my life.

I was still at the restaurant, but Dad was slowly coming back in more and more. I was surprised to see an energy in him return that I hadn't seen since Mom died and I think he was finally realizing how frozen he had been.

We'd had a lot of talks since the incident. He felt he'd betrayed me and maybe in a way he had, but he was still my father and as hard as it was, I had to forgive. My father hadn't been himself, he had given up. I knew that after everything that had happened to me, to my mother, he was trying—in his own way—to keep me from meeting the same fate as my mother.

Ford took a little more time coming around. He felt almost more betrayed than I did and I think it all went back to the fact that he felt my father had thrown me in the line of fire.

Like my thoughts conjured him out of thin air, Ford appears in the doorway to the restaurant. He would sometimes come in for lunch when he had the time, his partner, Wagner, always in tow. I like Wagner, he was a good guy, married for a long time and a guy who would always have Ford's back.

Today, Wagner is absent when I make my way over to Ford. "Where's Wagner?"

Ford smirks at me and I feel my body lighten at the sweet grin, his signature dimples on full display. They were something else. "I thought it'd be nice to have lunch with my girlfriend today."

I smile at him and nod. "Here?"

"I've got something else in mind, think you can sneak away?"

"Of course, she can." My father's voice comes from behind me, and I give him a grateful smile when he shoos us out the door.

We get into Ford's truck; one he'd bought for himself when he'd decided to stay here permanently.

Our conversation is about how our days have been but it's not long before we end up at a little strip mall just outside of town, we park and I look around at the restaurants, I point to a sandwich shop when we both step out of the car. "That place looks pretty good."

He opens the back seat door and grabs a small cooler and gives me a grin. I eye his suit that he typically wears to work and bite my lip. "On the other hand, maybe food can wait."

He wraps a hand around my waist and pulls me close, his lips grazing mine and says, "Don't tempt me, woman." Pressing a quick kiss to my lips he lets me go and grabs the cooler and a set of keys out of his pocket. Curious as to what he's up to, I follow him to a vacant storefront and watch him open the door with a stunned breath on my lips. "Ford?"

Not answering me, he opens the door for me, letting me step inside. Raising a curious brow at him I look around the empty room. There's literally nothing inside but I have a feeling about what it's supposed to be. "Ford," I say again, this time a little breathlessly.

"Laney." I turn to him and wait for the explanation. "I want to make all your dreams come true, and one of them was to open up a flower shop." He looks around and then with a wide grin, says, "This is yours, babe. All yours."

I let out a breath, trying to keep the tears that suddenly gather in my eyes at bay. "Ford, I don't know what to say."

"Well, I'd like to give you a name suggestion."

I smile and wipe under my eyes. "I'm open to that."

"I was thinking, *Annie's Flowers*."

I pause in my movement and press my hand to my chest. "After my mom?"

He nods and grabs my hands, pulling me to him. "I know how much she meant to you, I also know how proud of you she'd be." I hold a hand to my chest as if I can hold my emotions in. "And I think it'd be a really good way of honoring her memory."

"Ford, I don't know what to even—I can't even breathe."

He looks at me with worry for a moment and pauses. "Because you're…"

I scoff a laugh and say, "Because I'm so happy!" I grab his face and press my lips to his in a scorching kiss.

"Maybe food should definitely wait," he murmurs.

I laugh again and pull away. "Ford, I can't believe you did this for me. I'm just so shocked."

"Well, part of being your husband is making your dreams come true."

I quirk a brow. "Husband?"

"Oh shit, have we not done that part yet?" He feigns confusion and playfully grabs my hand, searching for a ring.

I laugh outright. "I think I'd remember that…"

He looks at me with so much love I swear my heart is going to burst out of my chest. He takes a breath, reaching his hand into his pocket and kneels to the floor, I hold one hand over my mouth to keep the excited laugh in. "Well, I think it's about time we do. Delaney Torrez, I am absolutely in love with you. I don't want to wake a single day or go to sleep a single night without you by my side. My dreams mean nothing without you in them. Would you please do me the honor of being my wife?"

I nod my head and gasp in air that seems to not be getting into my lungs fast enough. "Yes! Of course, I will."

With a brand new accessory on my hand, a brand new business to get up and running, and the man I love in front of me, I take stock and realize that life simply could not get better. After all the things we've been through, what matters is we made it. And I'm never, ever letting it go.

EPILOGUE

FORD

IT WAS THE grand opening of the new flower shop, *Annie's Flowers* and so far, the turnout was already amazing. We were selling today too, but it was mostly family and friends here to help us celebrate another milestone in our lives together.

We'd been busy since we started renting this place and not a second of it would I change. After I'd proposed, we'd both decided that we didn't want the hassle of a big drawn-out wedding planning process and so, six months earlier, with permission to copycat my brother's wedding, we'd been married in my parents' back yard with strung lights and a cleared-out barn for coverage.

It had been the night that changed it all for me. After months and months of rigorous therapy and insight into my soul that I was not prepared to see, I had a journal and a half full of stories and insecurities that were buried deep down. As part of my wedding present to her, I'd given my first journal to Delaney, telling her that there were no demons that I wanted to hide from her. It had brought us even closer together on our day.

That whole day, all I'd seen was the love and happiness that showed on Delaney's face. I didn't know if I'd ever seen her happier. And I couldn't believe that I'd been the one to do that for her.

I was beyond grateful that it was my life, that I was at this point of having my dreams come true, and every single one of them was wrapped up in the woman who was currently rubbing her small five-month belly right now.

Oh yeah, it didn't take me long at all to make that happen and though she'd protested slightly with the flower shop just opening, I'd managed to convince her.

"Hey, man." Liam walks through the door with Margaret in tow, and I smile broadly at the pair of them. They'd also flown down for the wedding and I was happy to see how well Delaney and Margaret had gotten along, so much so that Margaret and Liam both were in our wedding. I swear those girls talked more than I talked to my own wife, but it was nice to have friends to rely on. To have family to rely on. It'd been years since I was able to do that and I missed that feeling.

"Dude, thanks so much for coming out." I slap him on the back and hug Margaret, Delaney rushes over and her and Margaret squeal at each other before hugging, Liam and I just give each other a look and shrug. Girls.

"I'm so glad you're here!" Delaney says and hugs Liam quickly. It's a full house and we couldn't feel more support from our family and even the community than we do now.

When we'd told her father what the name of the shop would be, pride shown in his eyes and he and Delaney hugged for a long while. It took me some time to forgive Joaquín for the role he'd played in the Rafael situation but after much convincing, and actionable proof that he was trying to be a better father, I'd forgiven him, and we haven't spoken of it since.

I was happy, finally. And I wasn't about to do anything to jeopardize that.

WHEN THE PARTY starts winding down, I practically shove my parents out the door until the entire flower shop is empty.

"Whew," Laney says and leans against the front counter, her skin glows from happiness and the pregnancy and both of them make me want to bend her over the counter. "That was nuts."

She smiles when I approach. "It was amazing, babe. You did

great. But I think you need a break."

She moans when I rub her shoulders. "Oh yeah? What kind of break is that?"

I smirk because she knows me better than I thought and I head toward the back room, her hand tucked snugly in my own. I open the door and pull her in, shutting it behind me. In the corner is a convenient rocking lounger that I'd put in here at my own request, this room is for filing but half of it is converted into a small nursery of sorts, because if I know one thing, it's that Laney won't pause working for much, so with every security measure possible, this whole room was completely baby-proofed for when the little bun was here.

The chair was something I'd ordered special, and I was about to show her exactly why. I take my time showing her my love and unbuttoning the buttons that run the length of her dress, kissing her everywhere the dress exposes, down her shoulders and to her naval where I press a sweet kiss to the baby bump. Seeing her stand in front of me with my baby growing inside of her leaves me breathless.

So instead of talking, I lead her over to the chair and after quickly stripping myself, I guide her over my lap and show her how passionately I love her. How much I would do for her, how far I would go to prove it. And when we're done, she lays across me, catching her breath.

After a while of lying there together, she leans up and looks down at me. "Thank you."

I frown and smirk a little. "I think I should be the one thanking you."

She laughs and that sound makes my heart pound. "Not for that." She pauses. "Although, now the big chair makes more sense." I just keep my smirk in place and nod my head. "No, I mean, thank you for this. For the shop, for this life."

Her eyes shine, something I've become used to with the hormones in her body, and wait for her to say what she needs.

"I've never been happier. And it's because of you."

"I love you, Laney." I take her mouth with mine and sigh. "We got this, baby. All of it."

And isn't that the truth. When the trouble came, no matter how long it took, we always showed up for each other, and we always would. Forever.

The End... Almost

EPILOGUE #2

FORD

"ALRIGHT, THAT'S ENOUGH." My gruff voice is from being protective, it's not emotions. It's my manliness showing up. Dad instincts. Tough things. Guns, cars, women—well. Woman. Only one.

"Ford," Delaney says on a laugh. "She only got to hold her for a second."

"Yeah, and as best friend and auntie, I deserve more than one second!" Lizzie retorts with a snap of sass, her eyes never leaving the bundle of literal joy in her arms.

Madilyn Annie Gentry is perfection, just like her mother.

"Yeah, well I made her, so I get dibs." I say, edging closer.

"Ford Michael, I barely had a turn!" My mom's voice breaks into the space and I take a moment to toss her a glare. The room is full of our loved ones, my parents, brother and his wife. Liam and Margaret flew in once they heard that Laney was in labor. Delaney's dad is sitting in the corner taking in the scene with a smile on his lips.

Bobby is even here and since I've reestablished myself here again, we've grown back into the best friends we used to be before the fuckery that was my life happened. I'm grateful to have him back in my life.

"You already had two babies, you didn't get enough time cuddling us?"

Mom quirks her brow. "I also survived you both through your teen years, I deserve my baby snuggles." Before I can protest, Lizzie gently hands little Madilyn to my mother while I stand there gaping.

"Ford," I move toward Delaney, "We'll have plenty of time when she's up all night. They won't stay long." Her words are quiet, only meant for me.

"Yeah, well. I've been waiting for her for forever." Her eyes soften, just underneath are some dark spots. "You feeling okay?" She smiles softly. "I feel great. Tired, but great."

"You did amazing." Suddenly, I'm able to ignore everyone behind me—while keeping an eye on my daughter—and study the amazing woman in front of me. I've seen hard things in my life,

I've done some hard stuff too, but watching her go through labor was one of the most excruciating things I've ever seen. Women are warriors.

"That was… not easy." She chuckles.

"One and done?" I ask jokingly. She stares at me, contemplating my question.

"I don't know, I guess we'll see how we do with this one for a bit first."

I tilt my head. "How could you possibly want to go through that again?"

She shrugs. "Just look at her."

I do, Mom moves over to me and places her in my arms, I lean back in the chair I'm sitting in and look at her. I can already tell she'll have dark hair like her mom, then like a miracle, she opens her eyes and looks at me. I swear, my breath gets stolen from me. Little Madilyn looks at me with slightly unfocused eyes and I physically feel myself being wrapped around her little finger.

I look at Delaney again, "Yeah, okay."

"Knock knock." I look up and see Gemma James enter the room, a rare smile on her lips. She walks to Delaney and sets a bouquet on the table beside her. "Congratulations guys."

"Gemma, thank you so much! I didn't think you'd be able to come." Delaney gushes. They have an easy friendship that has been slowly come to fruition over the last couple years.

"Of course, can't miss seeing the next great FBI agent being brought into the world."

Her words have me pausing, "Boy, that's a nice compliment, Gemma. You feeling okay?"

"I was referring to myself." She says pointedly and reaches over to take Madilyn.

I study her, "You seem… relaxed?"

"Yeah… what is that? A tan?" Margaret jokes.

"Shut up," She murmurs without taking her eyes off of my daughter. Fuck. I'll never get tired of saying that.

"Seriously, what's going on with you? Did you close that case?" I only knew the barest of details of her latest case but someone being framed for serial murders is a big topic of conversation in our line of work.

"Of course, I did." She replies as if offended that I would doubt her.

"So, what is it then?" Liam pipes up, normally he wouldn't give two shits about someone's personal life, but over the years, the three of us and our extensions have become a tightknit group.

"Just took a vacation, what's the big deal?" She replies, it's silent for several minutes. Because Gemma James *never* takes a vacation.

"With who?" Margaret demands.

"Gem! I finally found a spot that wouldn't get me towed, you forgot the balloon!" A cheery voice pipes into the room and in comes a guy who looks at Gemma holding a baby like he just found heaven.

"Caleb! I told you to wait in the car!" We all swivel our heads back and forth like it's the most fascinating tennis match in history.

"Who's this?" I ask, putting a hard edge in my voice like the protective brother I am.

"Oh hey," He raises a hand and looks around the room. "I'm Caleb, Gemma's husband."

THE END

ACKNOWLEDGEMENTS

I will do my absolute best to not make my acknowledgements as long as this book, but no promises. Just kidding!

Always first is my favorite husband (you know who you are, even if you never read this). We've had some of the craziest times in our life this last year! We moved three times, I wrote two books, we had a new addition to the family. We left our home state and FINALLY purchased our farm like we've always dreamed. While we haven't always gotten along perfectly, or agree with each other, I never doubted your support and love. Thank you for supporting this crazy adventure!

To Harper, little girl, you will take the world by storm one day and I can't wait to cheer you on from the sidelines. Oliver, dude, you are awesome. You're only a little one now, but I can't wait to see what you do in this world.

To my favorite (work) wife, Avery James King. Dude.

"This is going to sound weird, but for a second, I think you took on the shape of a unicorn." I know we've yet to decide if it's a compliment that we can both quote Stepbrothers, but hell, if that doesn't bond someone, I don't know what will. You've been the sounding board for *everything* and I appreciate you more than you know, bitchacho.

To my freaking AMAZING editor. I'm so sorry. I feel like I say that a lot, but sometimes it's necessary. Thank you for being wicked awesome, you (Ellie) and Rosa are the bomb.

Beta readers, you guys read this for me TWICE. I know you all were happy with the first draft, but I was thrilled you loved the second (third? Fourth? It's been a long year.) I don't know what I would do without you.

To my fam, you guys have no clue what I'm doing most of the time, but that's okay, you support me anyway. Thank you.

Finally, to my readers! You guys, I'm honored that you read my books. I can't even believe it sometimes how lucky I am. I have THE BEST readers ever. You guys shared and loved my last release so much I almost cried (This is a big deal), thank you, thank you, thank you, thank you.

J.S. Wood has been writing contemporary romance for four years and enjoys giving you the happily ever after we all deserve, while at the same time delivering you humor and occasionally, some suspense. Her love of romance novels inspired her to write her own.

When she's not writing, she's playing with the family, hiking in the Rocky Mountains, or dreaming with her husband, two young kids and an abundance of animals. Their dream is to one day get their own fully sustainable farm.

"Nothing happens unless first a dream." – Carl Sandburg

Keep up with her at www.jswoodauthor.com

9 781737 419396